The Eye of The Sparrow

Flowing Mountain Press

KELOWNA, BRITISH COLUMBIA

Copyright © Mark Howard 1996

ALL RIGHTS RESERVED

No part of this book may be reproduced or transmitted in any form by any means, electronic or mechanical, or by any information storage or retrieval system, without written permission from the author, except for brief passages quoted in a review.
   This book is a work of fiction. Names, characters, places, and incidents are either the product of the author's imagination or are used fictitiously. Any resemblance to actual events, organizations, or persons, living or dead, is entirely coincidental.

Canadian Cataloguing in Publication Data

Howard, Mark, 1950-
   The eye of the sparrow

   ISBN 0-9681252-0-4

   I. Title.
PS8565.O8387E93 1996   C813'.54   C96-910595-9
PR9199.3.H66E93 1996

Published by
FLOWING MOUNTAIN PRESS
Box 31023
853 Anders Road
Kelowna, B.C.
Canada V1Z 1K2

Printed and bound in Canada by
MORRISS PRINTING COMPANY LTD.
Victoria, British Columbia

To Gudrun

ACKNOWLEDGEMENTS

I would like to thank the RCMP, Kelowna Search and Rescue, and Alpine Helicopters Ltd., for their advice and assistance.

The Eye of the Sparrow

David Ashton thrust himself from the back of his father's Mercedes and stared sullenly at his mom. Behind him, the bus to summer computer camp was about to leave. Its engine was running and kids were hanging out the windows.

David's mother was middle-aged, with a bright, worn look. She insisted on sounding cheerful. "Whew! We made it!"

He didn't acknowledge her smile. Her large eyes appealed to him. "David, we're sorry to send you off like this. Your dad was hoping he could postpone his meeting in Vancouver but it didn't work out. We'll do something special when you get back – I promise – "

His eyes had fallen to the asphalt. He shrugged.

"And don't worry about camp. We'll know you'll do just great."

He grabbed the strap of his duffel bag and jerked it off the seat. "Yeah. Right."

He sensed her hesitate. *Go on, say it. That I'd better not flunk like last year.*

"Take care of yourself, David. I love you."

She drove off. Shouts struck him from the bus. He watched the car for a moment, a glare of silver receding across the parking lot, then turned away.

"Hey – it's Snotball!"

"Aw. He misses his mommy."

"Their other car's a Vega."

In cold defiance he made no motion to board. Computer camp! The two words seemed to concentrate all he knew of anxiety and loathing into one lump in his gut. The bus said it all – puke-orange, black-lettered with "School District No. 23 Central Okanagan" under windows draped with assorted nerds, creeps, and mental defectives. The rows of keyboards and monitors lay in wait with their merciless logic. The lake was too cold to swim. The hamburgers tasted like regurgitated Cat Chow. Computer. Camp. What sadist had thought of combining the two?

Every kid on the bus, except one or two irretrievable hackers, shared somewhat in these feelings. Missing a week of summer in British Columbia's Okanagan Valley is something to regret. Cutting the dry interior plateau, it is a series of lakes wedged in a long, narrow scar of the last glaciation, extending from the U.S. border north for over a hundred miles, to about the town of Vernon. The valley, once seen, is not forgotten; it is one of those places that seems to rise from the imagination. In the north its power is the rugged plunge of the land for over seventy miles to Okanagan Lake, and the contrast of sagebrush and Ponderosa pine to the moods of an inland sea; in the south it is the vast contortions of rock between Skaha and Osoyoos Lakes, thrust to the very edge of orchards and vineyards. Everywhere there is a tension, a creative energy of starkness juxtaposed with peace; even the names of the towns – Osoyoos, Penticton, Oyama, Kelowna, Kaleden – catch at this unexpectedness of the land. And on that cloudless blue day in July, 1987, with a capricious little wind darting up Okanagan Lake from the south to toy with the sailboats off Kelowna, there are very few who would not have been sad to leave.

The bus driver was motioning to David, his other hand on the door lever. "Come on aboard, son."

I'm not your son. I'm nobody's son.

"Yeah, Snotball, come on. I got some paper for ya."

He mouthed an obscenity and shoved the duffel bag up the steps. The year before the kid – Alf something – had seen him pick his nose once and wad it up in a little bit of paper, and now he was Snotball.

Above him, in the aisle, an instructor was waiting. The one with the stiff little mustache who always wore tennis shorts. The recreation coordinator, Mr. Bruchard. Rick. Rick The Dick. So gung ho it makes you sick.

"Welcome back, Mr. Ashton. I hope you'll stay with us this year."

He stopped, one foot on the bottom step, a hand on the rail, his body tightening –

The man smiled again. "Stow your gear in the back, David. It's time to get rolling."

Confused, he did nothing; then he quickly made his way past him and down the aisle, not daring to look from the pile of luggage ahead. The bus started forward; he lurched, but wouldn't grab for a seat. Reaching the pile, he hoisted the duffel bag up and pretended to search for something in its pockets. *Hope you'll stay with us! They've got it in for you! All because you took off for one afternoon –*

His mind raced over the events of that day a year ago when, for no reason that seemed adequate now, he had ditched an afternoon canoeing session and wandered into the forest. He saw the place where the trunk of a great pine, gray with years, spiraled out of the rock as if something had twisted it until it snapped; the sun darting in and out of the branches of the fir; and that first uncertain glimpse, in the light of a sudden clearing, of the house –

He looked up. A car going the other way swept with redoubled speed into the distance. Mr. Mahon, the camp director, his round little head pinched and red, shouted accusations. He stood, lips quivering, hating each answer. But in the end they had agreed not to tell Dad –

I wonder if that old guy's still there. I wonder if I would find him mending a shirt, knowing I was watching him, like nothing in between had ever happened –

"Sit down, David."

He turned. The Dick was at the front of the aisle, elbows bent, leaning forward against two seats. Everyone was turning to look, eager stares grinning at the ends of twisted necks. *Why should I when* you're *standing? Can't wait to start turning stomachs with the rah-rah routine?*

"You have to be seated while the bus is in motion. I see a couple of empty places –"

Between your ears? "I don't want to sit."

Rick's camaraderie vanished. He straightened. He was even wearing a little gold neck chain.

"Either you sit or this bus stops."

"– That's fine by me. I don't want to go to your cruddy camp."

In the instant before Rick turned to the driver, David eyed the shocked faces in the aisle. They were gloating with relish. The bus braked; a paralyzing tightness spread from his chest. *They hate me – everyone hates me –*

The thing slowed and started to pull off the highway; at the noise of the tires on the gravel he fought not to panic. The air was prickly, too thick to breathe.

The Dick waited for the bus to come to a dead stop. The kid who called him Snotball gestured at him and, when he'd caught his eye, shoved a finger up a nostril.

Rick's voice rose. "Now, Mr. Ashton, if you'll kindly let us know how long we have to sit here."

"You don't have to sit here at all. Just let me off."

"Sorry, I get paid to take you to camp and teach you a few things and bring you home—"

He snatched at some words, recklessly. "So what do you want, a gold-plated whistle?"

Rick exploded. He advanced down the aisle, shouting. "What I want is for you to keep your rotten attitude to yourself so that those kids who do want to learn something and have some fun can do it! What's your problem? You'd rather do nothing all summer? So would everyone else—I'd rather be at the beach too! You think everybody's against you? I've got news for you—you don't have an enemy on this bus but yourself. And you're in for a rough ride till you see that. So if you want to make me out as a drill sergeant for caring about your safety, go ahead—just let the rest of us get on with life—"

The man was standing directly in front of him; his voice was almost boyish and it filled David with contempt even as he stared at the floor. But he hated, even more, his own smallness.

"Let me off."

"No."

"I'll go straight to the first phone booth—I promise—"

"And James, the butlah, shall pick him up directly," someone ventured.

"You're going straight to the first seat. Here—next to Carla. It's even by the window."

A few loud snickers came from behind and Rick regretted it. But he had to take control.

David glared at the man in hate. "You think I care if it's by the window?"

Rick looked at him, then turned, went back to the front of the bus, and said something to the driver. The machine rolled forward to turn onto the highway. A hot wadded mass rose in David's throat. *You dick. My dad'll get you. I'll run away and he'll sue you out of your shorts—*

The bus lurched onto the pavement. He caught for a seat and saw himself shoving the kid who called him Snotball and the others who were eyeing him in glee face-first through a window—

And then he had swung himself into the seat and was huddled in it, against the metal wall. *My dad will get you. You'll be using your stupid little mustache to wipe your butt—*

The wall darkened. *Why do you make me do this. So I can grow up to be a company vice president and spend my life in meetings?*

The vibrations of the bus shuddered and ebbed against him. At the thought of his father his emotions converged. It was he who made him go to computer camp; yet it was to him that he looked for protection and revenge.

Joseph Ashton was determined to arm and protect his only child. He would have been astonished if anyone had accused him of being dictatorial; he was seeing to it that his son got an edge in school. All boys wanted to loaf in the summer – that had nothing to do with anything –

At first glance he seemed to believe, above all, in wealth and success. He'd attained both; yet in his own mind they were means to a greater end, power. Power to decide his own fate, to not just survive at the mercy of others.

His youth had been very different. Joseph was himself the only son of wealthy parents. He had studied strenuously to please them at a liberal arts college of his choice in California, in the '60s, only to find himself somewhat lost after graduation. His ambition was to be a novelist, or playwright, or filmmaker; he'd expected avenues to open to him and when none did, he returned to Vancouver, found a low-paying job and a cheap apartment, and began writing at night. His parents were dubious, and tried to interest him in law school; he toiled and lay awake in desperate fear of being proven a young fool. Yet with growing excitement he found a story and pursued it, seeking out its substance and laboring to realize it from the myriad of possibilities in which it was held. The result was a pretty good novel; so good that among the rejection slips there was actually a note from a junior editor, with a few encouraging remarks. He revised, and revised again; sent off piles of sample chapters, agonized over covering letters – all with one result, a white envelope as silent and impenetrable as the words it contained. They would not read his book. Unfortunately it did not suit their program, their present requirements. It was not until the last polite little notice had dropped to the floor beside his bed that he wept.

He continued, after a time, to write; but a cold mistrust grew in him. Only schlock got published. Only the crassest, most superficial people succeeded at anything, and they did so with riotous contempt for the sea of fools who believed in hard work and ability. He looked on his classmates who were becoming dentists, lawyers, and engineers with envy and superiority.

He had no idea what to do. A small promotion at his job mattered little to him. This job was with a manufacturer of aluminum windows. He had no interest in the work, and when he received a second promotion he was startled; he hadn't brown-nosed.

He soon forgot to question it, however, because a few people were put under him and he discovered the love of his life: to exercise authority. A reversal took place. The average guy believed not in hard work and ability but in a free ride and coffee breaks. He would mold them to management's expectations; he would demand from them what he demanded of himself. His first zealous attempts at this earned him a black eye.

He learned and adjusted, and soon became adept at asserting his will without appearing tyrannical. He began to rise in the company, and as he did he came to see his new life as a mission. Everywhere decent, honest people were being shafted by suckholers, connection-peddlers, hustlers – and always the victims were told that there was nothing for it, that it was the eternal way of the world. But in one little corner of Dominion Aluminum Ltd., the tables would be turned. There would be pure justice.

Reward and advancement would be based strictly on merit. Employees who became too friendly he eyed with suspicion, and they soon learned to keep their distance. He accepted isolation as the price of his new order. He could be neither liked nor disliked, for no one knew him; but he was respected.

He met his future wife at a fund-raising carnival; she was the palm-reader. Barely twenty and veteran of a disastrous marriage, Elaine Dahl was in search of stability. Born in Singapore to remnants of the colonial aristocracy, she had acquired an appetite for hot foods, horse racing, mahjong, and diluted extracts of Buddhism before being forcibly abducted to Canada as a teenager by her mother (her first marriage was to spite her). She married Joseph to reform herself; his reserved nature was as penitential as the faded Victorian airs of Vancouver and at one point she had her ticket back to Singapore paid. The flight was canceled because of fog.

She stayed, waiting for misery to again get the better of guilt; to her surprise, she discovered that she did not dislike her husband. He was eminently considerate and fair; to the few people with whom he would drop his guard, he could be childishly playful. And, almost without her knowing it, what he might have been touched her imagination.

David was conceived soon after; in the years of his childhood his parents developed in directions that would have seemed impossible to them in their youth. Joseph grew comfortable with the success that had seemed so unattainable and tainted, and success changed him. He was transferred to Kelowna and promoted to vice president; his just, impersonal order seemed secure and his convictions lost their anger and their edge. Why had he been so negative? Had he not risen from laborer to the highest levels of management, without favoritism? He settled into the self that he had chosen; his hair receded and became tinged with gray, his suits were flawless, and in his eyes and his voice one could feel the weight and presence of the company. He wrote nothing. It was the demands of his position; he would take it up again when he retired. In reality he allowed the ache to die, because he had fulfilled himself differently. And the time would come when, if he thought of a hope-crazed young man in a cheap apartment at all, it was as a brief, vain, foolish interlude.

But he remembered enough of that young man's love and pain to fear them.

As he gained authority, he began to transfer some of its premises to his family. It was a subtle process; he was neither very stern with his son nor dictatorial to his wife; he appeared to listen to them; but his will always prevailed – for no other reason, it seemed, than that he believed this to be the natural order of things. Elaine was confused by it; her idea of conjugal injustice was hot-forged in the screaming brawls of her first marriage. This new domination seemed mild, and she learned to tolerate it as a consequence, almost a trapping, of her husband's status. His reserve, too, seemed suited to his position; but he could never turn it off. At the dinner parties, which she loved, he would study his colleagues as they socialized, speaking and laughing just enough that they wouldn't notice; once, according to Constanza, their Filipino housekeeper, he'd even come into the kitchen to take notes. It pained and baffled her that he could not relax around people; but this too she justified by success. Wasn't it lonely at the top?

She became aware, now and then, of dissatisfaction, and reacted sharply. She had security, affection – it was a lie of television and the movies that relationships had to be passionate. How many women, taken in, had ended up in something like her first marriage?

Her hands were strong and creative; she took up making jewelry and in time formed subtle, moonlit things out of jade, and dawn visions of agate. They sold so well through her friends that, with Joseph's grudging consent, she opened a small shop. It was on a busy street; but as soon as one closed the door, one felt a great distance. From somewhere amidst hanging plants, Chinese silk-paintings, and Malaysian tapestries, a clock ticked, slowly; the necklaces were not encased but lay against fragments of driftwood and stone; there was a hint of some sharp fragrance in the air. When David was in kindergarten he spent his afternoons there; it was his and Mother's special place, a labyrinth of curiosities. His young voice, rising unseen from the clutter of plants and furniture, would sometimes strike her in an instant as the cry of a tropical bird in a park she had loved in Singapore. She would seek him out then and hold him, with a closeness that came not to feel strange.

He loved to draw; she set up a desk in a corner of the shop where he would sit with his pencil, his feet not touching the floor, his face knotted in concentration. Joy and sorrow, anger and laughter seemed to well up from his hand. There were many pictures of the shop, and Mother making jewelry. They would work away, far from the rush outside, drawing on each other. He wanted to paint pictures when he grew up.

Young as he was, he remembered the time he announced that to his father – how his father's face went cold and he said nothing. He remembered his fear and confusion, that what he had said was so terribly wrong. Then his father smiled and said, "That would be nice, David," and sent him to bed. He lay still a long time; then he heard his parents arguing. His mother's voice was like the shaking of the pines in a high wind.

At Christmas of the year he turned ten, he got his own computer. At spring break, his parents took him to Disneyland – and came back with integrated software, a program to teach typing, a program to help him with his math, and a graphics processor so that he could draw. In June he got a "B" in math and Joseph, elated, added a high-resolution color monitor and a forty-megabyte hard drive.

But the following year the "B" did not move up to an "A." On the day he brought home the report card his father called him to his study.

David was surprised to see him standing at the window behind his desk.

"Come here, David."

He took a few steps towards the huge oak desk. His father was shadowy against the evening sun. The report card was nowhere in sight.

"No – come here. Come over here."

He hesitated, wanting the desk between them. "– Are you mad about my grades –"

"I want to show you something."

He approached the window. Okanagan Lake came into view, a piercing play of light curving off among the mountains to the north, four hundred feet below their home on Clifton Road.

"Look down there. What do you see?"

David shielded his eyes. "Just the lake—"

"No. At the house that's being built."

He studied it. It was on the other side of a vacant lot. He could look down on the roof. The workmen were putting their tools into a pickup, getting ready to leave. A dog was pacing in the back of the truck, eager to ride. They looked small.

"What do you see?"

His father's voice tensioned him. "Just some men and a dog—"

"They're not men." The gray eyes stared down at him. He started to look away. "Look at me. They're not men. They squander their hours on this earth, half-doing a job that means nothing to them, bemoaning their fate. What animal does that? Even before they die it's like they never lived."

He stood, still and afraid, fixed on the steel-gray depths of his father's being.

"If you do not have a plan for yourself the world will make one for you. And that will be it." The voice grew stranger—harsh yet intimate. "Listen to me, David. In the future—your future—fewer and fewer people are going to count. Incredible advances in technology are coming, that will concentrate power in ways that would have seemed unimaginable just a few years ago. Oh sure, there'll still be democracies and elections—but they will reflect, not make, the real decisions. The common man will enter into those decisions only as a factor, a quantity. The stakes will have grown too high for him to participate.

"With today's microcomputers one top-level manager, without leaving his desk, can access and analyze volumes of information that would have required twenty management personnel strung across three continents in the past. The sons of those twenty guys won't be managers. They'll be lucky to push a broom."

His father's eyes drove down at him. "More and more people are going to be left out, David—left out and left behind. I don't want you to be one of them, as I almost was. It's time you started working harder, started preparing to go after your goals. I'm not saying you have to be a computer expert. But you must acquire the skills early—get an edge. I've registered you in computer camp this summer."

He remembered how he'd stood, mouth open, trying to grasp the magnitude of the disaster –

"It's run by Futuristix Incorporated, a consulting firm out of Vancouver. I've checked them out, they're top-notch, the staff has five Ph.D.'s with experience in everything from chip design to artificial intelligence. The machines are Compaq with Intel 286 CPU's, 18 megahertz clock speed, a little slow but enough to get you going, networked with a printer for every five stations –"

He searched the lake, desperate to find an excuse, an objection. Far to the north, off Okanagan Landing, he caught a glint of something. It was a sailboat, tacking to starboard, the sun striking off the mast –

"– A bit of Quick Basic, but the emphasis on DOS and word-processing concepts leading up to an introduction to integrated software –"

His throat stiffened. He'd flunk. At computer lab at school he took the old disk out and stuck the new disk in and nothing happened. Was it Control-Open Apple-Shift or Control-Reset or Open Apple-Shift-Backspace? The other kids were already done and Mr. Macmillan was patrolling the aisle –

"I won't go."

His father looked at him, kindly. "I know it's a little intimidating, David, but the only way to conquer your fear of something new is to meet the challenge head-on. And when you do you'll find it's never as bad as you thought."

"You don't understand, Dad! I hate that stuff – I can't do it – I'm like a total geek as soon as I sit in front of the screen –"

"Then it's all the more necessary to go. Don't think of school. This is the real thing. Classes are in small groups and I'll arrange for a private tutor –"

"No! I'm not going!" Behind the rigidness of his father's face the lake scattered the remaining sun, unutterably calm. "They'll all be brains and I'll be the only one who doesn't know what he's doing!"

"David, I wouldn't send you if I didn't know you can do it. You're selling yourself short."

He fumbled at the keyboard. Mr. Macmillan came towards him. Fear emptied him and the words shattered. "If the future's going to be so bad I'll just be a reject anyway! How do you expect me to beat guys like Brent Foster – he writes programs for the teachers! Why do you even want me around –"

He turned away. His father's voice shot past him, beating him to the door. "We'll discuss this when you're in a more rational mood."

He was in the hall, wanting to say something back; then the stairs thudded under his feet. Below, in a corner of the living room, his mother stood. He met her eyes, accused her, and ran out of the house.

The other shore was lost in shadow. He zigzagged down the wooden steps and platforms to the swimming pool. To one side of the gate was a path. He took it, bitter that no one called after him, his feet striking the dusty indentations among the rocks and weeds.

The path came to an abrupt drop. He stared at the lake, hating how it went on despite him. He'd never be good enough. If he got a "B" in math then the next year it would have to be an "A." If by some miracle he got the "A," then he'd have to be a computer whiz. Why couldn't they give up and leave him alone?

You'll be lucky to push a broom. The lake blurred, the last light trembling. *Just because you're vice president in charge of production you think you know everything and everyone else is a dwip. You think it'd make the headlines if you were ever wrong!*

We'll discuss this when you're in a more rational mood—

He snatched up a rock and threw it at a pine below. It smashed into the trunk, leaving a naked wound. *I hate you! I hate your stupid swimming pool and your stupid Mercedes! I hate your guts!*

He dropped to the edge. His hand tore clumps of moss from the rock. Tears struck the pockets of dirt where they'd grown. Twilight wrapped the lake, darkness stealing from its great depths.

—There was a motion in the corner of his eye. He turned and stared down into the monotone of the street.

It was by the house that was being built. At first he saw nothing; then something moved against the softened angles. A shape wandered, huddled, around the barren yard, stooped over as if searching the ground. Twice it stopped and picked something up, with a slow, satisfied motion.

Recognition shot through him. It was that old guy who collected pop cans. He'd seen him before.

For a moment he was unsure; then the sight maddened him. *That's what* you *think I am! Just because I'm not good at the things* you *want me to be good at!*

His hand found a rock. The man's presence grew perverse, as if his father had arranged for him to be there, had known in advance that he would run from the room, had known even the path he would take. There, that's what'll become of you if you don't go to computer camp. A bum, a nobody, a loser, a zero.

If you do not have a plan for yourself the world will make one for you. And that will be it.

Something pushed at his throat. He fought it, his fingers tightening on the rock, but it came. *I'm sorry I'm just a stupid kid but why can't I be good enough why couldn't I be good enough just for one day—*

It hurtled into the twilight. There was nothing, then a thud. The rock clattered down the roof.

"Hey you!" The outline of the man faced him. His chest constricted. "What's the big idea?"

He couldn't think. He stood on the edge, his mind blank, poised to run, and yet at the same time, somewhere, imagining that he could tell him—

"How 'bout if I come up there and skin your hide? Then maybe you won't go chuckin' rocks at people who ain't done you no harm!"

The shape started up the slope. He turned and ran, stumbling up the path, the lights of his father's house blurring like rain.

Futuristix Incorporated operated its summer computer camp at Silver Lake Forestry Centre, on the road to the open pit copper mine above Peachland. The bus, having crossed Okanagan Lake on Kelowna's floating bridge, shuddered up the hill and past the scattered communities and orchards of the west side, towards the turnoff from Highway 97. On this stretch the highway is four lanes, shrill and utilitarian, intent on speeding past the pine-covered volcanic mountains with as little bother as possible; but after it leaves Westbank, descends into the valley of Powers Creek, and climbs past the Gorman Brothers sawmill, it enters a deep cut through the earth. For a time you are enclosed in masses of rock and shadow; then the lake reappears and the road plunges towards it, towards the great bend at Rattlesnake Island and the uninhabited mountains on the other side.

David stared, all of it hard and distant, dreading the moment the bus would turn off. They crossed a concrete bridge with a sign that said "Trepanier Creek" and entered Peachland. The town is right on the lake; and it is there, just as the highway touches the shore, that the road to the

Brenda Mine begins its long climb out of the valley. It's a refreshing drive after the fury of the highway, winding up through the gardens and flowers and hobby orchards of the town, the vast bend in the lake reforming below; but the grinding gears and stench of diesel punctuated David's sense that it was over. He would go to camp. Within minutes of the bus pulling up at the dead end, everyone would know of his humiliation. The Dick would pass the word. At the stuffy orientation session the instructors would eye him. Kids would gather in groups in corners of the bunkhouse, talking in undertones, and stop and stare when he came in . . .

His fist clenched. A week! He'd never make it.

Far below the highway wound against the steep slopes towards Summerland. He thought of following it, on and on. No one would know him, no one would bother him. He would find out what to do with his life without being told.

The bus hit the end of the pavement. The lake and the highway were gone and there was only the straining of the machine up through the dry canyon of Peachland Creek, a torpid wake of dust and the sun slanting down. The children were almost silent.

The Dick sensed his moment. He stood, tanned arms braced against the washboard jolts, his young face perennially enthused. "Listen up, people! We're going to be there soon. I want to take a moment to tell you about some of the recreational activities we've got lined up. Those of you who were with us last year know that camp's not all computers. We expect you to work hard and learn, but we also want you to have fun. Silver Lake has a soccer and baseball field, an obstacle course, miles of trails, and a sandy beach. And, contrary to what you may have heard" – he grinned – "it's not too cold to go in, right?"

Kids groaned. Dust rose past the windows. The Dick, relishing it, was about to go on when a voice commented, "Right mate, it's just tight on your balls."

Carla giggled. David recognized who said it. Jeff something. Most people thought he was Cool, especially himself. They'd even think he was Cool doing garbage duty.

But to David's shock, The Dick only gave him the evil eye, and went on. The outrage stuck in his throat. *I'm a little slow to sit down and I get crapped on in front of everyone, and* he *can say something like that.*

"Regular play in soccer is three games. Standings will determine the draw for the Jamboree, which is on the afternoon of the last day. Last year the Zerks beat the Zombies on a penalty shot in the last minute."

"And that's the last we want to hear of it," Jeff added.

The Dick tightened and shifted his position against the seats; but the next moment he was smiling. "You were on the Zombies, weren't you, Jeff?"

"Uh, was I?"

"Before the game you made up a chant and went around saying it. To the whole camp. I remember it —

> We Zombies aren't alive
> So we don't take no jive
> We're awesomely berserk
> The Zerks are just plain jerks
> Winning's not the thing
> It's how you play the game
> So we'll kick their bloody cans
> With the dead meat of their fans."

Jeff laughed. "Hey man, no fair."

The Dick smiled, a smile of the lips only. He began going over the rules for checking out equipment. The bus shuddered towards a piece of blue sky pasted above the next curve in the road; dust drifted around the curve below without settling.

David, huddled against the jolts, stared at The Dick in hatred. *Yeah, you would connect with that guy. You both think you're Joe Cool. Anyone who kisses up to you's got it made.*

Suddenly he felt cold, hollow. *Dead meat. That was meant for you. He's got it in for you.*

He fought away from it. It couldn't be like that. He was an instructor. He was supposed to be fair. *My dad will—*

There was no hope. The force of it bent his head to the black vinyl floor. Ancient pieces of gum and obscure filth bulged in the cracks. Even if The Dick couldn't rig things with the computer guys, he'd flunk. He'd flunk because there had to be losers and they were guys like him, guys who were Not Cool, who couldn't make jokes with The Dick and get away with anything, grinning. Guys who sweated and struggled and needed extra help and flunked anyway, while the Cool Ones faked it and treated everything really casual and passed.

He saw Jeff and the kid who called him Snotball grinning at him. Hey man, having a ball with your snot?

– Their heads were rammed between stakes. An instrument like a push broom was dipped in a bucket of sewage or vomit and shoved into their screaming faces, jabbed into their mouths and eyes and nostrils until they choked and bled –

His head twisted from side to side. The grooves in the floor swayed and dissolved into black. *Let me out. I just want out–*

A timid little noise came. Are you all right? Are you sick?

It was the girl next to him. She'd call The Dick. *They'll say you're a spazz. A mental misfit of a snot-eating spazz–*

He forced his head up. Without looking at Carla, he mumbled that he was OK. Then he fell back against the seat and turned to the window. He felt weak, shaky.

The jolts had stopped. They were back on a paved road.

He fixed his eyes on the mountains. Everything looked like it was made of metal, even the sky. If only there was a way to break through it – to just be allowed to live –

There is one thing. You could run away.

He saw himself climbing through the forest, to the cabin of the old man. He had seen it so many times that the fragments of memory, like seed husks in the darkness of the earth, had opened and become lost in a creation.

A soft mountain wind would just stir the tops of the pines. He would wander slowly up through their great trunks, his steps almost silent against the floor of the forest. Nothing human – no encrusted wrappings, no Styrofoam coffins of food – would litter his way. His path would be almost imperceptible – a mere thinning of the pine needles between the trees.

He strained to go deeper into the memory, to free himself from everything connected with the camp. He knew that the house was not locked in wilderness – that it was, in fact, only a hundred meters or so from the road; that he barely had to go through the forest at all but could follow the power line. But he needed to imagine it as a place where the outrage of the camp could never reach.

The old man, Mr. Black, would remember him, of course. He might even be expecting him. He would not be surprised, at any rate, to see him staring out from the undergrowth at the edge of the clearing.

It was necessary to do that. You couldn't just climb the steps and knock on the door. Mr. Black would be sitting on the porch, like he was the first time, doing some bit of work. He would pretend, again, not to notice him – but this time he, David, would smile and the old guy would say, "So it's you again, young fellow," or something like that.

The first time had been nervous. He'd come upon the clearing suddenly, and approached to its edge before he'd seen the old man in the shade of the porch. He couldn't back away and go around the place; the guy would hear him. He'd yell for him to get out, screech that he was trespassing.

He remembered thinking that he could say he was lost. But then he might make a big deal of it, take him back to the camp –

He stood a long time, watching, afraid to try to retreat. The guy was bent over something, working with repeated concentrated motions. He stopped now and then and rubbed his eyes.

At last he started to back away, touching his foot behind him, feeling for quiet. He was fully back into the shadows and ready to turn when the old man said, without looking up, "You sure weren't no trouble."

An impulse shot through him to run; but he didn't. He stood, staring at the shape under the porch, aware of his own breathing.

"Most people who come around here are just a nuisance. Hunters. Bill collectors. Dirt bikers. They make a lot of noise and leave. I run 'em off if I'm up to it, but more of them just come. What's your name?"

". . . David." The word sounded strange.

"David, uh?" He seemed to think about it, the thing he was working on folded in his lap. Then he laid it aside and stood. "I'm Harold Black. I live here with my dog and cat. We get along fine."

He didn't know what to say. He could only stare, uncomfortably, at the man's thinness. His pants were cinched and gathered at the belt. His face was still in shadow.

"I don't dislike no one. But the only people who come out here do it to make noise and cause trouble. In the summer they go up to Wilson Lake. I hear 'em screamin' at night, driving around piss-drunk, their faces blotched and red, the girls with their tits hanging out in the headlights. I felled a dead pine across the track once but they got chain saws and a winch. A couple of years back I had my fence broke down for firewood." The voice halted. "Before that I carved my name on a slab of yellow pine and hung it out by the road, all sanded and varnished. It said 'Welcome, Harold Black.' They left it alone for two whole weeks, then it got spray-painted. I sanded it down and revarnished it. They came back and hacked it to pieces."

He stepped forward, into the sun. His eyes struck David; they were deep blue, soft in leathered skin, not rough like his voice. He had a stiff mustache and stood painfully straight. "My dog don't bark so I got tin cans on the gate. I could carry on about it but it don't do no good. What brings you out here? You must be from that camp, Silver Lake, eh?"

". . . Yeah."

"You runnin' away, or you just decided to break out from the herd, have some time to yourself?"

He quickened. "They went canoeing. I'm tired of always being in a group, always being ordered around."

"Well I don't blame you about that. I see 'em marchin' along the trails sometimes, and some loudmouth stoppin' them to yak about this sort of tree and that, and how it profligates itself, and what sort of beetles and moths want to kill it, and I suppose those kids tromp home with a head full of facts. But they ain't learned nothing from the forest."

The old man took a step down from the porch. "Yeah, I've seen 'em lots of times. But they've never seen me." He peered at David. "Would you like to sit awhile? I'm done mending that shirt. I got up this morning and couldn't unbutton it; it was like my fingers weren't even attached to me. So I got mad and damn if I didn't rip the blasted thing off."

David hesitated. The man fascinated him and made him nervous. He was like no one he knew.

No. He'd turn out to be just another old person, carrying on endlessly about his troubles. Why sit and listen to it?

". . . I think I'd better be getting back."

"I got lemonade – and it's not that stuff they sell frozen in cardboard."

"Thanks, but I've really got to be going."

The man looked as though he were about to say something, but stopped. He stared at David for an instant in a way he couldn't understand; then, in a soft voice, he said, "Well, suit yourself," and turned and stepped back up the porch. He picked up the shirt and stood, bent over, searching for the needle and thread.

David told himself to go; but he only stood, looking out from the shadows at the man and the house in the sunlit clearing. Something was wrong. It had felt so solemn and exciting running off from the camp, the solitude of the forest closing around him; it had to come to something, something besides sneaking back to the bunkhouse.

He stepped to the edge of the clearing. The sun pressed gently on his face.

"Mr. Black?"

The man looked up.

". . . I guess I can stay awhile."

He waded through the dry grass towards the house. It was one of those old ranch houses that you see now and then in the valley, with walls of weathered boards, a steep roof, and a covered porch along the front. It was not particularly neat or run-down but to David it was like shacks he had seen from the highway.

Mr. Black pulled a chair across the porch. As David approached a beautiful dog, a golden retriever, lazily rose to his feet and sauntered down the steps to meet him.

"Jimmy's more accepting of strangers. I guess it's because he's a better judge of character. He knows what they've got on their minds before they open the gate. He don't bark, like I said, but if he doesn't like someone he'll come and tell me."

David held out his hand and let the dog sniff him.

"Come on up. I'll get us some lemonade."

He opened a screen door and vanished, an angular motion, into the dimness of the house.

David stared around the porch. A gray cat hung off the edge of a table, delicately washing a forepaw. David stepped towards her and noticed that her tail brushed the dogeared corner of an old book or pamphlet. He read the cover: "*Let the Dead Bury their Dead,*" by "Joseph Hutenbrunner, B.A., D.D." Beside it were others: *He Will Burn Up the Chaff with Unquenchable Fire*, and *The Trials of the Righteous in the Last Days*.

The screen door squeaked behind him; he turned, quickly. Mr. Black held out a plastic cup. His eyes took in David and the table. "Pretty meaty reading, eh? My brother sends me those from Calgary. They're real sharp, those preachers, they know what's goin' on, but by the time I'm done readin' I'm near sick at how godless and rotten the world's become."

David took the cup. A glossy mass of pulp floated on top. Mr. Black motioned towards the chair he had drawn up. Jimmy came back up the steps and lay down under the table, directly beneath the cat.

Mr. Black folded his long body down into his chair. It was stiff, wooden, straight-backed. Lemonade slopped over the edge of his cup. "Yeah, whoever said this world's goin' to the dogs had the right idea but the wrong animal. The dogs are doing just fine. It's man that's sick. Sick to death."

David stared down, embarrassed, at the floor of the porch. He should've left. Now he would have to sit and listen, maybe for hours –

"You don't believe me, do ya? That's 'cause you're young. When you grow up you'll find out."

He stiffened. *He's just like Dad. He thinks kids are idiots.*

"Hell, Vancouver's overrun with queers and drug addicts. You can get murdered for no reason at all and the undertaker will cheat your widow on the coffin. There's nothing done that's not done for a buck and the politicians just laugh, they lie right into our goddamn faces. Kids sue their own mom and dad. Old folks get beat up in broad daylight and nobody stops to help them. People drive like the devil's got into them –"

David started to drink his lemonade; at the first taste his face drew back from a sourness so sharp it stung. It was all he could do not to spit it out. He struggled to swallow, gawking at the old man, unable to talk.

"What's the matter? You all right?"

He forced some of it down, the sourness pinching his eyes shut. "– No sugar!"

"Huh? I thought I put some in. I guess I didn't. I'll go get it."

Mr. Black pushed himself up from the chair and stalked into the house. David rushed to the porch railing and spat. Jimmy's ears shot up and the cat tensed to jump. He swallowed, trying to suck the citric taste from his mouth. At least it was an excuse to leave –

The screen door shrieked open and Mr. Black stood over him with a ceramic canister in the form of a skunk. "Here, hold your glass up. I like my lemonade tart, like a good apple, but I know you kids are fiends on this stuff. Drat, I forgot a spoon. Well, just hold it up, we'll get it." He tilted the canister. It was shaking.

"I think I'd rather have some water, please –"

"Aw, come on now, I promised you some lemonade, better'n that stuff in the store, and I want you to have it. It's no big deal, we'll sugar it up, just put your glass under the rim here –"

David held out the cup. Mr. Black moved the canister over it. The skunk smiled up at them, coyly. "Easy does it now. I'm stiff after that sewin'. Let me tell ya, getting old's no fun. You lie awake aching at night, you wake up hurting and raw and you see all these ads saying you ought to be jogging and bicycling and playing tennis and climbing Mt. Everest and you feel like you're nothing. Like it serves you right. Some mornings I sit on my bed and think how I'm just taking up space –"

"Mr. Black, stop!" The canister had been shaking with nothing coming out; suddenly a big lump of sugar broke from the rim and cascaded into the cup. Mr. Black didn't notice or didn't think it was enough, and an avalanche followed.

"What are you doing!"

"Whoa – the damn thing's hard to stop –"

Sugar began pyramiding like an hourglass in the bottom of the cup and a ring formed on the porch floor. Jimmy leaped up and licked; the cat, in disdain, continued to wash.

"That's way too much!"

Finally Mr. Black raised the rim high enough. The skunk trembled. The old man stood there, clutching the canister like an animal that had gotten out of control. David looked up at him in amazement.

"Aren't you going to drink it?"

"It's half sugar!"

"Well taste it and see. First you're complainin' about how it's too sour – I know you kids are hooked on this stuff –"

He hesitated. "Could I maybe just have a glass of water?"

The old man didn't say anything; he stared at the cup in anger, and defeat. Suddenly, he turned away, towards the screen. "Sure. It's not fit for nothing. Throw the goddamn mess out." He started through the door.

"No – wait – it's OK –" David raised the cup, to swallow it in one shot. The sugar hadn't mixed and the lemon seared his lips, but he kept on, to the inevitable moment when the white mountain at the bottom slid against his mouth and the sensation turned sickeningly sweet. He gulped at the sugar, hoping Mr. Black wouldn't see, and wondering, remotely, how the lemonade had become so important, as if it would decide whether they could like each other –

He forced the cup back. Everything was sugar.

He couldn't swallow it all. His eyes opened.

Suddenly he realized that Mr. Black was watching him through the screen. He looked distant, shadowy, like someone he had met a long time ago, but couldn't remember.

The man stepped onto the porch. His anger was gone. He reached out, took the cup from David's hand, and stared into it. Then he looked at the boy, a ring of white ooze around his mouth. His face broke out into a sheepish grin. "Lord, I guess you do need a glass of water. Come on in here." But he didn't move; he only stood there. His voice grew light, agitated; he might have been about to laugh or cry. "I'm sorry, boy – I was all worked up – all that talk about politicians and undertakers and how lousy things are . . . My fingers are stiff, stiff from that sewin' . . . I'm real sorry –"

"It's OK."

"Hell, I was a diesel mechanic, I worked a twelve-hour shift, middle of winter, Mica Dam, then played cards half the night. I don't know what's happened. I'm a goddamn good-for-nothing old man."

David struggled to grasp it. He didn't say it, like an adult would, for sympathy.

The voice strained on. "It's real funny. You don't know how or when. It just creeps up. Or why. That's the strangest one of all. There ain't no why."

He was silent a moment; then, abruptly, he motioned David towards the door. "Come on in. I'll get you that water."

He remembered being a little afraid as he stepped past the man into the darkness of the house; yet he knew, then, that Mr. Black wouldn't hurt him. He found himself in a large room, lit only by cracks around the curtains, somber masses of furniture and a huge stone fireplace evolving out the dark.

"– Why is everything closed up?"

The voice moved past him, dimly formed. "Oh, that's just to keep the place cooler."

Water began to run in a sink; as David's eyes adjusted he saw that the kitchen was in a corner of the room. A wood stove stood in the middle, surrounded by heavy wooden chairs and a table, joined out of pine. The fireplace was of granite boulders, set on a slight incline and capped by a richly varnished mantle. The place looked neat, like a hideout in a movie.

Mr. Black handed him a cup and he drank. The water was as cold as if it had been scooped from a stream of melting snow. He swallowed deeply and wiped the sugar from his mouth.

"Yeah, it gets warm down here in the summer. I usually go to my summer camp up on Mt. Clements. I don't suppose it's too much higher, but you get a breeze coming down the valley –"

David finished the cup. "You go to a summer camp?"

The old man laughed. "No, son. Not like yours. It's a place I built in the bush. I guess you could call it a shack. But I like 'camp' better – because that's what I do. I go up there to camp out, get away from the idiots who come tearin' around here in the summer. Oh, it's not much; but it's all I need. Plenty of food, a table and chair, and a bed. In the evening I sit and look at Trepanier Creek way down below there. The trees are mostly in the way but there's one or two spots where the sun just catches the rocks of the streambed. I sit with Jimmy till the valley bottom gets dark, and the water turns to cold polished silver, going on forever. I like it up there."

"Are you going there this summer?"

There was a stillness. The form of the man seemed to contract. He felt afraid to ask again.

"– No. I don't think so."

He had wanted to ask why but hadn't, sensing some reason he shouldn't know.

Now, a year later, it was obvious. The guy was too old.

– The bus slowed, almost to a stop, and turned; he caught himself; a rough dirt road jarred everyone from side to side. For an instant he stared around, lost; then the sick depression came over him, as if it had never left. They were turning off to the camp. A few minutes and he would be in hell. The Dick would read out which bunkhouse they were assigned to and they would have fifteen minutes to tromp up to it and dump their stuff on the pee-stained mattresses and report to the lodge. At 15:00 the bell would go and the instructors would close the doors to the mess hall. And that would be it. One hundred fifty miserable kids shoved together on the benches, and when they were dead quiet Mr. Mahon would march to the front and welcome them in his fake voice.

Run away. You could run away. The words played in his mind, as if they really didn't mean it, but comforted him anyway. Mr. Black would hide him. There'd be fires at night in the big stone fireplace, Jimmy asleep on the rug and the cat purring, and they'd play checkers and dominoes and roast marshmallows, and Mr. Black would talk about all the neat things he had done, about the big diesel trucks at the Mica Dam –

The bus struck a deep rut and swayed out of it, undergrowth scraping its sides. *Idiot. Dad would kill you. You'd have to go back sometime.*

No. He wouldn't kill you. He'd call you into his study, and Mom would be crying downstairs, and he would be sitting behind his big oak desk, and first he'd make you walk up to it, and then he'd make you look at him, and he'd wait, wait until you were just starting to cry, and then he'd say, in that voice not exactly like a judge's and not loud, "David, words cannot express how deeply you've disappointed us—" And then the voice would come like through a storm, and he'd babble that he was sorry, that he would never do it again, not ever again, and still the calm sad all-knowing words would come—

—No. And he wouldn't stand in front of Mr. Mahon again either.

Then there is only one other thing. To run away—and not come back.

The jolts stopped. Ahead was the bar across the road and the parking lot, ringed with tall, scrawny pines. At first sight of it he struggled at the keyboard, afraid to ask for any more help, the kid next to him grinning in contempt. Invalid path or filename. Bad argument type. Syntax error. Escape. Control-C. Escape.

The bus pulled up behind another. Kids were crowded around the door and other kids were handing their things down to them. Some of them were even laughing.

The Dick stood, radiant at the chance to give orders. "Welcome to Silver Lake. When you've got your stuff I'll tell you which bunkhouse you're assigned to. In about half an hour a bell will go. That's your signal to report to the mess hall for—no, not food—orientation! For those of you who are new with us, the mess hall's in the lodge, the big two-storey building overlooking the lake—"

Kids stood and crowded to the back to get their bags. He turned away to the window.

—Mr. Black stood at the foot of the steps, shielding his eyes from the sun, the dog at his side, panting gently, golden. He hadn't said much when he'd told him that he had to go; but after he'd said goodby and started across the clearing, he'd called out, "You come back anytime— anytime." He'd turned and waved, and as he did an image of the man caught in his mind, standing thin and straight, as if his body by choice took less than what it needed from the earth—

"Come on people, stop shoving. There's plenty of time. Point to which one's yours and they'll pass it back to you—"

Come back anytime. Maybe he could help. If you went there and explained —maybe he would phone Dad. Maybe Dad would listen to another adult—

He strained to remember if he had seen a phone, but couldn't. The jostling and noise in the aisle scraped him. *Stupid creeps—can't wait to unroll your little Ghostbuster sleeping bags and start kissing up to your bunk captains?*

He pressed his head down against the glass, willing The Dick to leave him alone, expecting any second to hear, "Everybody out—David, that means you—"

His eyes shut. He saw the clearing and the house, dreamy in the late afternoon sun. He stood, knee-high in the dry grass, facing the porch. "Hello! Mr. Black! It's me, David!" He caught the silence, and listened. The screen door—

What makes you think he'll even remember you? Old people can't remember things for a week or even a day. It's been a year—

No! He will remember! He will!

No he won't.

His hand shoved the seat in front—

Everybody out!

His eyes opened, his fingers digging into the seat. *Shut up! Shut up, you butthole—*

He stared around in astonishment. The bus was empty.

Mr. Radcliffe peeled his collar away from his neck. Twenty-four kids in three rows peered at him from behind their terminals. Some were intent, some were bored, some were bewildered. "Now we come to the meat of the program. The principal, you'll recall, doesn't like the idea of Hot Dog Friday. He knows that the students must sell 80 hot dogs to break even on that item. He's decided, therefore, that the event will be canceled if less than 80 hot dogs are sold. Let's look at the next three lines and see how they test the assumption, that this figure of 80 hot dogs is a reliable indicator of the success of the sale:

```
230 IF Q1<80 AND R<M THEN GOSUB 1000
240 IF Q1>=80 THEN GOSUB 2000
250 IF R<=M THEN PRINT "NET PROFIT WAS $"; M-R; ".":
    IF R>M THEN PRINT "NET LOSS WAS $"; R-M; "."
```

"Can anyone tell me the purpose of the first subroutine?"

David tensed as the man's eyes moved along his row. They went past Michael of course and then there were only two more before Jeff and himself.

It wasn't true that the back row was the best. And it wasn't true, either, that you could just hide behind your monitor. They'd zero in on anyone who was trying not to be seen. Your best chance was to look like you might know the answer, but wouldn't be very good at explaining . . .

"Yes, Rebecca."

"It's if you sold less than 80 hot dogs, and want to know how much you made on each thing?"

"That's part of it, but there are _two_ conditions. Q1 must be less than 80 and R must be less than M. We just calculated R in the FOR-NEXT loop starting at 200, it's the total wholesale cost of all the items. M is our total gross profit. So we GOSUB 1000 if we sold less than 80 hot dogs, but still made money. Now, what happens when we get there?

David stared at the lines following 1000. They were more of those FOR-NEXT loops, one inside another. Last year Jeff had made a joke about them. Swenson had caught him not paying attention and snapped, "Perhaps you'd like to explain what a FOR-NEXT loop is – Jeff."

He'd shot his head up, pretending to be startled. "A FOR-NEXT loop? Oh – uh, that's just a little prayer."

"What?"

"Yeah, uh, it goes in a loop like this: 'For God's sake don't pick me next . . . For God's sake don't pick me next . . .'"

He stole a glance to the side. It must be neat to have guts like that. But he didn't even get in trouble, really. They didn't hold it against him. They made him a bunk captain. *He can make perverted jokes on the bus and be a bunk captain. But if I had said that –*

"David?"

His name fell through him. He looked up, his mind blank.

"Care to take a stab at it?"

There was a muffled snicker.

He stared at the sweat stains around the armpits of the man's shirt.

"How about line 1150? PRINT "AMOUNT MADE ON "; N$; " WAS "; (Q*P-W/Q1*P1-W1)*(-100); "PERCENT OF LOSS ON HOT DOGS." Print statements give it away every time, right?"

The man smiled at him. *You think it's funny? Give what away? Give what away? I'm supposed to understand this?*

"OK. What we're doing is sorting out those items we made money on, taking each of those profits, and expressing it as a percentage of the amount we lost on the hot dogs. That way, when the principal says, 'You didn't sell 80 hot dogs,' we can answer, 'No, but we recovered 45% of our loss on the milk, 87% on the chips, and 136% on the ice cream.' Get it?"

He stared at the man bitterly; he was talking to everyone.

They don't give you a chance. They stop just long enough to show everyone you don't know.

Radcliffe picked up a piece of chalk, but didn't draw anything. "It's tough getting back, isn't it? This is not a hard program. It looks hard, because it has a lot of variables in it. And because there are a lot of variables, we need devices like arrays and FOR-NEXT loops to efficiently process the information. Can you imagine what a mess this thing would be if we had a different variable for each item – if the quantity of hot dogs was H, chips C, milk K, ice cream E, and so on? Instead we have an array with one variable, Q, representing logically related data that can be processed sequentially in a FOR-NEXT loop. That's what I want you to get out of this, not the arithmetic."

David shoved his hand across the keyboard. *If that's not what you wanted, why did you ask?*

It's tough getting back.

He's heard. He's been laughing about you with The Dick. They slurp coffee and laugh about you.

"Let's look at the second subroutine. We branch there if Q1>=80 – that is, if we sold 80 hot dogs or more. It has the same sequence of nested FOR-NEXT loops as the first: FOR Q=1 TO S: FOR P=1 TO S; FOR W=1 TO S. We're taking the same data, the quantity sold, price, and wholesale cost of each item, and processing it differently . . ."

The voice drifted off beyond the rows of keys. Shiny from the sweat of his hands, they glared at him in their insane sequence. *Nobody wants you here. You're just a nuisance. You'll never get anywhere and everyone knows it –*

Something touched him. He jerked away from it, turning to look.

Jeff was holding a folded piece of paper out to him, offering it to him with a grin.

He took it, then wished he hadn't. *It's about you. It's one of his perverted jokes.*

I'll kill you –

He unfolded it and read, warily:

>   970 DO SUBROUTINES LEAVE YOU SOBBING?
>   980 DO ARRAYS CAUSE YOU DISMAY?
>   990 JUST INTERFACE YOUR BUTT WITH A GREENIE
>   1000 AND OUTPUT YOUR TROUBLES AWAY!
>   ON A SCALE OF 1 TO 10 I RATE THIS POEM A –

The paper crumpled in his fist. He glared at Jeff in hate and turned away, the lines on the monitor blurring past him in amber madness. *Leave me alone! Is it my fault I can't understand this stuff? Is it my fault I'm forced to be here? Leave me alone or I'll –*

– The thing was shoved into the bucket to recoat it and then lifted, thick and dripping –

– *No! Just leave me alone!*

"Come on, guys. Look carefully at lines 230 and 240. There's a condition for which we haven't tested. What is it?"

The voice jarred him. He saw himself stumble for the door –

"We've tested for having sold less than 80 hot dogs, and for having sold 80 hot dogs or more. What's wrong with the program? Any ideas – Jeff?"

Jeff studied his screen. "What's wrong with it? It's . . . uh . . . unfair to vegetarians."

The room exploded in laughter. Even Radcliffe leaned the hand with the chalk up against the blackboard and laughed, shaking his head. But despite this, and the envious grins on all the faces turned towards him, Jeff stayed deadpan.

Radcliffe waited for the uproar to subside, then looked intently at Jeff, smiling. "Very true. What else?"

"Well . . . uh . . . what happens if Q1 is less than 80 but R is greater than or equal to M?"

Radcliffe rapped the chalk on the blackboard. "That's it! If we sold less than 80 hot dogs <u>and</u> lost money, we don't branch to either subroutine. All we get is a statement of the net loss. And that's too bad. Can anyone tell me why?"

Rebecca put up her hand. "Because if we looked at where we lost the money, we might find that the hot dogs weren't really the problem?"

"Exactly. And that brings us to your homework assignment for tomorrow – to find the simplest way to do that. That's always what we're after – the most efficient, economical way to get the results we want. I'll give you a hint – you don't have to write a new subroutine." He put the chalk down. "This sheet explains the assignment. Take a good stab at it. Getting back into programming's not as tough as it feels, you just have to stimulate the nerve endings. See you tomorrow."

All around him kids turned off their machines and gathered up their stuff. He sat, ignoring them, his eyes fixed on the screen, the amber lines blurring and coming back into focus. It would be worse than last year. *You just have to stimulate the nerve endings*! That's like saying you already know it –

He would fail. And the Cool Ones would hover around him, drawn to the spectacle, watching and relishing it day after endless day –

DO SUBROUTINES LEAVE YOU SOBBING? DO ARRAYS –

His hand hacked at the switch. The screen went dead.

Mornings were classes and labs, afternoons were sports and recreation. The schedule for the first full day matched David's bunkhouse – No. 7 –

up against No. 5 in soccer. Jeff, as bunk captain of No. 7, had forced everyone to agree to his name for the team. The Zorgs. He said it was from a really cool arcade game called Blood Alley. The Zorgs were lizards who came out of trap doors in a warehouse and tried to spray you with dioxins. If you didn't jump out of the way you turned into a lizard too and they ate you. While you were being eaten your eyes popped out and blood squirted from the holes.

One kid said it was dumb, just like the Zombies, but nobody listened to him.

The soccer field was north along the shore of the lake from the camp, and separated from it by a wooded area. At the end of the game David walked slowly towards the edge of the trees, his T-shirt clinging to his back and stomach. The Zorgs had won, and he had scored a goal. And not a garbage goal either, but a hard rising shot to the far corner –

Everyone had cheered and crowded around him. He'd felt like he was lifted off the ground. When he'd come off the field, even The Dick had said, "Way to go, David," and smiled at him. Why had he done that?

The sun played on the lake, a texture of aching light. Ahead the leaves of the aspen stirred, fragile against the mass of pines. Maybe The Dick wasn't so bad. Maybe if he could get some help everything would be OK –

"Hey, that was a wicked shot. You oughta turn pro." He glanced back cautiously. It was Paul. He was all right.

He smiled a little. Paul jogged past him, towards the path into the trees.

He started to call out but didn't. His steps slowed as the words rubbed him. *You oughta turn pro.*

For scoring one lousy goal? He said it to put you down. So you don't think you're something.

At the edge of the forest the path went down, into a little ravine. He stopped, debating what Paul had meant, trying to recall just how he'd said it.

The undergrowth was still and hot. Patches of light lay on the trodden ground and on the thicket. Voices sounded through the trees, idle and happy, rich with the contentment of a summer afternoon.

A strange idea came over him. *Suppose he did mean it as a putdown. What about it? You still scored the goal. Does it matter so much what other people think – if you've done something, and you feel good about it?*

He stood lost in the strangeness of it. He scored a goal. Alone in the middle of the lake, a canoe glided. On the far shore the tall trees sought the sun.

"What are you trying to do, burn a hole in the goalie's gloves?"

It was Jeff. He drew in, rushing to defend himself, everything swept back to its distance. He waited for him to come up. He was sporting a soccer ball.

Jeff grinned. "Well?"

David faced him coldly. "The goalie wasn't wearing gloves."

"He would've, if he'd known we had someone who could drill it like that."

He looked away, unsure how to react, afraid to give him an opening.

"I'm going to move Brent to center. Can you do that from the other wing?"

"I don't know."

"Well if you can it would sure give us a powerhouse line – you, Brent, and Roger –"

"Look – I scored one goal – OK?" He made as if to go.

"Wait a minute! What's eating you – is it that note I passed you – that dumb poem?"

David only looked at him.

Jeff laughed. "Hey man, you gotta lighten up! That was just a joke. In Radcliffe's class you have to do something or you'll die of terminal BOREDOM. I wasn't trying to haze you."

He stared at the ground, unsure. The path was pounded smooth, worn to bare dirt. Suddenly he looked up. "It's not a joke to me. I hate that stuff! They go too fast and they don't explain! I'm going to flunk and my dad's gonna kill me." His voice stumbled. "I hate this place! You're a bunch of showoffs and nerds!"

He turned and started down into the ravine, his body taut at what Jeff might say. A voice broke through the blunt rhythm of his steps. "You want some help?"

He stopped. It wasn't Jeff's usual tone. As he turned a thought came, that he did not really want to pass . . .

"What sort of help?"

"Programming, DOS, database – whatever you want."

"You know it all?"

Jeff ambled towards him. "Boy, you don't make it easy, do you?"

He didn't answer. *If you pass Dad will say he was right all along. That all your pleading and arguing not to go was crap.*

But to flunk. To understand less with each lesson, and so to be questioned more. To be sent for special assistance. To do different stuff than the rest of the class, hunched before your screen to try to keep them from seeing—

He looked on, confused, as Jeff approached.

"I wouldn't mind helping you. We could do it after supper. Besides, I don't think you're so bad off. You've just got to document your program more, make a chart of it, keep track of the variables."

Jeff stopped in front of him, spinning the soccer ball on the tips of two fingers. "A couple of sessions and you'll be right in there with the rest of us nerds. One of Radcliffe's Robots."

"No I won't. I'll be the same flunker I am now."

"You can't flunk. This is summer camp."

"Oh no? Mahon will call your mom and dad and tell them you can't come back."

"Relax. He didn't even do that to Rudy Janson for breaking into the course evaluation survey." He switched to a pompous drone. "Please. Rate. Your Instructor's. Enthusiasm. (A) Deceased. (B) Comatose. (C) Needs CPR. (D) Unsatisfactory."

Jeff twirled the soccer ball. David's gut tightened. "You smart guys can do anything you want. But if the rest of us tried it they'd can us! You make a joke of everything and still get certificates—"

Jeff laughed. "On genuine parchment no less, suitable for framing or wrapping fish . . ."

He glared at him, bitterly. "My dad asked me why I didn't get one. Then he phoned Mahon right in front of me. I begged him not to—"

Jeff seemed taken back. He stared at the ground a moment, then looked at him, seriously. "Who are you living for, man? Yourself or your dad?"

The question threw him. He looked at Jeff as if he had spoken in a foreign language. "What do you mean? Does your dad let you do anything you want?"

"No."

"Then what do you mean?"

"I mean, if computers aren't your thing, maybe your dad will just have to accept that."

A cold, sarcastic laugh broke from him. "Are you crazy? You don't know my dad."

Jeff almost said something, but stopped. There was a silence; then he said, "Look, do you want me to help you or not?"

David avoided his eyes. Insects flitted through the underbrush.

"OK."

"Tonight after dinner?"

"No – uh – I've got kitchen duty."

"OK. Tomorrow then. The sooner we get you on track the sooner we can take a little dribble down Blood Alley."

"What?"

"The Zorgs, man! I want to have a few practices before we play the Reptiles. They'd be fun to snuff." He spun the soccer ball into the air and caught it on three fingers.

David eyed him warily. "So tomorrow after dinner in the reading room."

"Rightey, mate." Jeff dropped the ball onto his foot and kicked it back into his hands. Grinning at David, he seemed to hesitate, as if expecting something, then tucked the ball under his arm. "Well chow, arrivederci, and all that."

David nodded faintly. He watched as Jeff strolled down the path until he could only catch glimpses of him, and of the soccer ball as it was spun into the air and caught.

He thinks you're stupid. He's only doing it because of soccer. Because you scored that goal.

A sick feeling came, weighing him. *There's no such thing as friends. Not really. People just use each other.*

He stood a long time, not wanting to return to the noise and jostle of the camp. The playing field was deserted. Here and there through the undergrowth there were flashes of blue water, steeped in sun.

At the far end of the field was a path. What was to stop him from going that way, on and on? No one would care, except his mom and dad.

As he plodded back voices sounded through the trees, a remote, happy garble.

He came out next to Bunkhouse No. 8. Kids were strolling in groups down to the mess hall, yakking about this and that, wondering what was for dessert.

Dinner that night was spaghetti and meat balls, and dessert was only jello. Nobody would admit to knowing what kind of meat the balls were made of, and, as if in frustrated curiosity, a lot of dissected remains had been entombed in the green depths of the jello. It was a grim night to have kitchen duty.

As the mess hall emptied David stood waiting at the sinks with two girls. They were still missing two boys and it was decided that they would scrape and wash. The last kids turned in their trays and hurried out the double doors to freedom.

They'd watched the stacks grow in miserable disgust.

"If they're not going to eat it they should at least have to scrape it into the cans," one of the girls said.

"We'll be here all night," said the other.

"Hey, you kids get going in there!" It was George, the cook. He advanced on them from the kitchen with a huge wire whisk in his hand. "Read what it says! You can start washing and when them other guys come they can dry."

"It's no fair! They're late, just so they won't have to wash!"

"Holy smokes, I've been cook here seven years and that's the first I've heard of it! You don't worry about them, you just get busy." He winked. "You're only late once in my kitchen."

He grinned at them and went back to his work.

Over the big triple stainless steel sink was a sign which said, "Fill first sink with hot water and two-thirds cup detergent. Fill second and third sinks with hot water only. Scrape plates thoroughly before washing and double rinse after."

One of the girls turned on the taps. "Amanda, I'll wash and then we'll switch."

The other girl laughed. "Susan you rat, that means I get the dirty water."

David glared at them. *So you expect me to scrape. Thanks for asking— You're only late once. I hope it's good. It had better be good.*

He sickened with anger. Globs of sauce-encrusted noodles oozed out between the plates. Someone had even stirred his jello until it was almost liquid and added it to his milk. *They should feed from a trough. Why is it always me. Why should I get kitchen duty tonight. We have a Mercedes and an Acura and a heated pool and a Jacuzzi and I'm sent here to scrape shit.*

"I can start washing now," one of the girls announced.

He turned on her, savagely. "Do you think it's right that we have to do this?"

Susan was startled. "But the cook's got it in for them."

"They should have to scrape too!"

"If we don't get to work we'll catch it," Amanda said.

"I don't care! It's not right. We shouldn't be dunked up to our elbows in this crap, for not being late!"

"It's not a punishment. It's just the dishes."

"Yeah, right! You made sure you didn't have to scrape!"

Susan slapped her wet washcloth down on the sink. "All right, let's trade! I'll scrape and you wash!"

Suddenly it didn't seem so much better. It would take longer and he'd be stuck between two jabbering girls.

He turned away, grabbed the big spatula, and yanked the first plate down to the rim of the trash. The yellowed edge of the spatula rammed at the mess. Bits of spaghetti splattered the black plastic lining; sauce trickled, glistening, into its folds. He shoved the plate towards the sink without looking.

"Amanda, do you have Swenson for database?"

"Yeah."

"Isn't he a geek?"

"Oh, I know. It's so stupid, the way he grows his hair long at the sides and combs it back over his bald spot!"

The contents of the next plate slid over the rim. Everything in the world was trash, would someday be trash.

"And his jokes, they're so dumb! Like today he says, 'If a byte is eight bits, what's a "zyte"?'"

"Oh, sick!"

"And then the boy behind me, he leans forward with his bad breath practically in my ear and whispers, 'Hey Susan, what's a "tyte"?'"

"Oh! What'd you do?"

"I turned around and smiled at him and stepped on his foot. Swenson thought he was laughing."

"You did not!"

"Did so!"

Scraps of wilted lettuce fluttered into the black depths. A glossy mass began to form in the bottom and he scraped faster, aiming the drops to befoul as much of the can as possible. So what if they ignored him. The stuff they talked about was so dumb anyway.

"I can't stand Radcliffe either," Amanda said.

"Well you must admit he's kind of cute."

"He's so hard! Like that program about the hot dog sales? I got so mixed up with all those loops — I felt like I was lost in a bowl of spaghetti —" They both laughed.

A cry came at him, a surge of excitement and shock; but he said nothing.

"And he's such a nerd! I mean, the way he stands up there and leans against the blackboard like he invented computers or something and you're thinking is this English or what?"

A glob of spaghetti struck the wall and hung. He raked stuff down on it to dislodge it, wanting only to be done, to be away from their yakking and the feel of her taking each plate from him as if he were a machine. Shiny with grease and streaked by the spatula, they passed from indifferent hand to hand into the sink.

Fewer and fewer people are going to count.

"And you know what happened last year? He wore this really pukey tie, it was greenish gray with these black squiggles on it, and we started making fun of it, like someone said it was an autopsy on the brain cells of a dead hacker, and he started getting all red, so he says, 'I didn't know you liked it so much, it comes in yellow too,' and he pulled it out of his shirt and his tie clip goes flying across the room and hits this guy on the chin, and everyone starts cracking up, and when we stop laughing he says really serious-like, 'Things could be worse. I could be your surgeon.'"

Susan leaned over the sink, shaking with laughter, the plate she was washing bobbing in and out of the water, her long brown hair falling forward into the suds.

"Jeez, Susan, it's not that funny."

"Things could be worse! Oh shit!"

Amanda started laughing. "Get a grip on it, Sue!"

"What a spazz! It comes in yellow too —" She dissolved into uncontrollable laughter.

David turned to look. He was holding out the next plate and was getting angry that she didn't take it. *They'll blame me that we're so slow —*

— The girl was holding on to the edge of the sink, her eyes glistening, soap bubbles clinging to the tangled ends of her hair. His anger vanished —

Amanda was turning red. "Hey Sue, it's not shampoo!"

Susan flicked suds at her; they struck and ran down her cheeks, sparkling.

"You rat! I'll get you for that!"

"You don't have any bubbles!"
"I'll tell Radcliffe you think he's cute!"
"Don't you dare! Seriously, I'll kill you—"
"You're serious, all right—"

Susan scooped up a handful of suds and flung them at her. Amanda dodged, reached into the sink, and splashed her. Susan swept a wave over the side of the sink, soaking Amanda's pants and shirt.

"You geek! Look what you've done!"

Susan eyed her grimly. "Amanda?"

"What?"

"How many fits are there in a fight?"

They broke into hysterics.

David looked on, the dirty plate forgotten in his hand. A voice urged, *Splash her. Let her have it*, and he saw Susan, her face flushed, her long hair tossing and dripping, recoiling from his attack, her eyes wide with shock and then wild with an incredible joy—

The plate slid into the sink. He reached, slowly, for the largest island of bubbles—

Suddenly they were facing him. Amanda was talking, breathlessly. "Don't mind us, we're just—"

He flung at them, splashing them both, the suds white and streaming on the redness of their faces, and then he was laughing that it was as he imagined it would be, Susan's eyes darkening in wicked delight while Amanda screeched. He stepped back, comically brandishing the spatula; there was a swirl of long hair and motion and he was struck in the face with the dishrag.

He wiped his face with his sleeve, unsure, ready to hurt.

She stood before him, soaked, tangles of wet hair in her eyes, the dishrag raised to strike. Behind her, Amanda shrieked, "Cream him, Sue!" There was a moment in which they hung on each other's being, taut with uncertainty; then he laughed.

She laughed back. "I guess we're wet enough."

". . . Yeah."

"What's your name?"

"David."

"I'm glad you could join us."

All three dissolved into fits. And he was swept up in astonishment that they accepted him—

"What the bloody hell's going on here?"

They turned, the voice stopping the rush of their blood. It was George. There were two boys with him and he was furious. "You think I don't got enough to do, is that it? These two punks skip out and I go round 'em up just so you don't have to do it all, chasin' after them all the way up to Bunkhouse 5, and when I get back you're trashing the place! Look at this! You've hardly done nothing! You kids nowadays make me sick you're so goddamn spoiled! You know what you woulda got when I was your age – a leather belt across your wet little butts! Shit, I got half a mind to do it, I'm so fed up! I used to get a half-time helper and this year even that got cut! But you brats won't ever have to worry about that, will ya –"

The voice blurred past him into noise. One of the two kids standing behind the cook, smirking at him in glee, was Alf, the guy who called him Snotball.

"And after you're done moppin' up this mess you're gonna wash some walls in the kitchen. Or maybe you'll help with what I had in mind for these guys. Cleaning the exhaust grills. Just gettin' them down is fun. The edges are sharp and the rancid grease drips in your hair."

Amanda began to cry. David's throat tightened; suddenly he heard himself blurt out, "We'll clean it up, but we shouldn't get their punishment too!"

The man ignored him. "This has been a long time comin'. Every year – shit, every week – I get a sloppier job in here. It's time I gave you kids something you won't forget. I been to Mahon but he could care less. It's time I really laid it on –"

He felt small and afraid in the grip of the man's anger; but his outrage broke over it. "None of that's our fault!"

"Then how come there's water all over the floor and crud stacked up here to the ceiling? Huh?"

He waited just long enough to triumph in David's silence. "You kids could bullshit your way to China and back but it won't do you no good. I've had it. You girls had better do your hair up."

"I didn't start it," Amanda sobbed. "We were just having fun."

"I started it," Sue said.

"I don't care. You're both gonna finish it. Get going on the dishes. You" – he thrust his hand at David – "come with me."

He didn't move. It wasn't right. He didn't deserve their punishment.

The engine of the bus was running, the air bitter with diesel. He got out of the Mercedes. *Hey Snotball I got some paper for ya –*

"Did you hear me? By God I'm going to do something I'm gonna regret . . ."

He stood, stiff with hate, a remote tingling in his legs. It wasn't right. It wasn't right—

Amanda raised her hands to her face. "Please, go with him—"

The cook grabbed him by the arm. His grasp was incredibly strong; he cried out and it tightened on him. He heard Sue pleading, "Stop it! I'll clean the grill—" and then he was flailing wildly, the man dragging him towards the kitchen, his hatred of the place filling him to choking. He felt himself pulled like an animal past the kid who called him Snotball; the pimpled face spread into an evil grin—

He swung with his free arm and missed. The kid came at him, the eyes turning vicious—

"Hey!"

The cook grabbed Alf and yanked them apart.

"I seen you grinning at him! I'm not taking no more crap! I've had it up to here!"

"Let go! My dad's a lawyer!"

"Shut up and get in the kitchen or you're gonna be here till midnight."

"You can't make us do anything but the dishes!"

George didn't answer. He jerked them the last step into the kitchen and glared around. "Where's the fucking step ladder—"

The kid trained his cold blue eyes on David and rasped under his breath, "You're dead, Snotpicker."

George thought it was meant for him; he spun around, clamped each of them on the neck, and began hurrying them back through the alcove. The other kid shrieked. "Let go! My dad will sue you!"

The cook said nothing; David struggled to keep up, the sensation of the man's fingers on his neck searing, the shocked faces of the two girls careening into sight and vanishing, the violation of his spirit too sudden and violent to fully hate. They burst through the double doors into the shadow of evening; but it was light enough that they would be seen and recognized and he found himself thinking, with remarkable detachment and even relief, that Mahon would phone Dad to come pick him up and it would be over—

The man hurried them down the wheelchair ramp and up to the road, the kid who called him Snotball spewing protest, as if to guarantee that the whole camp would know. On one of the trails up to the bunkhouses a group of kids stopped and stared at them. As they came towards the director's residence Alf grew frightened. He dropped his lawsuits. "Please don't tell Mr. Mahon! If I get kicked out my dad will kill me! I'm sorry I skipped out. I'll clean the grill—"

The cook was silent, and his silence was more terrible than anything he could have said. There was only the strike of their feet on the road and the quickness of their breathing. They came to a set of steps that went down to the director's house, a modest log building. The man let go of them. David walked down to the door, his heart pounding but at a distance. High overhead, in the aura of evening over the lodgepole pine, the first star was out.

The cook knocked. There was the sound of a television. They waited; the other kid tore a splinter from the end of a log and fidgeted with it. The cook knocked again just as a dull tread of shoes approached the door.

Mahon stood before them, stout and rumpled in his suit, his expression turning peeved. "Yes?"

"Uh, sorry to bother you, Mr. Mahon"—George hesitated. "Things just aren't working out in the kitchen. Two kids skipped out on me tonight and I had to go chasin' after them, and when I run 'em down and haul 'em back I find the ones that did show up having a blasted water fight! I got all I can handle! I just don't have time for this—"

The words swept up against the director's managerial stare. Somewhere behind him a buzzer went off on a game show.

"You left the mess hall unsupervised?"

The cook's voice became edged with defiance. "Yeah."

"You know that's against policy."

"Well what am I suppose to do? I don't have any help left!"

"You could've assigned them kitchen duty for the next two days."

"What about the other three? It's not fair to them."

"You mean the ones who were having a water fight?"

The television audience cheered.

"They wouldn't have done it if I had a helper to keep an eye on them! Look Mr. Mahon, it's bloody ridiculous! I can't clean up in the kitchen, plan for the next day, and keep the dishwashers on the straight and narrow all at the same time! If I had that half-time helper back, crap like this wouldn't happen!" The cook glared, barely controlled, into the director's impassive face; and David, looking up at them in the harsh light of the doorway, saw his father and knew that to Mr. Mahon George's anger was meaningless.

"The staffing allocations are fixed. I told you that. We have to operate within them. I don't intend to discuss it further."

The cook seemed to swell with rage; behind them a siren wailed on the TV, the audience applauded wildly, and a woman began shrieking, "Oh, I can't believe it! Oh!"

Mahon wanted to get back to his show. David felt his little eyes studying him. "Why have you brought these two here?"

George stepped forward. He was a good six inches taller than Mahon. "You don't intend to discuss it further, eh? All right, I'll let them half-wash the dishes and sling crud all over the kitchen, and when the health officer shuts us down and all them richos keep their little darlings away from <u>your</u> diseased camp, <u>then</u> maybe you'll listen!"

He turned and started to go, thinking he'd scored heavily; but when he was halfway up the steps and there were still only fading bursts of laughter and applause from the director's TV, he began to slow. At the top he turned back, halfway. "That one in the plaid shirt skipped out. They were mouthing off and fighting. I don't have time to put up with it, not with all I got to do."

Mahon was unperturbed, his voice flat. "George?"

"Yeah?"

"Don't leave the mess hall unsupervised again."

The cook glared at him and stalked away.

The game show broke for a commercial. David suddenly felt more vulnerable with the cook gone. Before Mahon could clear his throat to go at them, the kid who called him Snotball began talking furiously. "Sir, I didn't skip out! I started getting a stomach ache at dinner because of the green pepper in the spaghetti sauce and I told the guys at my table I was going back to my bunk to lie down but I guess they forgot to tell the cook like I asked them! I felt like puking sir, honest, just ask David! He was sitting at my table. Isn't that right, I felt like puking, didn't I, David?"

He turned on the kid in disbelief. Despite his voice the eyes were cold and threatening.

"And we weren't fighting either sir! We were just horsing around like the other kids. I was a little ticked that he forgot to tell the cook that I left 'cause I felt like puking, that's all."

Mahon smiled at him, thinly, and muttered, "Felt like puking, did you? An old schoolboy trick!"

"Sir?"

"Never mind. David, what do you have to say about this?"

An incoherent mass of things came at him; and out of them, for an instant, he actually heard himself telling Mahon that he had been at the kid's table and it was true; it was followed by the briefest image of the two of them walking back to the kitchen together and Alf saying, with a kindness he had never heard in his voice, how sorry he was that he had ever called him Snotball –

Are you out of your mind? The words hit like a shove. The pimpled face leered at him from the bus. *You're dead, Snotpicker –*

He heard his voice breaking from him, stiff, determined, passionate. "He's lying, sir! I wasn't at his table. He's a liar and a cheat, who thinks other people should do his work. Now he's trying to threaten me into lying for him! George saw him grinning at me because I was going to get his punishment. Ask him, sir! That's what started it."

Alf glanced from him to the director, wildly. "He was sitting right across from me! Swear to God!"

"I wouldn't sit right across from you! I can't stand being in the same camp with you!"

"All right! That's enough!" Mahon assumed his most feared voice, a barbed, cold speech that crumpled kids up and disposed of them, instantly. "I've had trouble with both of you before. If either of you is brought before me again, I'll be phoning your parents to come pick you up. There are a hundred and fifty students in this camp and probably a hundred and forty of them don't want to be here. But for the vast majority it becomes a positive experience. I suggest the two of you try harder to make that happen. Fast." A mosquito drifted past him into the house. He didn't react. "David, you can go back to the kitchen. And you" – he thrust the judgment at Alf – "go back to your bunkhouse. Your stomach ache, I'm afraid, is chimerical – that's right, look it up. You should've told George. You didn't. You could've gone to the infirmary. You didn't. And you weren't exactly recumbent when George found you. I wish you a speedy recovery. You'll have kitchen duty tomorrow night and the night after that. Now good night – and remember. You're both on Zero Tolerance."

The kid gawked up at him, open-mouthed; then he turned away and said, bitterly wounded, "So much for telling the truth." He slugged up the steps to the road and was gone.

David stood lost in turmoil; then out of it a fierce sensation swept him, engrossing as a dream. Liar! Faker! They didn't fall for it! He'd be punished. To see him report to the kitchen, pimpled and scowling; to spy as he stood sullenly being told what to do! Imagine having it on video —

"He won't bother you. Now get back to the kitchen — and no more water fights."

He didn't realize the director had spoken to him until Mahon started to close the door. Then he burst out, "Thank you, sir!"

Mahon smiled discreetly, and the door shut. He was alone. Insects swarmed around the porch light in the onrush of dark. Noises of the game show came in frantic, garbled spurts.

He stepped back. A delicate crescent of light lay tilted in the sky. He stared up at it, lost in gratitude. There was justice. The scum would be punished. They would pay for their lies, the insults and putdowns they had heaped on him. He would see and feel and taste them suffer.

He saw the kid's pimpled face again as he lied, lied that he had sat across from him at dinner and asked him to tell the cook that he felt like puking. How could people be so bad? What had he ever done to him — nothing! And all to get out of work — so that he and those two girls would have to do his share!

Dad was right.

A voice drifted through him, stealing through the muffled blare of the game show. *You must become powerful. That is the only way you will not be stepped on. You must become like your dad, like Mr. Mahon. Then they will fear you. Then they will leave you alone.*

He climbed towards the arc in the sky. The night was soft around it. Dad was right, so terribly right. *He sent you here to arm you against the scum and trash. It was not just to learn computer stuff; it was to put you in with the liars and bullies, to teach you to want power.*

He stopped at the edge of the road. High and cold and far away, moonlight touched his face. Tears welled up in his eyes. *He loves you. Dad loves you. Only you have not understood. And wasn't that the greatest love of all, to go on even though you didn't understand, even though it caused you pain —*

He lowered his eyes, closing them against the dim earth. He wouldn't fail. He would study hard, harder than he had ever studied. He would learn the tools of power. The liars and bullies who lorded it over him now would end up like George. George! No one would call David Ashton by his first name.

He took a deep breath. It would be hard. But if he would just remember, when he got discouraged, this calm, far-off light —

His father stood on the far side of the room. His expression was subdued, but there was something in it, behind it, of incredible intensity –

He waited, eyes lowered, his body tremulous, daring to hope. The time had the strain of years.

When it seemed he could bear up no longer, a voice came. It was his father's, but it was not from him. Rather it seemed to come from a great distance. It said, "David. You are worthy."

He buckled to the floor and wept.

The next morning was vibrant with the stillness of a world creating itself. David awoke feeling cold, the night troubled. He tried to think why, but the light stealing in around the plywood shutters of Bunkhouse No. 7 distracted him. It cut in sharp lines across the sleeping shapes, as if to startle them back; and he thought how strange it would be, if he could see the dreams of all twenty-two kids in the room. Would they be totally unrelated?

He turned on his side, treasuring the quiet, the stillness of the double bunks turned this way and that along the wall. Soon they would wake up, and everyone would instantly start being himself. But what were they now? Were they bullies and liars, Joe Cool and Snotball, now?

He glanced at Jeff, a nondescript lump huddled in a sleeping bag like the others. To him it was all so effortless, so casual. He could never be like that. They could never be friends. But if Jeff was using him for soccer he could use Jeff to pass.

On the other side of the wood stove someone pulled a blanket over his head to shut out the light. The bareness of the place began to ache. How many hundreds, or thousands, of kids had slept here?

He saw his room at home, the walls glaring with Lamborghinis and race cars and hockey players. On his dresser were his shin pads that he hadn't put away, a board game that he'd gotten for Christmas and never played, and a sketchbook his mom had given him. The last drawing was of the bus on its way to camp. It rounded a curve and the road just stopped and it plunged off a cliff. He'd started to draw kids screaming and falling out of the windows, but erased them. Instead they sat, staring straight ahead as if nothing was wrong . . .

And why shouldn't they? No one cared what they felt.

He saw himself back in his room. Mom and Dad didn't know he was there. He listened to his walkman and crunched ketchup-flavored chips and drew dazzling birds in a jungle.

But once the door opened. It was Mom. She didn't see him. She stared around vacantly.

He caught his breath. She looked twenty years older.

An alarm sounded. He startled.

"Seven o'clock! Rise, you swine!" It was Roger. Jeff was training him but he was over-eager. Jeff himself turned indolently at the alarm, just enough to indicate his indifference.

Slowly the lumps stirred. It was like that movie, one day in the life of Ivan somebody. Another day of camp. Prisoners.

He sat up. The morning light scratched at the graffitied rails of the bunks. Somebody coughed hoarsely.

Why did the world you wake up to always have to be the real one?

The day did not go well. David struggled at the homework for Radcliffe, and it frustrated him worse than before. Somehow, from the moment he'd agreed to Jeff's help, he'd thought it would be easier. In database they were supposed to learn how to insert and rearrange categories and he'd kept getting files mixed up with fields. Finally he'd gotten it straight. If Joe's team was the Hawks and his position was outfielder and his ERA was .203, those were all fields in Joe's file. And if your name was Snotball and your team was the Cruds and your position was Condemned Dishwasher and your IQ was six-and-a-half—

He'd thought about it all day. He'd used it to pull himself on. Alf wouldn't be late tonight. As the mess hall emptied he'd watch from a strategic corner; he'd see him stand before the stacks of hardened slop, murderous hate and misery in his eyes—

And at first it seemed that this would happen. David positioned himself on the side of the mess hall with the alcove, but back, towards the lake. Dinner was Sloppy Joes, or Slimy Georges as they were called, and green beans and some sort of apple thing for dessert and he ate it quickly, indifferent to the lifeless sweet or salty taste, anxious for kids to start handing in their trays. At last the mounds began to rise; he glanced around for Alf and saw from the plates of the kids near him that it would be a good mess, that the soggy hamburger buns would flatten and bulge under pressure, forcing sauce to the rim. But if there were too many green beans on the plate the pressure might be reduced. Eat your vegetables—

Gaps appeared, then whole tables were empty except for a crumpled napkin or stain; three of the dishwashers stood waiting. He glanced up and down the rows, searching. Alf couldn't skip out. He'd be expelled—

He stopped, shocked. At the far end of the mess hall, by the stairs up to the reading room and the labs—he was talking to Jeff! Jeff! What could he want with that lump of shit—

Jeff said something and Alf laughed. They looked relaxed, like good friends.

His hands slid down the sides of his tray. Why would Jeff have anything to do with that scum? What if they were talking about him?

The green beans lay dead on his plate in a soggy chain. Jeff would help him. He would pass. Alf wouldn't get in the way. He almost mouthed the words across the hall at them, without looking up.

The ring of milk was dull and warm on his cup. Why did everything always go against him? Why couldn't he, just once, be the winner?

As if in answer the kid grinned at Jeff and made some sort of gesture in the air. Jeff laughed and waved goodby and Alf began strolling towards the alcove, his pimpled face spread in a leisurely smile. When he got to the dishwashers he greeted them and picked up the top plate on a stack. He held it as if it were a Frisbee and he was going to wing it into the kitchen at George. They all laughed.

David sickened; but the next instant he caught himself. *How could you be so dumb? It's all an act! He knows you're watching!*

The idea relieved him immensely. Alf would suffer. He could put on a show but it would die in the filthy gut of the stack, and when it did his pleasure would only be keener. To see the smile fade, the laughter stop . . .

But he had to meet Jeff!

He stared around. The mess hall was almost empty. It was time. And he had to turn his tray in! He'd have to go right by them. What if Alf said something?

Jeff had gone up the stairs. He was waiting. He stood and began moving towards the alcove, the tray light, shaky in his hand. How had he gotten into this?

It was because Alf was late. Because he was talking to Jeff. What was he up to?

He came towards the dishwashers. It felt like he had no body, only his arms and the tray. *If he calls you Snotpicker what will you—*

The sun sifted down through layers of forest to settle on the aspen by the lake. Why was his life so different? Why was it one long war –

He put the tray on the stack without looking and turned to go. Alf was standing right on the other side of the garbage.

"Hey! What's your hurry? Don't you wanna stick around and watch me grovel in this slop?"

He stopped and faced him. "I don't care." It sounded fake.

"Oh yeah?" He picked up David's plate. Something shot across it and flew at him, striking him on the side of the face. He leaped back, wiping at it. A lump of the apple thing fell to the floor in a splatter of brown sauce.

The other dishwashers had turned to look. The kid glared at him. "You care about that? Huh, Snotpicker?"

He couldn't speak. He stood, suspended against a huge force. It towered towards him. Something forced its way past his throat. "I – I'm going to kill you."

There was an explosion of laughter. He walked away quickly, straining not to run, the words raging, cavorting wildly on the other side of possibility. Kids gathered in the bunkhouse, calling him chicken. Figures like charred sticks fled against a red horizon. Alf's head was lifted and dropped and he took aim again –

He turned a corner. It was the stairs to the reading room. He groped for the railing. The stairwell was thick with a muffled noise. He fought for air. He'd kill him. He would. They'd heard him say it. They'd laughed.

He clutched the rail. Something would come now. Something would tear through it all, hurling it away, and he would be free –

He started up the steps. Suddenly it was incredible that it had just happened, that the kid had thrown crap on his face and that he had said what he did; it seemed like something he'd imagined, and now he should be on his way to Jeff, worrying about files and fields –

But the next instant it was vast and unendurable.

He turned at the landing. He didn't know or strain to know what he was going to do. There was only rage welling up through him, seeking an act.

The reading room appeared, books and tables arrayed before the lake, silver merging to gold in the evening sun. Jeff was sitting at a window, flipping the pages of a book. He fought his way past the intervening tables.

Jeff looked up. He was going to speak but he cut him off. He stood over him. "Why were you talking with that shithole?"

"What?"

"That guy downstairs –"

"You mean Alfred?"

It threw him. Jeff picked it up. "Poor guy, he's called Alfred E. Neuman all the time. It got to him for years what with his face and all but now he carries a clip-on bow tie. He's not a shithole."

"Are you friends with him?"

"Sort of. What's it to you?"

"I'm – I'm going to kill him."

Jeff breathed out and put the book down.

"I mean it – I've never done anything to him and now he's thrown crap on my face – I'm sick of being shitted on –" The words swept him on, stumbling. "I don't care if the whole world – No one wants me here. No one wants me at home. It's going to end – it's got to end –"

"Calm down, man. What did he throw on you?"

"Some junk off my tray."

"Why'd he do that?"

"He skipped out on kitchen duty last night and Mahon gave him double. Is that my fault?"

"Did you haze him for it?"

"– No."

"Then why did he throw stuff on you?"

"Because I wouldn't lie to Mahon for him. Because I wouldn't say he skipped out because he had a stomach ache." The words charged him. They sounded so real, so true. The shithole had planned it since last night –

Jeff tipped his chair back. Something about it antagonized him. "Look, this is none of my business, but I don't think Alf would actually throw something on you, just for that."

He gave way. "You're calling me a liar! I can't believe you'd even talk to that scum, much less stick up for him –"

"Look man, why don't you sit down and try to get a grip on yourself –"

"Why? Because you're just like everyone else! You think I'm a joke, a loser! You wouldn't be caught dead with me if it weren't for your retarded Zorgs! Think I don't know that? A stupid ball dribbles to one side of a post and you're OK – sort of. But if it goes to the other side you've missed the cut, you don't rate. It's barf."

Jeff stared up at him. "Man, no one stands a chance with you, do they?"

He swept past it, enraged. "I don't need your help. I don't need your retarded poems, either, which was all I was good for before I scored that stupid goal. It's all barf and shit. The guys who make it are guys like you – the Joe Cools, who gel their hair just right. You can do anything and the instructors just laugh it off. But no one's going to be laughing – no one's going to be laughing soon –"

"Look – I'll talk to Alf about it."

"Yeah. You'll be rolling together on the floor of the bunkhouse."

Jeff slammed the book shut. "All right. I came here to help you. But you're past help. So just do me one favor, OK? Keep your freaky world to yourself." He stood and started gathering up his stuff.

David stared at it. There were pencils, blank sheets of paper, a sketch of a flow chart –

He pushed it way, maddened. "You're the freaks. All of you. You invent all these rules but they're not the real ones. You put on this big show of being hard on Radcliffe and all the rest but you're really their suck."

Jeff's hands stopped on the papers. He looked at him, stung.

A thrill shot through him. He had rattled Joe Cool. "That's why you can say anything you want. Why you can call The Dick your mate and talk about your balls on the bus. You're their suck."

"Shut up."

It wasn't Jeff's voice. It was dark, hurt, angry. He exalted in it and it swept him on. "You're pissed that someone figured it out, aren't you –"

"You're going to be a lot worse than pissed if you don't shut up –"

"What're you doing to do? Write a poem and pass it to Alfred?" He watched, carried recklessly on the surge of his triumph, as the kid, no longer Cool but ordinary and vulnerable, glared at him in hate.

"Man, you must really want to be trashed."

He heard himself laugh. "Get lost. Without The Dick and Radcliffe you're just a little jerk."

His fist tightened as he said it; but to his shock Jeff picked the junk up from the table and walked away.

He watched him go. Vast things moved past him. He'd exposed and humiliated them. Now he'd be respected. Now he'd be left alone –

A shadow came between him and the window. He turned –

The rows of empty chairs, arrayed peacefully in the evening sun, swept him to their vanishing point, somewhere in the forest on the other side of the lake.

Night was reaching up from the forest by the time David returned to his bunkhouse. From the mess hall he'd wandered out past the parking lot. A rough dirt road branched off and followed the slope above the camp to the power line; he'd trudged along it, masses of darkness closing over him, his elation turned cold. No one would help him now. If he passed, he would do it alone.

But there was worse. Jeff was his bunk captain. He could lie. Then he would be expelled. Zero Tolerance.

He was also the sort who could talk kids into things. Like Alf. Every minute, for the rest of camp, he would have to be on alert.

Suddenly he'd stopped. He couldn't do it. He couldn't study, struggling in front of Radcliffe, all the time knowing that they were plotting. He'd crack.

Below him, through the trees, he'd caught the outline of the nearest bunkhouse, huddled around a feeble light.

– The power line might take him close enough to the clearing to see the glow from the windows. He'd approach the porch, his chest straining –

The steps wouldn't creak. Through a gap in the curtains he'd see the big pine table, Jimmy asleep on the rug in front of the stone fireplace. But he couldn't see Mr. Black –

He'd stood suspended on the road in the obscure growth of the night. He didn't know when his hands grasped the rail of the fence and he pulled himself over it and struggled through the underbrush towards the camp. And it was not until he reached the porch of No. 7 that he thought about how quiet the bunkhouses were. Usually there were bursts of laughter and loud talk, sudden and ugly in the dark.

He stood at the door of the bunkhouse. Mr. Black wouldn't remember him.

He opened it. The Coleman lantern cut the bunks into jumbles of shadows. Why were they empty?

He advanced into the room. There was a movie tonight in the mess hall. Everyone was there.

He went over to his bunk. His body slipped into a heap on the edge. He struggled for a moment to think what sort of position it was in if they came at him but gave up. He fell back onto the mattress and closed his eyes. Waves shuddered into the dark—

Nobody loves me. No one at all
Sprinkles my ice cream, asks to play ball.

They were the words of a poem from school. A dumb poem. Sprinkles. Who'd want them anyway?

There was nothing to do but fight on. Against everyone. To the end. He curled up on the bed, his fists clenched.

"David?"

He shot up from the mattress. The voice came from the back corner of the room, somewhere behind the stove.

"David? Is that you?"

He peered into the corner. The voice was faint, like that of a sick child. He fought to hold back a vague fear. There was no shape visible in the shadows—

"David, it's me, Greg. Didn't you like the movie?"

Greg. He swung his legs to the floor. His body slumped, the tension draining. Greg was a wimp. He hardly knew him. He barely said anything and he was lousy in sports. He was small and had really pale skin. Kids teased him for it.

"I didn't go to the movie." It sounded like he felt. Like he didn't want to talk.

"Oh. I was hoping you'd tell me about it."

"I said I didn't go."

Something creaked. A little face jutted from the darkness of the corner. "Why didn't you?"

His hands stiffened against the bed. "Look, I really just want to rest, OK?"

Greg stared at him from his bunk. He had soft, bright eyes. They unnerved him. "Are you too tired to talk? Even for a little while? I need to talk to someone."

Great. I've got enough troubles of my own. "Why do you need to talk to someone?"

The kid hesitated, his face white against the dark. "It's this camp . . . I don't like it here. I want to go home."

David laughed, a dry little laugh. "Join the crowd."

There was silence, then the voice struggled. "But you really don't like it either, do you? That's why I wanted to talk to you. It's not that kids are mean to me, I'm used to that. It's this computer stuff. My parents say just to try hard and have fun but they don't mean it. Last year when I got home they asked all these questions about the other kids. I did OK but this year it's harder. I'm not an egghead. Today a guy called me that and I said I wasn't and he said, 'Well if you're not an egghead what are you?'"

David clutched his gut.

"Everyone knows what I should be. Only I don't. Is it the same with you, David?"

He stared at the concrete floor. His voice sounded strange, as if he were talking to himself. "Kind of . . . I like to draw so my dad's afraid I'll be an artist. He wants me to be in business. But I don't want to always fight everyone else . . . always try to beat everyone else . . . That means I'm a loser."

Greg stared down into the shadows below his bunk. "I guess I am too. Or at least everyone's trying to make me feel like one."

There was a long silence. It seemed that nothing more would be said; but suddenly, Greg leaned forward, out of the huge dark. "David, what do you suppose it would be like, being dead in Zanzibar?"

He laughed. "What do you mean?"

"Just that."

"But if you're dead you're dead. It doesn't matter where."

"Are you sure? If living in a place is different, couldn't being dead there be different too?"

A few moments before he would have called him a little weirdo; but now, he tried to grasp it. "You mean you're not really dead? – like heaven or hell?"

"I don't mean heaven or hell. I mean Zanzibar."

His gut tightened. "I don't get you."

The kid peered down into the shadowed channels of the floor. "I've never been there of course, and I never will, but . . . there must be a place, where all this stuff doesn't matter –"

David struggled with it. Suddenly, to his surprise, he felt angry. He imagined getting out of the bunk and going over to Greg and looking down at him and saying, "I'll tell you what it's like being dead in Zanzibar! You lie by the side of the road with flies crawling all over your face and all these people walk by laughing and talking mumbo-jumbo and hardly noticing you. And finally someone rolls you down into a ditch with a push of his foot –"

He didn't say it. In a moment the anger was gone and he knew only that he was tired and didn't want to think.

The kid was watching him, expectant, the light of the Coleman deep in his eyes –

He heard himself speak softly. "Don't worry, Greg. We'll be all right –"

The little face broke into a smile. A calm sort of warmth spread over him. What if it could be true. What if, in a way he couldn't understand, everything would be all right –

The door of the bunkhouse opened. They both turned towards it, startled. A fat kid stood in the doorway. He was chewing gum.

"David Ashton? Is David Ashton here?"

He didn't answer. He strained to place the kid but couldn't. The name Darren or Daryl came into his head, and the lower bunkhouses, maybe No. 2, but he wasn't sure.

The kid glanced from one of them to the other, jaws flapping. When he spoke the words tightened between chews. "Isn't one of you guys David Ashton? Mr. Mahon wants to see you in his office. Now."

So that was it. The end. They'd made up some lie and he was expelled. It was a cinch, if you were a bunk captain, a top student, and a suck –

He pushed himself up from the bunk. There was only emptiness, and a sniffling little grief that didn't matter, and the blank front of a massive desk . . .

"Mr. Mahon wants to see you. Now."

"I heard you."

He would not submit. He would not. The power line arched into the dark –

"Don't go with him, David! He's lying! Mr. Mahon always watches TV now!"

"Shut up you little cat turd!"

Suddenly he understood. They were waiting in ambush. They'd bribed the fat kid with gum or hockey cards –

"I'd hurry up if I were you. Mahon looks like he's gonna blow a bird."

Greg sat up in his bunk, half lost in shadow. "Liar!"

The fat kid stepped towards him. "How'd you like your nose flattened?"

"It's OK, Greg. I'll be OK."

He watched as the fat kid's expression changed to a relieved little smile. Suddenly it seemed logical and inevitable that they were waiting, and inevitable too that he would go. He felt a surge of energy, through a dull fear. There would be an end. At least they would be expelled. He stared at the fat kid in contempt. "You go first."

The kid laughed. No fat shook. "Sure, man. Afraid of the dark?"

"Don't go, David! He's lying! I can feel it!"

He turned to the little splotch of flesh in the corner. "You're right. He's lying. Goodby, Greg."

The fat kid stiffened. "What sort of crap is this? All right, I don't care if you believe me. Just wait till Mahon –"

"I can't hack this place, Greg. I want it over. If it's not now, it will be tomorrow –"

He would remember Greg's face, the soft eyes questioning. He jerked his hand at the door and the fat kid, chewing harshly, turned and stepped into the dark.

He followed him through the porch and down the path to the washrooms. A yellow, insect-splattered bulb glowed at the entrance to each can. He imagined them crouching there, breathing in the night odor of urine. Or they were behind the first aid station. Between the two buildings was a bare rectangle of earth, a lurid arena.

His legs tightened and he almost stumbled on the slope. The fat kid walked faster. He stopped. To go between the two buildings, that was the trap –

He saw the bulk of the kid stop and turn. "Hey man! Come on!"

The voice had lost its indifference. Yellow haze outlined his head. He'd stopped chewing.

"I'm not that stupid."

The kid threw up his arms. "Jeez, are you paranoid or what? Want me to tell Mahon –"

"Tell Mahon anything you like. Tell him to suck a dick."

The dark sphere of the kid's face stiffened; then he actually glanced towards the entrance to the boy's can in desperation, and a thrill shot through David that it was all just as he had guessed, that it really was over. A wad of something pushed against his chest.

For a moment everything hung suspended, the fat kid standing miserably at the edge of the piss-colored light, pushing the dirt with his foot; then a shape emerged from the can.

"Get out of here!"

The fat kid started to protest.

"Can't you hear, dumbfucker? Beat it! And if you say anything—"

"Then tell Alf not to call me 'half-ton' any more!"

The shape took a step towards him. Yellow glare slashed down its side. It was Jeff.

The fat kid bleated, "Don't call me that any more," and stumbled across the bare place into the dark.

Jeff turned to him. His hair was wild and he looked like he'd spent a night in the can. For an instant he exulted that this was Joe Cool; but the voice stopped him. It was crazed. "We're going to trash you, man. We're going to trash you like no kid in this camp's ever been trashed. You're a fuck-face snot. A total zero. Getting expelled wouldn't teach you anything. We're going to show you what everyone in this whole camp thinks of you."

He caught a movement at the far corner of the first aid station. It was Alf of course; they would've come at him from two sides and the fat kid would have stepped back, chewing.

It seemed to inflame Jeff's rage that he didn't answer. "No one can stand you. You go around thinking the whole world's out to crap on you. Well here we are. We're Silver Lake's angels of mercy and you're going to eat shit. Right up your fucking nostrils."

As if on cue, Alf stepped out from behind the porch of the first aid station. His face, in the yellow light, was pasted in an idiotic grin.

David scanned the slope in front of him. There were lots of rocks; but there would be time to throw only one, maybe two.

Jeff's voice halted. "I tried to be nice to you—Yeah, I wanted you on the Zorgs. But I also felt sorry for you. After we talked I knew it was tough for you here—that you were getting screwed around by your dad. I wanted to help—"

He seized on it. "Leave my dad out of this! It's tough here because of all the sucks like you! No one who's straight stands a chance—"

"Shut up, fucker!"

"Say anything against my dad and I'll take your head off!"

Jeff came towards him but stopped at the base of the slope, his body backlit by the glow from the can. "No one calls me a suck—no paranoid little freak like you—"

Alf started across the arena. *I'm going to kill you.* The dishwashers laughed, their mouths gaping. Slop struck his face, again and again—

He summoned up the hate, drawing on it. Noting the position of the nearest good rock, he stared down into the ravaged shell of Joe Cool. His legs tingled and far away a dapple of light touched a stream.

"You suck brown—"

Jeff started towards him; he scrambled down the slope towards the rock, into the last instant before the fury. He felt the thing cold and angular in his hand and flung it, the kid almost on him. There was a sound like a catching of breath; Jeff's hands jerked to his face and he stumbled forward. Alf came up behind him, his crazed grin like a mask; blood seeped from between Jeff's fingers, he couldn't see it but he knew from the way his head rolled and he touched it, and something screamed at him in his nerves to finish him, to rush the last few steps down the slope and kick him in the head and face only one attacker.

But he didn't move; it wasn't remorse but raw shock at what he had done, at the sight of the kid fallen to his knees, contorted against the piss-yellow glare of the can. The thing screamed again—

Something rushed at him; he raised his arm. Alf's eyes drove at him and in a shred of an instant he knew the delay was fatal. There was a massive blunt outburst of pain and his back struck the ground. The night exploded with screaming or swearing and a huge ugly weight came down on him. He struggled to shield his face, his cheek searing.

Fuckin piece of shit Blows pounded his wrists against his face. *Get your hands away snotpicker* He arched and twisted, trying to throw the kid, his head battered against the ground. *What makes you think you're so much better than me, huh? I'm expelled but you're fuckin dead*

He struggled in the mute onslaught of panic; suddenly a hand clamped one of his wrists and tried to pry his arm away. It gave; but as Alf tried to push it against the ground David sensed, quicker than thought, that he was off balance. He lurched up, twisting; with his free hand he shoved the kid's shoulder. Alf fell; it seemed unbelievable, the hideous weight lifting, the gaudy yellow sting of the light striking him as he wrenched his arm free and rolled and strained to his feet. Shadows whirled around him and he started up the slope, his legs slipping from under him. He would remember thinking how it would be dark and safe in the forest—

The ground started to level; the black peak of the bunkhouse jutted over him. He sensed escape when there was a rapid burst of thuds behind him. His lungs ached against the pounding; he'd barricade himself inside—

He'd almost gained the black rectangle of the porch when he was shoved from behind. The ground gave out and he struck. He started to writhe; his arms were jerked behind him and pinned and he was yanked to his knees. He cried out.

Fuckin chickenshit. Now you're really gonna die
Hold him! Fuckin hold him while I trash his face

Jeff came up, the dimmest vestiges of light from the can catching the blood down the side of his neck. He raised his fist. *You're gonna die man. I'm gonna bloody hell pound you till you're dead*

Help me The cry broke from him even as his body tensed for the blow. His head snapped back, tearing; it dropped through a raging night. He groped for breath –

Now who's the suck now who's the suck
There's someone down there man get the shit
You won't be calling me that any more, will ya
Did you hear me man? There's someone down there
Say 'I'm a suckhole.' Say it! 'I'm a suckhole'
Jeff! Someone might've heard him
Say it or I'll ram this bloody fist through your face
Stuff it, Jeff! Do you wanna get caught? Get the shit

The black shape throbbed, its fist raised towards him; suddenly it turned and hurried towards the cans. The piss-colored light bulb below pulsed against the gash in his cheek. Blood ran and hung from his lip, a warm current of pain in the dark. He waited, gathering his breath, until it seemed Jeff must be far away; then he yelled.

Help me! Someone –

With a scream he was jerked clear off the ground by his arms then back; the night blotted and Alf's breath raked the side of his head. *Guess you won't try that again fucker*

Let me go Mahon'll kill you

The kid cinched him tighter; savage hate spewed in his ear. *Think I give a shit? You put me on his hit list, when all you had to do was BS a little and we both would've gotten off easy! And then you sit all grand in the mess hall like you bought your ticket and you're waitin for the fuckin show to start! Well the show's here, and knowin how you love crap, I snuck down to the cans and clogged a toilet*

No! Let me go!

Look – here it comes – a gorgeous bucketful – and you're gonna wallow in it, shithole, you're gonna wallow in it up past your fuckin eyeballs

Jeff came out of the cans. He hurried towards them, holding something out from his side. At the sight of it David struggled; the yellow glare swung and exploded. He tried to twist free or to get one knee up and stand; the kid bore down on his arms and they skidded sideways together in the dirt, his mouth gaping, his being overwhelmed by the depth to which it could be violated.

Hurry up man we've got to get out of here

Jeff came up. The thing was placed on the ground and with a savage heave he was lined up with it. The acid stench of urine cut the night and Jeff's voice heaved. *You're condemned to die man. You're gonna drown. You're gonna suck it down your throat*

Someone's comin up here I heard em

It's too bad man but you asked for it

Will you stop yakkin

Terror seized him, a terror through which only feeble shreds of pleading could break, a seizure of the mind and body that knew only one thing, escape. Hands clamped his neck and began forcing his head towards the bucket; he gave way slowly, the night breaking apart in gasps. *Please don't . . . please . . .*

We don't have time for this bullshit

Something rammed his back; he jerked forward and his head plunged into liquid. In the first shock it was only cold and thick; then the foulness of it bathed him and his eyes and mouth and nostrils tightened shut. They churned him up and down in the filth and he knew that he would give out and try to breathe. His mouth burst and his nose filled with the fluid. They brought him up. Rivulets streamed down his face, entering his lips as he fought for air, running from his chin. He shook in their grasp, sobbing, plunging through the dripping stench to the limit sought by all torturers.

Hey shithead how does it feel

Come on Jeff we got to get outa here

I'd kill for a flashlight

There's still time to get back to the movie let's dump him and split

What's the matter you loosing your cool

I keep hearing things down there

I don't care what you hear we're gonna bloody hell carry out the sentence

Look Jeff

The voice cut him off, a brutal parody of Joe Cool, bunk captain of No. 7, leader of the Zorgs. *Just do it*

The hands tightened on him. A voice shouted at him to resist but it died in a quivering emptiness, a far dark place where the only will left was to submit completely. The fluid burst over him; his head was rammed up and down in nauseous waves. His lungs screamed and he sought death. His mouth would open and he would choke –

Suddenly it stopped; his head shot out of the bucket. For a moment he knelt, shaking, barely aware that they had let go, cries and noises piercing the streaming filth; then the idea of escape hit like a shock. He swayed to his feet and lurched away from the noises; a crack of light split the black mass of the bunkhouse and he veered off.

A shape appeared, a squat thing. He'd started to turn from it when recognition shot through his nerves. The fire barrel – it stood, unnoticed, to one side of the bunkhouse, full of stagnant water –

He rushed up to it, flung the cover off, and plunged his head in. Cleansing waves enveloped him and he thrust himself deeper, embracing the metal drum with his arms, his hair tossing from side to side, swirling in the delicious currents. When his air ran out he came up, sucked in the night, and submerged again, wanting never to stop –

He came up. The stench no longer lay thick on the night but lingered in the wet clumps of his hair. He could sneak into the bunkhouse and get his shampoo and towel –

Shouts broke out. He turned in terror. The log buildings lay huddled in yellow glare, beyond them darkness and noise. He stared for an instant at the ugly puddle of humanity; then he turned and plunged towards the forest.

It started just behind the bunkhouse. Vague masses of undergrowth blocked him; he pushed and trampled his way through, branches flying back, the brush of the leaves hateful against his wet clothes. There were no more shouts, only the grief of his breathing. Already, from filthy mouth to mouth, the whispered delirium spread; the movie would hardly be out before the whole camp would be infected. *Oh Jeez who was it you know that David Ashton kid the jerk who wouldn't sit down on the bus Oh yeah him –*

A branch struck his forehead. He grabbed it with both hands, bending it double, but it wouldn't break; it split into twisted fibers. Sap smeared his palms; he bore down on it, trying to make it snap.

Oh yeah him. The guy who picks his nose and keeps it. He shoved the branch back and forth, aching sobs of hate breaking against the dark shudder of the leaves. *You're a fuck-face snot. A total zero. Everyone in this whole camp everyone*

The tree flailed in the night, helpless, disgusting. *Hold him. Fuckin hold him while I trash his face*

He pushed the thing away. His knees struck the earth and he clawed it. God would punish them. God would burn them alive for all eternity. There had to be something like that. There had to – or how could anyone stand it –

He was swept into the depths of it, his forehead touching the dry crust of leaves. *Shithead shithead shithead*

His body trembled as he wept. There was no relief, no limit but exhaustion. Hands dug into his neck. They shoved him down through black endless oceans of shit and piss. He would never come up, never. In all the world there was no word, no lie, that could ever bring him up.

The earth crumpled through his fingers. They took everything. They took basketball and hockey and cheeseburgers and Nintendo. They took his friends, his family, his mom and dad. They left nothing.

Except rage. He treasured it up as he wept. Without it he was nothing.

Ages passed. The night grew cold. He struggled to his feet and stumbled into the bush.

Mr. Mahon leaned forward. His shadow, distorted by the one light he had bothered or chosen to turn on in his office, swallowed up the mess on his desk. "I'm running out of patience. Your actions weren't those of innocent bystanders. I suggest you tell me what's going on, now – especially you, Alfred."

The two kids stood before him, rigid, determined in their innocence. He knew the look well in all its variations – the bunk captain and top student almost defiant, the other one tempted to plead. And he knew, too, that they were lying. Behind them, Rick Bruchard stood at the door, the boyish brightness of his face gone.

Jeff stared down at Mahon. The noise and feel of his victim as he struggled, the stench and the blood on his forehead dazed and battered him. He'd never imagined that they would be caught, that an instructor would shout at them as they fled. Why had they stopped? Idiots! He couldn't have recognized them. It was like they were hypnotized.

And now, to stand here, bloody, stinking, and guilty –

Stay cool, man. Just stay cool . . . "We've told you what happened. We left the movie early because we were bored. My folks have it on video. We were going back to our bunkhouses when we heard the cries for help. We started to go up there but got scared and decided we'd better come back and get an instructor. That's when I fell and Mr. Bruchard started yelling at us."

"You weren't coming towards the lodge. You were heading for the maintenance sheds."

"We were scared . . . we got turned around in the dark."

"If you were looking for an instructor, why did Mr. Bruchard have to shout three times before you stopped?"

Jeff thrashed around the objects on the desk. "I don't know – from the way he was yelling, we knew he was going to blame us for something. Just like you're doing."

Mr. Mahon studied his paperweight. It was a plastic golf ball, all dented and patched, with the words, "Old golfers don't die. They just get teed off."

He spoke abruptly. "Rick, could you go up there and have a look around? Check on David Ashton in No. 7 – see if he's OK."

His eyes moved to Jeff and he knew. Rick went out. He slumped a little in his chair. "I didn't know you and Alfred were friends."

"Well, uh, sort of."

"Well, if you're sort of friends, you probably know that Alfred had a little run-in with David last night."

Jeff hesitated. "Yeah, uh, he mentioned something about it."

Mr. Mahon's voice relaxed. "You know, David's a hard nut to crack. He's capable of doing much better academically. He's got an attitude problem of course, but it's hard putting a finger on it . . ."

I can finger him, man. The words lurched up inside him; he glanced at Mahon in panic and then away. Alf looked like he was bursting. *Hold it man, stuff it – can't you see this is all a trick, to get us to talk –*

"I know that parental pressure's involved, but there's more to it. I wish I knew what's driving him. He's making this place hell on himself, and it's no fun for the rest of us –"

"It sure isn't, sir!" Alfred leaned over the desk, his pimpled face red and clammy. "You know what he did when you gave me kitchen duty? You know what he did? He stayed in the mess hall after everyone else was gone, just so he could watch me doing the dishes! It's bad enough he gets me in trouble, but then I'm supposed to stand there in all this muck with him grinnin' at me? No one should have to take that, sir!"

Mahon's nostrils tested the air. The kid stank. It was sweat but mixed with – it was like he'd done something in his pants. He'd been vaguely aware of something but it hadn't hit him until Alfred leaned over . . .

"That must have made you pretty mad."

Shut up, man! Jeff stepped on his foot. It was corny and stupid, like Laurel and Hardy. Like slipping off the edge of a cliff, one finger at a time, in an old cartoon . . .

"Yeah, uh, it made me mad. But I didn't do anything to him! If he comes in here it's all a bunch of lies like he told last night!"

Mahon was tempted to ask what was a bunch of lies. He contemplated the golf ball, a battered little globe.

The kid's bare arms. That was what stank. What the hell had he done?

He shifted to Jeff. "I've been meaning to talk to you about David. I was wondering if you, as his bunk captain, might have noticed something – if he might have said something –"

"Could we sit down?"

"Sure." He motioned to two chairs behind them, against the wall. They slumped into them.

Jeff felt less cornered. "It's like you said . . . He thinks everyone's out to get him. He gets on lots of people's bad side . . . I wouldn't be surprised if he was the one calling for help."

"Did he get on your bad side?"

"No. Maybe on my nerves a little."

Mahon pressed his bulk forward in the chair. "Good, because I've been meaning to ask you – since you're in the same bunkhouse and in Mr. Radcliffe's class together, I thought you might be willing to tutor him."

The boy jolted upright. "I tried –"

"You tried what?"

"– Nothing."

"What did you try to do, Jeff?"

The man stared into him with the weight of authority and the hardness of middle age – and yet, there was a hint of compassion, of understanding. *Tell him – tell him how you felt sorry for him . . . how you tried to help him, and you were shitted on and called a suck . . .*

"What did you try to do?"

The room seemed to move inwards, straining to the breaking point against the silence. *It's over, man. Tell him. Maybe it won't be so bad when they hear what a shit he was –*

The voice tightened. "David got on your nerves more than a little, didn't he, Jeff?"

He faced the director dead on. A voice shrieked, *Look, why don't you just accuse us? Why do we have to play this asinine –*

There was a knock at the door, so faint that it might go unnoticed. His heart raced. Mahon didn't react – or was there, in the calm relentlessness of his eyes and voice, a stronger hint of mercy if only he would confess, that is, confess immediately, before the door was opened?

"Come on, Jeff. You tried to help him and he rejected you, didn't he?"

Rejected me? Is that what you call it? I had our books out, paper, everything – I drew a flow chart –

The knock came again, timid, unsure . . .

"It's time you came clean, guys. You both stink like an outhouse."

Tears welled up in his eyes. He stole a glance at Alf. He'd crack any second.

You told him over and over you could pull it off. That it would be your word against his. That there would be kids who would swear you never left the movie.

There was a third knock. Jeff clutched the chair. Who the hell was it? Why didn't he answer? Could it be, that the whole thing was arranged –

Mahon stood. Alf gave way. "Sir, please listen to me – I couldn't take it – My dad will –"

Jeff cut him off, frantic. "We didn't do anything! We've told you the truth! If Ashton says anything different he's lying!" It sounded fake, stiff as though squeezed through the cracks of an idiotic mask. He could not be expelled, he could not be punished –

Mahon went to the door. Jeff strained to meet Alf's bitter glare. *Listen to me, man! It's not over! It's still our word against his –*

His dad picked up the phone. He watched, his chest a shell; but his father's expression barely changed. He couldn't comprehend what he was hearing. It was a mistake, a sick joke. His son, the honor student, the class leader, suave, unflappable –

The door opened. The fucker would stand howling in shit –

It was dark in the hall. On the other side of the door, a little white face perched atop an insignificant body.

Mahon was startled. "Greg?"

The kid stepped into the room. He looked at Alf and Jeff; his quiet shining eyes ravaged them. "Mr. Bruchard sent me here. I didn't go to the movie. I saw what you did to him. All of it."

Jeff buried his face in his hands.

As David struggled up the slope from the camp, only the need to find a way through the brush kept his mind from shearing into fragments. Mom and Dad pressed him in their arms, their voices a warm, cleansing sea; Dad stepped to the phone and set in motion gargantuan forces of revenge. On the first day back at school kids gathered in knots on the playground, talking about their summer; he went up to them, relaxed and happy –

Branches shuddered in the dark. As he shoved through them they whipped at his face and neck and his head twisted to escape. *Hey there he is — David Ashton. You'll never* bee-leeve *what happened to him. Not in a million years*

You can't go back, man. Ever. You're branded. Like an animal. Shithead shithead

He slowed, fighting to keep his mind above madness, to think over the noise of his breathing. It was not the darkness of the brief summer night but of the forest, obscure channels dissolving into impenetrable shapes. Terrors could be waiting – ghosts, murderers, aliens – he could be kidnapped aboard a space ship and wake up naked, attached to instruments in a laboratory –

He forced it to stop. There had to be a place where he would be safe, safe from everyone, so he could think.

He could go to Mr. Black. He wouldn't have to tell him what happened. He could say he'd gotten lost on a hike –

No. *He'd smell you.* Then he'd carry on about it; maybe he'd even laugh –

But where else was there? He was getting cold. To lie in a pile of leaves scratched together in the dark –

A noise seized him – a muted bristling of the air, somewhere over the trees. After an instant of fear he recognized it. But not from that evening. He saw himself plunging down a tangled path, giant towers rising into the late afternoon sun . . .

He ran forward, into the shallows of the dark. Something low and angular blocked his way. It was the fence, the fence he had climbed just that night.

What an idiot he'd been to go back. To think he could escape them, and not get expelled, and even pass –

He pulled himself over the rail and stepped onto the road. Ahead, over the black solid of the trees, he caught it – the hum of the power line. He ran until the towers came into view, huge and obscure in the night.

He stopped and listened. High over him the wires swooped in invisible arcs, surging with energy. They could take him to Mr. Black. He would be safe and warm. As he stood the sound became almost hypnotic. He was meant to go back.

He found the path or overgrown road that wandered between the towers and started along it. But as he struggled with the turns in the trail, doubts weighted him. He would stand, filthy, cold, and small, before the lighted windows under the porch, clutching the courage to knock. At long last a curtain would move; then the door would open, just enough to reveal a tall, narrow form on the other side of the screen. It stared down at him, cold and suspicious. *The only people who come out here do it to make noise and cause trouble.*

He slowed. The chill of his wet clothes and hair pressed against him. The night blurred. *Please God . . . please help me . . . please make Mr. Black remember me . . .*

High over him, the air vibrated. Vast currents shot through the night. Slowly, through the sheer act of putting one foot in front of another, he gained hope. Mr. Black probably wouldn't recognize him at first, how he was. But he couldn't have forgotten completely. He'd remind him how he'd been sitting scrunched over on the porch, sewing, and had pretended not to notice him; how he'd stood with the dog at his side and called out after him to come back anytime. And if all that drew a blank, he'd mention the lemonade and sugar . . .

"Well if it isn't you again! What took you so long? Come on in!"

He entered the room. From his place on the rug in front of the big stone fireplace Jimmy rose slowly, wandered over, and sniffed him. Below one of the pine chairs the cat's tail switched. Mr. Black went to the cupboard. "You look hungry. I got some real good cookies . . ."

It would be like that. And, if Mr. Black was grouchy at first, that was just how he was. He didn't like many people. That's why he lived all alone.

The idea gripped him; he slowed. The towers stood thrust into the night sky, below a scattering of stars. The cut on his cheek pulsed and the encrusted collar of his shirt rubbed his neck.

Mr. Black would understand. He was the only one who would. He knew how cruel and evil people were. Hadn't they torn down his fence— hadn't they hacked his sign to pieces—the sign he'd made himself that said "Welcome"? He could tell Mr. Black what happened—him alone, of everyone on earth. He wouldn't make excuses. He would say it was all just like in those pamphlets of his.

It struck him with the force of a revelation. His body trembled as he tried to tell him and then he felt the man's gentle hands on his shoulder. "Easy boy . . . you're safe here with me . . . they can't hurt you no more." Love bathed him. He threw his arms around the thin form and pressed his face to him and wept. The voice seemed to well up deep inside him. "God loves you, boy. God loves you all the more for what they did to you. His Wrath will consume them. Oh how I long for that. I came out here to get away from the idiots, the scum who did this to you. I – I never was happier than that afternoon. Stay with me, David. I've had a lonely, bitter life – I've gotten all dried up inside. But you and I – we're alike . . . We'll get along just fine . . ."

His hand clutched for a branch. The air was charged; currents surged through him, breaking over the pain. How could he not have seen it? Mr. Black had suffered too. He knew the truth about people, the terrible truth. He knew God would punish them.

He started moving faster. Mr. Black needed him. Now, more than ever, they could be friends. And how wonderful it would be – just the two of them, and Jimmy, and the cat. To not lie awake in the bunk thinking about the assignment and the sweaty feel of the keyboard, to not pick at George's slop, hardly caring what it was, the approaching start of class like lead in his gut. It was gone forever. He was free.

His feet pushed against the trail; he forced himself on, anxious, as if the power line were the ramparts and watchtowers of a fortress and he was seeking the door. It seemed much further in the night. Could he have missed the little clearing to the side, where you could see the house?

He fought the cold stiff touch of his clothes and the strangeness of the night. He was starting to shiver. Soon he would see it – the first glimpse of the porch, the glow in the windows –

But nothing broke the wall of the forest. He searched the memory. It had seemed so fast, coming back – running half out of control between the towers, careening down through a tumble of sun. It must be soon.

He struggled on, peering for the slightest opening in the trees, the night air raw on his cheek, his breath laboring. As his anxiety grew the thing came at him. The bucket was brought up. His arms tore at his shoulders as Alf's body bore down on him, riding him. *You're gonna wallow in it, man –*

No!

He stopped; he'd said it aloud. The sound of it jolted him, stark and cold in the dark. It had power; suddenly he drove the words at them. "You're gonna die! You're going to eat it!"

The earth was yellow and cracked, the air dead still. Stinking, bleeding, faces crazed, they were dragged towards pairs of stakes –

It pounded inside him and he had to force his breathing past it. His eyes swept the night, panicking. He had to find the way –

A strange thought seized him. What if it had never really happened? What if the whole thing, the house, the old man, had been the wild flight of a summer afternoon – or if the house were there, but a stranger opened the door, and said no Harold Black had ever lived there?

Don't be stupid. He started off again, his steps forced and uncertain. Maybe he'd already passed it –

You're gonna wallow in it up past your fuckin eyeballs

His lips quivered. They deserved to die – he couldn't be left totally alone, hated and ridiculed by everybody –

We're Silver Lake's angels of mercy

His hands started to contort against his face; suddenly, something moved against the forest.

He turned. There was nothing –

Then he caught it, a fold in the dark wall of the trees. It couldn't be the way; he remembered a little clearing.

He approached. It seemed to be a trail. But should he follow it, when if he just went on to the next tower it might all be as he remembered?

He stood, confused, the night bearing down on him. He couldn't get lost on the power line. But what good was that, if he couldn't find the house?

He started into the trees. Brush closed around him and then the stars were gone. None of it looked familiar. He knew he should turn back.

What will you do

Sneak back to the bunkhouse and kill them

The dishwashers' mouths gaped –

"Stop it!" His voice shot into the night; then he was rushing through undergrowth, his being crying out for escape. Somewhere he warned *you're going to get lost* but it didn't matter. In all the world there was nothing left, nothing but the light in the window and the violent unburdening and the old man's fierce embrace . . .

The trail widened. He sensed something ahead and worked his way forward. The trees fell away on each side, dissolving into an open space. He couldn't see all of it.

Something rose in his throat. There was a house.

It came into view slowly, an angular intensity of darkness. Slowly it took on depth – a gabled end wall, a low-sloped roof over a porch. But there was not a light anywhere. Its darkness filled the clearing. It had the deep stillness of something abandoned and forgotten.

He came to a stop, unable to comprehend. It couldn't be Mr. Black's house. It was some sort of barn or shed, or a place the people had moved away from.

He took a few steps into the clearing. The stars spread out, faint against the solidness of the thing.

Yes, it was different – the roof went a different way. He tried to picture the house in detail but couldn't – they would not relate, the house dreamy in the late afternoon sun, settled softly in time, and this black shape –

He went closer. On the other side of the silence something grew, enormous; his body tensed. He caught a dim suggestion of steps onto the porch, and wooden posts; and still he was carried towards them. Lots of old places had that.

The steps just touched the gentler night of the clearing. He hadn't come down them at first. He'd folded his sewing away and stood, his face still in shadow as he spoke. *I'm Harold Black. I live here with my dog and cat.*

But it wasn't the same! It couldn't be! No one lived here. They weren't gone, or sleeping; the loneliness weighted the air as if no morning would lift it.

He advanced to the foot of the steps, his whole being suspended. The dog had come down to sniff him, beautiful, lazy.

He peered into the intense darkness under the porch. Without stopping, he went up. The wood was dull, almost silent under his feet. He tried to remembered how many steps there had been but couldn't.

It was like stepping into nothing. He advanced one foot at a time, his arm in front of him; at last his fingers brushed something. It was fine, metallic. It bent under his touch.

His hand slid down and closed on a handle. The screen door.

Come on up. I'll get us some lemonade. He'd closed his eyes. The world had gone white. When he opened them the man was standing there, watching him through the screen.

He pulled the handle. Hinges squealed. He felt the door open, its mesh vaguely scratching the dark.

The real door was locked. He knew it before he felt for the knob. It clicked tightly, indifferent.

"Mr. Black?" The words were soft but behind them there was a rushing. He ran his hand over the door. It was a featureless slab. He backed away and began touching the wall. The screen door slid shut.

"Mr. Black!" He couldn't have moved away.

But didn't he have a brother in Calgary – a preacher or something? No. He wouldn't have gone to the city.

But what if they forced him? What if they came and took him away to an old folks' home?

No. It couldn't be. His hands scoured the dry boards. He moved along the wall, not knowing for what he was searching.

His side struck something waist-high. He felt it. It was a wooden table.

A vast desolate grief swelled out of hearing. It was the table the cat had sat on, with the pamphlets. He remembered standing over them, reading their covers, and the screen door opening behind him . . .

"Mr. Black!" The cry seemed swallowed up in the night, its bewilderment and anger surging back through him. He moved around the table, following its edges with his hands. He would find a way in –

He touched the wall. It was wood but not the boards, not so dry and old. He ran his hands over it. There were no joints. It was a solid sheet –

"Ow!" His finger caught on a nail. Some idiot hadn't driven it in all the way –

His hand found an edge and moved along it. The knowing spread through him, silent, unstoppable. It was a window. The windows were boarded up. He moved to the next one, to where he saw it in the shadow of the porch, its curtain closed, the room on the other side dark and cool –

It was boarded up too. The sheet was crooked. He saw them, like shadows – people who didn't know Mr. Black or care. They came and slapped the plywood on, banging it up in a hurry, and left –

So it was over. Just like that. His only hope.

He pressed his head to the plywood. For a moment it seemed distant, practical, a matter of deciding what to do next; then he saw the old man standing a few feet from where he stood now, holding the shaking jar over his cup, and it shattered. He clung against the boarded-up window, crying the man's name, the abandonment incomprehensible, the fury growing to find an end. Alf leered at him. His pimples were red and swollen. *Hey shithead. Try the bell!*

He drove his fists against the board. Jeff regarded him studiously. "You know, Ashton, the problem is that basically you're a zilch. A nothing . . ."

"Mr. Black!" The name exploded off the sheet. He'd stood in the sharp light of the clearing, the dog beside him, and said come back anytime –

Nobody loves me. No one at all
Sprinkles my ice cream –

The fat kid recited it in a mocking voice. The bunkhouse roared and he grinned between chews . . .

He slumped down against the wall, his chest heaving, his mind tearing through layers of exhaustion. There was no end, no limit.

Aw, he misses his mommy
Please let me live. Please just let me live . . .
Even before they die it's like they never –

He huddled against the boards and wept. The intense night under the porch closed around him. It was the same house but it was not. This was the real one. Not the old man shielding his eyes in the slanting sun, the dog at his side, but this. Empty. Boarded up. The final indifference of all things –

Suddenly he did not know whether his eyes were open or shut. He saw, or sensed, a person. He was lying somewhere in the dark. It was all dark around him, yet he could see him.

Without moving, he came closer. It was like being across a room but there was no room.

It was Mr. Black. His eyes were closed. He was dressed in a suit. His arms were folded on his chest.

He came closer still. He did not look dead. His hair was neatly combed, his mustache trimmed, and his skin warm, like when he'd first come down the steps into the sun.

Mr. Black . . . The words trembled on the verge of sound. His cheek stung, wet –

Then he cried out with his whole being. "Help me . . . I love you –"

The shape didn't move or hear. Somewhere a pounding began.

He was about to cry out again but the muscles stopped. Mr. Black's face changed. The color faded. Slowly it turned gray . . .

The pounding grew closer, muffled –

Then he was staring straight down at him, and he knew that the warmth had been a trick. Mr. Black was dead. He would never move again or speak. The weathered skin of his brow, the lines around his lips and mustache, were terrifying for what they had been. People said stone cold dead, but a stone had never laughed or wept –

The pounding swelled, and now he could tell it was beating against something wooden and he could hear a boy crying out, very close but dulled and made strange by the wood. *Mr. Black—*

Fists struck the other side of the plywood, but the eyes, the lips would not move.

The cries rose to a frenzy, battering the sheet of wood, but the stillness endured.

He listened, afraid. Gradually the weeping subsided, the pounding diminished and stopped. He caught a faint noise of the boy sniffling in the dark but that too ceased.

The people left. Their steps faded into silence.

And then there was only the profile of the man's face.

Mr. Mahon started to reach for the paperweight again but stopped. He could see his watch; it was five minutes past ten. He got up from the desk to go to the window; through the open door of his office he saw Jeff's and Alf's heads shoot up. They followed his movements with the wary eyes of prisoners. He'd put them out into the hall because they stank; after he'd heard what they'd done, it had seemed to hang in the room.

In all his years this was the worst. There had been fights, pranks – some of them pretty cruel. But not this. From the way Greg described it, it wasn't kids at a summer camp at all. It had the lurid brutality of a movie . . .

He stared out the window. There was not much to see, just the slope above the lodge and the lights of the washrooms. It looked deserted, as if nothing had happened, but Rick and three other instructors were searching. He no longer heard their calls. By now they must be at the fence or past it. Surely they'd find him soon.

He pulled at his collar. It should have been over by now. Jeff and Alfred were expelled. Their parents had been notified and would pick them up in the morning. And David should have been found huddled somewhere crying, and he would have dealt with it and by now he'd be showered and settled in front of the television with a drink.

He smudged the dust of the window sill with his thumb. Not with David. Not a chance. He should've seen it would come to something; that David would lash out at the wrong kid and there'd be a mess. But what warning had there been except the dishwashing? A lot had happened between that and this.

He stared at the bare earth below, desolate in the light of a sixty-watt bulb. What do you do? You know a kid's hurting but you don't know how much, and it works from day to day without a sign, and you've got a camp to run, but all the while it's building towards an end. And then you deal with it.

He searched the dark. There were no flashlights.
You'd better phone his dad soon.

Mr. Mahon shifted uncomfortably. Joseph Ashton was one of the few parents who unsettled him. He still remembered, vividly, the phone call he'd gotten from him the year before, demanding why David hadn't gotten a certificate. *If David's performance is that far below his potential, then that's a sorry reflection on the competence and/or dedication of your instructors, is it not sir? I expect that to be rectified next year.*

And in the background he could hear the boy pleading.

His eyes fixed on the two little yellow lights of the cans. *It's going to be bad – if they find him. If they don't it's going to be bloody awful.*

Suddenly he saw the kid facing him across the desk. It was so vivid that he almost turned – but it was the year before, that afternoon he had ditched camp and run off into the forest. Through the boy's sullenness and fear he had sensed something remarkable – the afterglow of a tremendous exhilaration, a quickening of the soul, as if for a few brief hours he had known what it was to be free of a hopeless burden. The sensation of it was so strong that he'd had trouble chewing him out. He hadn't seen David like that before or since.

And that's why you didn't tell the parents. Why you threw administrative procedure and prudence out the window. Because in the joy of that escape you saw what the father had done to him, and you didn't have the heart to make it worse.

He smiled to himself, grimly. Heart. He'd never heard of it, in any administrative binder, seminar, or conference. If a student runs away from camp the parents are notified. It was a mistake. *And don't be so righteous about it. If you had told them maybe the dad would've eased up on him, and it wouldn't have come to this . . .*

He weighed it, intangible as the dark. Some fathers, yes. But not Joseph Ashton. His gut response had been right –

But still it was a mistake.

A flashlight moved down the slope; he drew himself up. Even from the speed of it he guessed. The shape entered the outermost reach of the light, striding towards the door of the lodge.

He turned back to the room. Jeff and Alfred didn't notice. They sat slumped in their chairs, legs spread, staring at the wall or floor. Something of the stunned disbelief that had spread across Jeff's face when he'd told him that he was expelled lingered in his unfocused eyes.

One of our top students, a class leader, reduced to a thug. Why? We teach them database and spreadsheet, word processing and programming, but we don't teach them to get along. To not be threatened. How do we do that?

He stepped back to the desk. Jeff looked up; his eyes moved away at once but it was enough to see the misery in them. *There's no bucket in the world deep enough Jeff . . . We'll miss you.*

Footsteps sounded on the stairs. Jeff and Alfred sat up. The three of them waited, all silently knowing.

Rick strode down the hall and stepped past the boys into the room. His hand gripped a flashlight. "He's not in the camp. We've searched everywhere, from the entrance to the end of the playing field."

"Did you search the wooded areas, the brush, above No. 7?"

"Yes. Really well."

"He might not answer."

Rick twisted the flashlight in his hand. "If he was inside the fence we would've found him . . . I think you'd better phone the RCMP."

Mr. Mahon looked away, past the scared faces of the two kids to the darkness of the window. That afternoon David had skipped out – something had changed him. Where had he gone? He'd said he'd only wandered around the woods and along the power line. But he'd sensed that he was hiding something –

You're grasping at straws. Call the police.

Rick watched him, impatient. He turned back to him, almost appealing for understanding. "Rick, I've got a hunch. Go up the power line, towards the road. He went that way last year when he skipped out. I think there's a house or two in there."

"Are you going to phone the RCMP? You've got to think of our liability."

Mr. Mahon hesitated. "I've got to phone the parents. I don't want to tell them their son's missing if he can be found quickly. Come back in half an hour – twenty minutes."

Rick didn't move. "You said he might not answer. If that's the case one guy isn't going to find him up there in twenty minutes. Phone the police, Ed. You've got a kid who must be in terrible shape, alone in the forest at night. It's no time to Mickey Mouse around."

He stared at the desk. He'd cleaned it during the waiting; it looked blank, efficient. *He's right. You can't afford a mistake.* He saw the phone in his hand –

But where had David gone that day? Where?

"Sir?"

He glanced up, startled. Rick turned around. It was Jeff. He was standing at the door, gripping the jamb. He looked older than his years. "Sir – uh – could I help look?"

He stiffened. "You've got to be kidding."

He couldn't answer. He could only stare at the director, raw with fear, the realization that they had gone too far.

"And it wouldn't change anything. Both of you might as well go back to your bunkhouses. I expect you here at eight o'clock sharp with all your gear."

Alf smirked.

But Jeff took a step into the room. "– I'm not trying to get out of it. I only want to say – we didn't want this –"

"Then maybe you should have thought about the possible consequences of your acts."

The kid faced him, the cut on his forehead ugly. "Let me go up the power line with Mr. Bruchard."

Mr. Mahon planted his hands against the desk. "No. Mr. Bruchard's right. I'm calling the police."

With a strange sense of going back in time, he reached for the phone.

Joseph Ashton stood below the vaulted ceiling of his living room overlooking Okanagan Lake. A scattering of lights defined the far shore, brightly at Traders Cove and ever more faintly to the north, but he didn't notice. He was preoccupied with a piece of paper in his hand, which he held as if he were about to crumple and throw away.

"I'm going to have a word with Trisha. This is the second time this month she's done this to me."

Elaine glanced up a little from her magazine. "What?"

"I've got to change planes twice – in Seattle and again in Chicago. If she'd routed me Vancouver to Dallas it would've been just one change. Last week she made me sit on the ground in Calgary. Optimistically the plane will be twenty minutes late landing at O'Hare, twenty minutes late taking off, and I'm stuck there three hours. She's under dreadful pressure, filing her nails and touching up her mascara . . ."

"Who?"

"Trisha. Sometimes I think she does it on purpose."

She tried to picture her from the Christmas party. "Oh, I doubt that."

"Why?"

Elaine looked at him, puzzled.

"Why do you doubt it?"

"Oh, well, why would she?"

"Because she had an easy time of it in Sales. All she had to do was flash her legs at Bob and take the rest of the day off. It doesn't work with me."

Elaine laughed. "Doesn't it? Not even if I tried it?"

Joseph drew himself up. "You're not an employee."

Then why do I feel like one?

The thought shocked her. It was too sudden, too blunt. She fought it, afraid . . .

He seemed to notice. "I know you think I'm paranoid. But some of these girls are really very clever. They resent that the company is run by men . . ."

"Then they should start their own." She put the magazine down. "I run my own business, why can't they?"

The telephone rang.

Joseph eyed it sourly. "I'm not available. It might be that asinine neoprene salesman. He called Phil at home."

Elaine started towards it. "I forgot to put the machine on."

She was almost there when he motioned for her to stop. "Wait. If it is him, I'll tell him to take a hike."

He walked over and picked up the phone. His voice changed. "Hello?"

Elaine stood beside him, staring at the lake. For a clear night it was dark. The moon brushed no path on the water.

He listened a long time. Nothing in his expression indicated it was not business; yet she did not return to her chair.

Finally he spoke. "I want him found – quickly. What is the name of the officer?"

They would come to remember how calm it sounded.

"Joseph – what is it?"

He motioned at a note pad.

"What's wrong?"

"Inspector Burton?" He shot a glance at her. "Write that down.

"I'm leaving now. I should arrive within the hour. I expect a complete account of this – this incident –"

He listened briefly then interrupted. "How will I interfere with the search when there is no search? Is that not correct, sir – my son's been missing two hours and no one is looking for him?"

He stiffened as the woman clutched him. Her cry sliced through him. "David!"

Before the dawn there is an easing of the night, an hourless world in which the darkness above the trees softens imperceptibly, and a dim aura of change seems suspended over the chill of the earth. High over the clearing, one could have seen range upon range of mountains emerging from the east, not shrugging or stirring, but reassuming the massiveness of their forms. The valleys with their lakes and rivers waited. It was as if the night grew opaque, suggesting the form of what it concealed, a stark profile of the land devoid of details. The Rocky Mountains, the Purcell and Selkirk ranges, the Monashees and at last the Okanagan highlands – the night paled against their ridges and summits, thrusting the successive folds of the Cordillera towards the distant curve of the dawn.

From the depths of the clearing only the circle of the treetops was more sharply defined; and, to someone who had been awake, that hint of day would have seemed to have stayed a long time without changing. It was not until long after the first softening that the trees took on form and the dry grass etched the nearest trunks. The dark mass of the house turned gray and angular. So gradual was the change that the world seemed suspended in a dull memory of itself; but abruptly the process quickened. No light struck the highest tree above the clearing; but the sky overhead glowed. The world was on the verge of something.

Nothing moved under the porch. On one of the hastily boarded-up windows, a sign was just readable: FOR SALE PEACHLAND REALTY 767-2744. The grass was long in front of the steps. In the gray end of night the house lost its ominous darkness; its desolation became ordinary. The pounding and the cry of the man's name were as a dream.

David slept. Cold had driven him finally to stumble around to the back of the house in search of a way in. Mr. Black did not believe in waste and there was a collection there, of old boards, pipes, stove parts, and apple boxes. Groping in it, his hands had closed on a scrap of shag carpet. He'd yanked it out, choking on the dust, and dragged it back to the porch.

There he'd rolled himself up in it, scrunching deep in the tube to try to shut out the cold. It lay heavy on the top of his head and his shoulders. At last he'd shoved the end against the wall. It was strange that, of all the images he battled before exhaustion took him, that of Greg looking at him out of the dark corner of the bunkhouse unsettled him the most.

He awoke in the blue-gray silence to a noise. It was like a movement in the dry grass; but as he struggled out of sleep he sensed that it had not come now, but some moments ago. He lay still, listening, not daring to wiggle his head out of the carpet. Maybe they were coming to take him back to the camp. He told himself to get up, to squirm out very quietly and get ready to run; but he did not quite believe it and nothing moved.

He was on the verge of slumping back against the floor of the porch when the sound came again. It was a swishing through the grass; in the silence after it he caught a panting, like a dog's. He forced himself out of the carpet, his head bleary and the night air raw in his throat. Didn't they use dogs to hunt criminals?

He saw himself led back to the camp. Mr. Mahon and the instructors were drawn up in a row in front of the lodge and he had to walk between all the kids. Their faces were blank from a distance but as he came closer their mouths curled in silent jeers.

He crawled to the railing and stared out across the field. There was nothing at first, only the grass which seemed higher and more like weeds than he remembered. Then he saw it – the head of a dog. It was standing in shoulder-high grass in the middle of the clearing, just looking at him.

A thrill shot through him. He pulled himself up on the railing. "Jimmy!"

The dog regarded him, eyes bright, overjoyed and puzzled to hear his name.

He hurried down the steps. "Jimmy! Don't you remember me? Come boy!"

He motioned with his hand. The dog seemed about to retreat.

"No, Jimmy! I won't hurt you! Come, boy!"

Still watching him, Jimmy lowered his head, unsure.

He stepped towards him. "I won't hurt you, promise!"

Slowly, the dog ambled towards him. He broke out into a smile, he was so beautiful emerging from the tall grass. He thought of his own dog at home and ached.

As the dog came up he held out his hand. Jimmy sniffed it. He was dirty and unbrushed and thinner, but not starved. David moved his hand carefully and stroked his head. "Good boy, good dog. What are you doing here? Who's taking care of you?"

In the dog's very stillness he sensed him wanting and seeking his touch; he saw himself stumbling away from the bunkhouse and then he had dropped to his knees and his arms were around the animal's neck. He pressed his cheek into the golden red fur, the air close and rich with dog-smell and the animal's heart beating. His head moved with his breathing and for a long moment he couldn't speak.

When he let go Jimmy was smiling at him, contentedly, in the bright panting way that a dog smiles.

He brushed his eyes. "I'll take care of you, Jimmy. Would you like that?"

To his surprise the dog turned and walked away from him a few steps, then turned back.

"No, Jimmy. Stay with me. I'll take care of you." He hesitated. "Who's been feeding you? Is it Mr. Black? Where's Mr. Black?"

Jimmy showed no reaction and he realized that Mr. Black wouldn't have called himself that. He wouldn't have called himself anything. He stood and pointed at the house. "The old man, Jimmy. Your master. Where is he?"

Jimmy turned and walked away again, and again turned back, eager for David to follow.

Could it be? Wasn't Mr. Black dead? In the night at the foot of the boarded-up window he had seen the unmovable ridge of his face, he had cried out his name and heard it muffled through wood. How could he doubt it?

Yet he did. By day it all seemed exaggerated and suspect. It was like a nightmare, nothing more. A lot of things could have happened. Mr. Black might be in an old folks' home. He might be living in Peachland, or with his brother in Calgary.

He told himself to keep a clear head, to listen to reason. Someone was feeding Jimmy. He should go with him and find out who.

He almost started off but didn't. That someone wasn't Mr. Black, or he would be here. What if they turned him in?

The sun setting across the lake inflamed the finish on the massive oak desk. His steps halted at the door. Downstairs Mom was crying. Her sobs shuddered through him as he stood, filthy and small, eyes lowered.

At last his father turned from the window. *David words cannot express how deeply*

"No, Jimmy! Where do you want to take me? Which way, boy?"

The dog panted at him happily, then turned and trotted off through the grass. He called out for him to stop but he didn't. He caught glimpses of his head and started after him. "Jimmy! Wait!"

The dog stopped at the edge of the trees. David came up. His head ached and his stomach complained and he realized that he would follow. But he didn't want to leave the house. It seemed strange that Jimmy showed no attachment to it.

He stared around, trying to think. They were at the end of the clearing opposite the road. There were no houses this way, nothing but forest. He looked at the dog as if he expected him to answer. "Where are you going, Jimmy? Who's feeding you?"

His tongue draped over his teeth, Jimmy wagged his tail at him and disappeared into the bush.

He glanced back. The light of early morning was cutting the tops of the trees and in the brightening below the house looked small and spent. The plywood on the windows stuck in his mind and he turned away and started after the dog.

The edge of the forest was thick with aspen and at first he didn't realize there was a path; as he entered among the pine and fir the undergrowth thinned but it was like stepping back into the night. It was cold too and he tried to hurry, anxious to catch sight of Jimmy. A voice shouted that he was crazy, that he would soon be lost, putting his trust in an animal . . .

The path straightened and he spotted him up ahead, trotting along. "Slow down, boy!" The dog slowed and he caught up to him. He started to ask him again where he was going but didn't. He wouldn't just lead him into the bush, would he?

An image overtook him. He saw himself climbing the driveway of his house towards the front door. It opened and Mom ran to meet him. He strained towards her, dirty, tired, and hungry.

He could do that. There was nothing to prevent him from going back to the house, and from there to the road, and one of the mine workers would give him a ride, and Mom would come pick him up. It would be hard with Dad at first but when he heard what they did he would destroy them.

And instead he was following a dog into the bush.

His steps faltered but didn't stop. It seemed to him that he was captivated by the dog and the strangeness of it; but beyond that the huge shadow drove him. It was always there, its images suspended, pulsing. There could be no peace, no rest until they suffered. He must find some place and plan it. Then he could go home.

He walked faster. Jimmy looked up at him, pleased, and ran ahead a little. Then he trotted sideways, glancing back as if he wanted him to play or toss a stick.

They must suffer horribly; and they must know that it was he, David, who was doing it, who was controlling them. They would taste what they had done. In blood and vomit. That was the only way. Go somewhere and plan it.

The trail was monotonous. It sloped gently down through lodgepole pine and fir, passing nothing memorable. There were little clearings but they never gave a view of the distance. It had the feeling of being lost, of wandering through a vast northern forest like on TV, a fearful endlessness of trees. He watched Jimmy nervously every time he ran ahead. There was no way to tell direction except the sky. He was moving towards the growing day.

A cloud passed over, the morning sun shining through its edges.

The encrusted rub of his shirt and the ache of his stomach tightened. The trees closed in and the path seemed to grow fainter. What if it stopped, and Jimmy took off through the bush and he couldn't follow? Or what if he came around a turn and there was a bear?

No. He would die of cold and hunger. He would get weaker and weaker and finally lie down on the cold floor of the forest. Jimmy would stand over him, whining, nudging him, but it would be no use. He wouldn't want to leave him but at last he would go for help.

He would lie and stare up at the tops of the trees, far away. Pieces of clouds would drift by and vanish. They didn't care about him but that was all right. He would feel no bitterness towards them. As the trees blurred and the feeling went out of his hands and feet he would think about many things. Things like the smell of his mom's perfume and the ring of an old telephone at some house in Vancouver and a toy in Mom's shop, a crystal that you could shake and flakes would swirl around inside, slowly drifting down like snow . . .

And that's how they would find him. Jimmy would be in the lead, panting along the trail, the rescuers struggling to keep up with their radios and stretchers. But it would be too late.

Jimmy would approach, cautiously, then crouch, with a high-pitched little cry. The men would just stand there. For a moment they would feel useless . . .

It was only in old movies that you closed your eyes.

What a triumph! Then they would suffer! Mr. Mahon would call everyone together in the mess hall to give them the news and some of the girls would cry. Classes would be canceled and they would all walk around stunned, talking in hushed groups. No one would go near Jeff and Alf. But when the men came down the slope from No. 7, bearing the stretcher, someone would see them clinging to the wall behind the cans.

And he had only to put one foot in front of another, on and on.

He stopped. He could see further down the trail than usual but Jimmy wasn't in sight. The forest was silent against the distant chatter of a bird. He sensed that there was something off to the left, that Jimmy had wandered off the path. He saw himself going there, catching up with him just in time –

His confusion grew. He could go a little ways, and if he didn't see Jimmy he could come back. He took a few steps off the path.

"Jimmy!"

His voice startled him. It sounded small, afraid.

There was no answer. The bird had stopped.

He had to decide. He had to catch up. He saw himself plunging into the bush. Shafts of light lay staggered across the trunks of the pine –

He moved; for an instant he didn't know which way. Then he was back on the trail, hurrying to where it vanished, his heart racing. He came to a turn; a fragment shot into view and then another and there was no Jimmy. He called out again, frantic –

The trail twisted through a thick stand of pine. He came out of it and stopped, shielding his eyes, the sun hot on his face. Ahead, the forest opened up and in the obscurity of the grass the dog stood, waiting.

"Bad dog! Slow down!"

Jimmy stared at him, happy and puzzled. He went towards him, feeling silly that he'd gotten so scared; he tried to sound angry. "Stay with me! Understand?" Jimmy lowered his head just a little, then looked at him as if wondering whether he would go on.

"Bark if I call for you. Bark if I yell Jimmy! OK?"

Jimmy seemed agreeable. He smiled at him and said "Good dog," and they started off again, Jimmy trotting along with the confidence he'd shown from the start, as if he'd been on the path many times. But as David followed he remembered the house and how he'd first come up to it and something Mr. Black had said. Something about hanging tin cans on his gate, because his dog didn't bark . . .

He was glad the forest had thinned. The trees were spaced out, with sunny patches between them; ahead there were even meadows. He could see further but there was still nothing distant against the sky. The trail narrowed and he wandered past dead branches, decaying trunks of fallen trees, and glacial boulders. There was not a sign of human presence except the path. When would he ever come to something?

Once he was dead they would really start to pay. Dad would sue Jeff's parents of course. He'd take their house and their cars and their boat and their condo at Big White. Alf's parents he didn't think were that well off. In that case maybe his dad could be lured into taking a job with someone Dad knew, and when he'd gotten a big mortgage and bought tons of stuff on credit he could be fired –

He caught himself. If he died, Dad wouldn't know what they'd done – unless someone in the bunkhouse snitched –

He walked faster, agitated. He needed a place to think. A place with food and water . . .

The earth glared like chalk under a lethal sun. Jeff and Alf were dragged across it, too frightened to resist. The air smelled of stagnant water. Ahead, there was a sort of pit.

A man was standing over it, reading something. He heard his name. David Ashton.

He approached the thing. The voice kept reading, solemn, profound. He looked down. Jeff and Alf were sinking into a thick, glossy brown fluid. It swelled and heaved through its broken crust, making a sucking noise around them as they struggled. They looked up at him, mouths gaping in little moans. Tentatively at first, then with growing abandon, he laughed. His voice was swallowed in the superheated air . . .

He startled; the place was gone. Jimmy had gotten ahead of him again; but this time he could see him. The land sloped away faster and he was standing at the edge of some tall pines.

What good did it do to imagine things?

He walked quickly towards the dog. What could he do, alone? Play a prank? Throw a rock? It would never be good enough . . . it would never be like that . . .

As he came up to Jimmy his nerves tightened. Brokenly, through the trees, he saw that the land dropped. There was a distance. He ran ahead. At last he would see where he was.

It came into view all at once: a deep, narrow valley. The mountains on the other side were scarred by ravines and rock slides and barren places. The morning light cut sharply across the larger ravines, leaving shreds of darkness on their eastern sides. There were no roads or houses, unless they were hidden in the trees at the bottom.

Jimmy smiled up at him, all tongue and canines.

"Are you crazy? That must be down a thousand feet!"

Placidly, the dog went on.

While David slept, the glow that had sharpened the circle above the clearing was noticed in Mr. Mahon's office. The director and Joseph Ashton sat on opposite sides of the room, a shattered no-man's-land between them. It was four hours since he'd arrived at the camp, the Mercedes befouled with dust and dead insects, and still, incredibly, there was no search. He had raged, argued, insulted; their shirts clung to their backs and their collars chafed their necks. They ached for sleep and their thoughts stumbled away from them but they held in, determined.

Joseph Ashton glanced at his watch. Its face had become hateful. Hateful too was the feeling of not being in command, of being dependent on people and circumstances he could not control. So what if many of the Search and Rescue people were on holiday. So what if the RCMP's dogs were being used in a criminal investigation. His son was lost. He had been beaten, humiliated beyond words. He had to be found. And then there would be hell to pay. By the whole bloody incompetent indifferent lot of them.

He stared at Mahon in contempt, at the rolls of fat at his waist and the bags under his eyes. He was to blame. Completely. By his own admission he knew David was in trouble yet he did nothing. Why was he not notified? What were thugs like this Alfred Spittal even doing in a camp that he had been told was for the brightest, most dedicated students?

A typical self-important little bureaucrat, coasting to retirement.

He stood. It was intolerable. Where was Briehoffer or whatever his name was, the Search and Rescue leader? It was getting light. They must start with the people they had.

He stepped past Mahon to the window. He sensed the man stiffen as he came near, saw the red veins in the corners of his eyes, and if it weren't for David he would have laughed. He had seen it in the board rooms a thousand times. The terrible moment when a strutting fool realizes he's outgunned.

Yes, the moment David was found . . .

Below, shadowy in the onset of day, the searchers were gathering. They stood in little groups, talking, yawning, awaiting orders. He counted them. Thirty-seven.

David. There should be an army.

A man came down the slope towards the lodge. The groups stopped talking and gathered around him. It was Briehoffer. He spoke to them a long time, gesturing quietly, the faces of the searchers intent. Joseph Ashton wondered briefly who they were, why they had come from their warm beds into this grayness.

Briehoffer finished. They divided into groups and started up the slope. At last something was being done.

Briehoffer continued into the lodge. Joseph Ashton stepped away from the window.

The director's voice surprised him. "What's happening?"

His first impulse was to not answer. He didn't turn from the door. "They've condescended to look for my son."

There was a silence. "You've got it all wrong."

He reeled on the man in cold fury. "More wrong than you, sir – more wrong than a place where this could happen? Where children are beaten and scarred for life?"

"One child, Mr. Ashton."

"Are you implying –"

Briehoffer entered the room. Joseph Ashton bore down at the bloodshot eyes, the sweaty jowls. "If you're implying that my son is to blame, I'll have your head on a stake."

"Uh, gentlemen? We've started a preliminary search –"

"It's bloody hell time."

Briehoffer didn't seem upset. He was a tall, slight man with glasses. There was a calmness about him that sometimes reassured, and sometimes came across as too casual. "Our goal is to cover the road, the power line, and some of the main trails before more people get here –"

"And when will that ever be?"

"I've notified every Search and Rescue unit from Vernon to Osoyoos. By midmorning I should have well over a hundred people."

"By midmorning I want David found! Where are your dogs, helicopters? What are the RCMP doing? You should be hitting this with everything you've got, now!"

"The air search will start when there's enough light. Dogs from Kelowna and Penticton are being used on a case. Corporal Reddick's getting fresh dogs from Vernon. He hopes to have them here by six o'clock."

Joseph Ashton advanced on him. "Do you realize, sir, that that's nine hours since my son went missing?"

Briehoffer unzipped his vest. "It's one of those things. But it's also one reason I haven't started."

Joseph Ashton waited for him to explain.

The man's eyes didn't move from his. "This situation's not like most. David didn't wander off on a lark, or get lost on a hike. He ran away. He ran off bloody and beaten and stunned. He's filled with rage and humiliation. He can't think straight. What I'm trying to say is, he might not be ready to be found. If we'd crashed around at night without enough searchers and no dogs he might've taken off on us. I don't think he's gone far. I think he's near the camp, within a half mile say, trying to stay warm and get a grip on himself. I want to go easy. I've told my people to call out, to reassure him, to tell him he can come home."

Joseph Ashton stood tensed in his wrinkled suit, trying to overpower him. "You had better be right."

Mr. Mahon felt his mind slip into a throbbing fog. To stay warm. Where would he go? What would he do?

There are one or two houses in there . . .

He stopped himself. It was a wild guess, nothing more. And if he was wrong—

It swept back into the storm of possibilities.

From its headwaters north of the Brenda Mine, Trepanier Creek carries the snow melt of the high country eastward until, below the mine tailings, it flows in a steady course southeast towards Okanagan Lake. Its valley, where David came upon it, is somewhat over two miles across and two thousand feet deep. The creek itself, in July, can be crossed on stepping stones.

Day was breaking through the cold shadows of the valley bottom by the time David and Jimmy came to the creek's edge. As he'd descended the dry mountain slopes he'd seen it below: not the water itself, but the thickening of the undergrowth. The fir had an unhealthy look, drooping and moss-covered, and fallen ones lay entangled in the thicket. The path gave out and he had to choose his way, over and under and around, the place so clogged with leaves and trunks and branches that for the first time since losing sight of Jimmy he was afraid. He struggled on, wondering how or when it would end, until a fir stopped him, its downcurved spines hung with yellow wisps of moss. In the silence he heard the rush of water.

They came upon it suddenly. Jimmy immediately waded in and drank; but David held back. He descended the low bank and stepped out onto the rocks. He could cross it easily; it was less than a foot deep and there were places where he could jump from one stone to another.

He stood, sweaty and cold, staring down the dark course of the stream. Just before it disappeared into the aspen, the morning sun broke through, pouring onto the surface. A strange thrill warmed and lightened him. Whatever creek it was, it flowed to the lake. It could take him home. He wasn't lost; but not only that, he could not be lost anywhere in this valley. He could climb high, and watch and wait, like a hawk gliding the crest of a ridge. He was free –

Free. And hungry and cold.

He knelt at the edge, his knees raw on the stones. He scooped up water in his hands and tried to wash them. It was clear and cold and when he drank it shocked the soreness in his throat.

He thought of camp, of the kids just getting up, and lining up in the washrooms, and filing down to the mess hall to eat George's pancakes. Rubbery pancakes, half submerged in syrup, stacked four-high, with two sausages.

Food and warmth. He had to find them, before another night.

Jimmy crossed the stream. He stood on the edge, the wet fur of his belly dark and dripping, looking at him as if he were ready to go on.

David sat. "I need to rest. How do I know you're not just wandering around, anyway? There's not even a trail anymore."

Jimmy panted happily.

"Stupid mutt."

A wind stirred the trees, high up in their tops. Jimmy trotted up the opposite bank and waited; when David didn't move he took to sniffing the bushes. Now and then he would glance at him hopefully.

David closed his eyes. The soggy half-eaten pancakes were sloughed into the trash and the kids took their places in front of their machines. Radcliffe waited for silence.

He stared down the rows in confusion; there was no empty seat. It was as if he'd never been –

His eyes shot open. Light glanced off the rocks; the undergrowth shifted.

The dog was gone.

He struggled to his feet and started to cross the stream, leaping once in the middle, the air swift and cold on his face. He reached the other side and began pushing through the brush. The branches were thin and springy and as he shoved and trampled them he heard himself cry, *What are you doing? He'll lead you around till you drop. Let him go – he's just a crazy lost mutt –*

He grew afraid. There was no end to it, no sign of any trail.

Go back to the stream and think. This is how you die. Go back and think –

He'd almost stopped when he saw it ahead – a fragment of bare earth. He moved towards it. There were markings. As he came closer it seemed impossible. They were tire tracks.

He came out onto a rough dirt road. It curved into the trees in each direction.

He stood, his mind jarred almost blank by it.

He could be home in a few hours. Mom would run a hot bath and Constanza would fix a double-deck cheeseburger and fries. His stinking clothes would be ripped to shreds. Maxwell would come bounding towards him . . .

He took a few steps, a huge ache inside him. It could all be over, in the past, if he could just make it so —

He entered a room. There were rows of tables and windows and through them a lake, adrift in the evening sun. He advanced slowly, afraid, the palm of his hand sweaty against the books he was carrying.

A figure was seated at one of the tables. It was Jeff. He was waiting to help him pass.

He advanced to within a few rows. Light stabbed off the water at his eyes. He heard his voice. It was thin, hopeful. "Thanks for helping me. I've gone over and over it. I just don't get it."

Jeff didn't speak for a moment. His voice had a deep calm. "There's a condition for which we haven't tested."

"What is it?"

"Being dead in Zanzibar."

He swallowed. "— Are you nuts? What does that have to do with the assignment? What does that have to do with anything? Some geeky little guy made it up. A nothing, a loser. Like me."

He waited. "Aren't you going to tell me that I'm not a loser?"

Jeff said nothing.

"Go on, say it — like all the rest of them! All I have to do is try harder, right? — chin up, nose to the grindstone —"

He moved up to the next row. "Come on! I'm selling myself short, right? I just have to stimulate the nerve endings, don't I? Come on, say it!"

Jeff looked at him. It wasn't pity or hate. Then he stood and started gathering up his stuff.

It maddened him. He blocked the way. "You think you know everything! Well you can cut all your calm sad crap and get this straight: I'm fed up with being your patient — your case!"

Jeff turned away from him and walked down the aisle towards the windows. He shouted after him, "Just leave me alone, all of you! That's all I've ever wanted from anyone —" Bursts of light came at him, glaring off the lake; Jeff passed into them. He watched in triumph as he retreated, the outline of his body fading.

He turned away to the stairs. The dirt road wasn't well traveled but it wasn't overgrown either. Someone could come along it.

He stopped at the first step, sensing something. There was someone else in the room.

He knew who it was. It was Dad, standing at the window, his back to him, looking out over the lake.

His body turned light and cold. In the next instant it would come – the summons, calm, unanswerable. He would stand, everything shrinking inside him, and when he had become small enough he would submit –

But there was nothing. High in the tops of the big pine, a wind stirred.

He peered back into the glare, his eyes almost shut. A hollow place grew inside him. It ached. The ache swelled and suddenly he saw that there were two figures, standing together. He strained to make them out –

His fingers groped for something, something to snap, to break. The aspen trembled. His father stood with his hands on the boy's shoulders, looking down at him in pride. He had proven himself. He was worthy –

A cry stopped in his throat. It couldn't be. And yet, he was the honor student, the class leader, everything Dad wanted and he could never give –

He turned and started stumbling along the road. Tears welled in his eyes and the hollow thing pushed up inside him but still he could see it – his father standing over Jeff, the future manager, while he would push a broom –

His filthy shoes kicked up dust; it rose blinding into the pain. He cried out at the rocks and weeds as they jolted past. "You don't want me . . . you never wanted me . . ." The trees jostled the desolate road. Jeff tossed the keys to the Mercedes into the air and laughed. He would lounge by the pool, not bothering to do his homework until ten minutes before class –

The ground moved faster, a blurred rubble. His voice slashed at it. "I'll never be what you want, not ever! But now I won't be any more trouble . . ." The aspen swayed. The road curved into nothing. Dust whipped across the tire tracks; his feet struck them like dead weights. He saw his mom and shuddered that she would grieve –

There was nothing left; and yet the next moment came. He slowed and stopped. The wind tore a few dry needles off the pine. He closed his eyes, his hands clenched at his sides. Jeff was the son he'd always wanted. Smart, aggressive, a leader. Adults said he would go places.

He wiped the mess from his eyes. "Then I'll go too."

He stared around, lost. At first there was only the wind in the grass –

Then he saw Jimmy, standing in the weeds at the side of the road, as if waiting for him. He had the same contented look. He started towards him.

"Jimmy! I'm sorry I called you a mutt!"

The dog ambled towards him. Suddenly he was running and then he'd dropped to his knees and his head was against Jimmy's neck, breathing in the richness of his fur. "Where are you taking me, boy? Please let it be somewhere – somewhere I'll be left alone . . ."

The dog waited until David released him, then looked up at him eagerly and started into the bush, away from the creek. He followed, trampling the smaller saskatoons, trying to avoid the brittle low branches of some of the fir. It was the same pathless flat as on the other side but there was something that kept him from being afraid. Jimmy made his way around the decaying trunks and across the tangled hollows with a kind of briskness, as if he were getting closer. He sensed that they would come to something.

The land began to climb. He saw it from a distance and remembered looking across the valley as he'd come down, at the ravines and rock slides etched into the forest by the morning light. A thousand feet – it numbed the aching pit of his stomach. But he would be safe. It was a place where no one would go, no one would look. He would have time to rest and think –

He started up, and with the effort of the first steps he fought himself. What would there be to eat? To drink? How would he not freeze in the night – this time he would not even have a scrap of rug –

The forest changed abruptly. The dense undergrowth of the valley bottom stopped. The steep slopes were covered in short dry grass and there were big open spaces like meadows between the trees. The red, wrinkled trunks of the pine were tall and straight; their tops leaned in the wind. Only the lowest branches of the fir were dead. The openness comforted him.

He struggled to keep up with Jimmy. The dog went straight up slope, panting hard. They had to be close –

He set his eyes on a tree, a pine that rose very high before it had any branches. He labored towards it, promising that he would rest there. The ground was covered with little plants, some with red leaves and others dark green and jagged like holly; he watched them appear and vanish under his feet. He looked up to see how close he was getting. Clouds were being driven on the wind, from left to right. They were white and billowy with dark undersides.

He thought of resting before the tree. The slope above it came into view and it was just as steep. His legs strained up but Jimmy wouldn't stop. The muscles of his forelegs worked hard from side to side. The animal's determination pulled him on.

He reached the tree and called out. Jimmy looked back as if appealing to him not to give up. He stood leaning against the trunk, looking back down at the valley. He thought it would be far but they were barely above the bottom. The dense forest of the other side rose over him. Tearings of clouds drifted across its sunlit surface.

He breathed in deeply. To sleep in his warm bed, after a big trip to the Dairy Queen. A double bacon burger and a hot fudge brownie delight . . .

His eyes ached shut. He mustn't think about it. It was all gone. There were only these empty places, silent except for the wind . . .

He started off again, picking another tree. The mountain grew steeper and it seemed that he lifted his whole weight with each step. The dog's back labored. He wondered why he would go straight up, not across the slope. He had to be hungry too. There had to be food, shelter. Why else would he come up here?

His legs wavered as if they would buckle at the knee. The second tree receded up the plane of the slope, tossing. The cool mountain air pushed at his chest.

Alf lounged against the wall of the cans. His pimples were bright red and he picked at a scab with his fingernail. He grinned at him evilly, saying nothing, yet he heard his voice. *Out for a little fresh air, shithead? After your brownie delight?*

– The kid started to look up; there was a white explosion. It blinded him; Alf's body burned an image into the glare. Slowly it faded and he saw.

He wasn't a charred corpse. He stood, alive, holding his blackened seeping arms out from his side, the air nauseous . . .

His feet dug into the mountain. He thrust himself up the slope. There had to be something – there had to be –

He reached the second tree and stopped, his chest heaving. He heard his voice. It was calm, cold. *They did this to you. Your empty stomach. Your thirst. Your sweat and exhaustion and your filthy clothes. Your being alone, so alone. They did it all. And you must make them pay. If you are a man you will make them pay* . . .

Jimmy waited ahead, eyes bright, tongue idling furiously. He provoked a strange thought. What if it wasn't an accident, meeting him. What if he was sent here by someone, to help?

He tore a piece of bark off the tree. Sent by who? God? The Care Bears?

He fired the bark over the dog's head. Jimmy looked at him to see whether he should fetch it. He almost laughed. "No boy, I'm not that mean." An image struck him. He broke a dead branch off the tree and held it out. "Hey boy, can you bite? Can you bite? Come on, grab hold!"

Jimmy didn't move. He thrust the stick out and urged him again but still he didn't understand.

The thing choked him. "Bite it, you stupid mutt! Kill it! Kill it!"

Jimmy looked at him, eager to please.

He threw the stick away. It hit a trunk and snapped. Jimmy struggled up the slope after it. He called out but the dog didn't stop. He rummaged through the grass, head low to the ground.

"No, Jimmy! I don't want it!"

He lifted his head, a piece of the stick in his mouth . . .

David took a deep breath. *What's the use. His bite's the same as his bark.* "Forget it! I just thought you might be good for something, besides leading me halfway to nowhere."

They started off again. It was steeper. There was no end, no easing. He raised himself a step at a time, no longer aiming for a tree in the distance but for the closest one. The wind dried his sweat and big clouds passed over effortlessly. His chest rose and fell hard and he wanted to stop every few steps but didn't; in the exhaustion there was a numbness. Time wore thin; it seemed hours ago that he'd stood at the creek, then only minutes. There were no landmarks; the open places with their solitary pine faded into the trees ahead, and when he'd entered among the fir, new meadows opened, leading off in obscure paths. Only when he stopped and looked back across the valley could he get a sense of how far he'd climbed. He was still below the long ridges of the other side, but now the tops of big trees rose shear below him, arched in the wind. The creek was far below him, hidden. The shadows of the clouds moved sharply over the land. For a moment he felt the exhilaration of climbing. Maybe he was the first person ever to have stood here, ever to have seen this.

When he turned back to the mountain, his eye caught something. It was the trunk of a big pine, broken off about six feet above the ground. He started towards it. The rest he had taken was superficial, of the lungs only, and his legs fought their limit. He knew each step.

One side of the trunk was blackened by fire. As he approached it he noticed others that were charred. They stood scattered among trees that showed no damage. Maybe the fire had been a long time ago.

He came up and touched the burned wood. He imagined lightning striking it, a white explosion, and the fire racing across the dry grass. Branches snapped into a swelling rush of sound. When it was over they stood smoldering, dead.

His father placed his hand on Jeff's shoulder. Alf swayed a few steps and fell. Dirt stuck to his burned flesh –

He sought Jimmy. The dog stood, waiting patiently as always, up the slope.

He strained towards him, through a rush of light and shadow –

Suddenly, up through the trees, he saw a mass of gray rock. A foreboding came over him. He forced himself on.

The muscles of his legs tightened in pain. They gave out short of the last tree but he could still see it, the size of it. It was a rock slide. He had seen them from across the valley but not up close. The mountain above him was heaped with angular chunks of stone, weathered gray boulders played on by the passing sun and cloud, bare to the sky except for a few bushes. Here and there rich brown and black fragments of dead wood thrust out of the rubble, caught in it and carried down. It was like an avalanche, but in another measure of time. There seemed no way around it.

What now?

The end of the road.

He dropped to the ground and stared at his feet. There was only his breathing and the dog's panting and somewhere in the big trees below him the hush of the wind.

His hair clung to his forehead. He wiped it aside. His mind was almost blank.

In the far channels of the night his hand brushed a screen door . . .

He startled. Jimmy was standing before him, his muzzle wet and glistening. He was ready to go on.

"You're crazy! We can't go up that!"

Jimmy was unperturbed. He walked to the base of the slide, placed his paws on the first rocks, and jumped up. Then, carefully selecting each foothold, he began climbing from one boulder to the next.

"Hey! What am I supposed to do!"

Jimmy turned back to him, hoping he would follow.

"I'm not risking my neck!"

To his surprise the dog made a sound. It was like a moan but not low. He stared at him, at his wondrous eyes and his beautiful golden dirty fur.

It was insane. But what else was there?

He tried to stand but his body wouldn't go through with it. He fell back and closed his eyes. He saw himself at the top, all the valley below him, the rock slide a forbidding wall . . .

He felt warmth, a rhythmic closeness. He looked. Jimmy had come back down. Their faces were almost touching.

"I don't think I can get up that."

Jimmy's tongue barely pulsed between his teeth. He made the sound again.

He heard his voice stiffen. "What's it to you? What do you want with me? I'm no good to you! I don't have anything! Go find someone who can take care of you."

He saw in the animal's eyes that it was useless. He breathed in deeply. "You're just a dog. That's why you like me . . . You don't know any better. I'll try to climb up there. If I break my neck, who cares?" He smiled faintly. "It doesn't matter, pooch. Not anymore. I'm losing it . . ."

He stood. The muscles of his legs trembled, depleted. The cold water of the stream eluded his throat. Only the wind was cold on the collar of his shirt.

He began to climb. It was harder than any slope. There was nothing secure, nothing fixed. The chunks of stone slid out from under his feet. He caught at the rocks to hold himself; the dislodged pieces crashed into the brush below but he couldn't look. With every step up he slid back almost as far. Soon he was on his hands, testing each rock before he tried to pull himself up by it; still they came loose, bashing his fingers. Sweat filled the corners of his eyes as he searched for the next hold; above the cracked, dust-covered stubs of his hands the mass of stone filled the blurred limits of his vision.

Jimmy stayed close to one side. As his arms and legs emptied of strength he became more unsure of each step. Some of the pieces were dark, lichen-covered boulders bigger than he was, poised on top of the debris. What if he brought them down?

How dumb it would look from a helicopter. A little ant of a kid, lying there squished, where only an idiot would go –

He found a good hold and let his body lie against the slope, an edge of a rock jabbing him with each breath.

He looked down. A giddy motion rose through him. The trees where he'd rested – their tops curved in the wind straight below. How would he ever get down?

He looked back. The end of it was in sight but he'd never make it. He'd slip. He'd lie injured, twisting in pain, the sky and clouds jutting over him. No one would hear his cries. No one would laugh.

His fingers tightened on the rock. He felt it loosen, the sensation of it giving way; he saw himself swept down the slope in a mass of rubble, arms flailing at first then battered as though dead.

He felt cold. His heart beat inside a shell.

You're stuck on this thing. You'll never get off it

He turned his face from the dog. *So this is it. The stupid end to your stupid life—*

He clenched the stone tighter, tears cutting the dirt on his cheeks. It was all nothing, most of all the pain—

Just climb

He stopped. Things moved past him. He held onto the rock in confusion. Had he said that? It had come from within, but as if he hadn't thought it—

Don't be crazy

There. That was him. But the other—

Just climb. He looked up at the slope. In a long plane above him the stones lay broken and heaped on each other, swept by passings of clouds. At the very top, where it ended, a tall pine stood against the wind. If he could just make it there.

He raised a foot and pressed it against the slope. It slipped and held. He searched with his other foot—

The body rolled down, jolted by the rocks it struck, doll-like . . .

He fought to clear his mind of it, to think only of the next step. The Dick stood to one side, shorts immaculately white, poised with his clipboard—

He thrust it away. His foot pushed against the rubble. The step held, and the next. He kept his eyes on the slope, searching for the best route. One of the large boulders was above him; he began to work his way around it. Climbing faster, he pulled himself up; the entire mass of rock under him started to slide. He scrambled sideways and up, outrunning it; the silence was broken by the impact of stones below. He breathed in, trying to keep the fear back. The big pine was getting closer.

Then he saw it. There was something tied to one of its branches.

Someone's been here It ran through him with the quickness of a dream. *Someone's been here!* He peered up at it, streaming out from the branch, clouds rushing overhead; it was a piece of faded yellow rope, nothing more.

His hands gripped the rock, stronger and more sure. He turned to Jimmy. "I knew you were taking me somewhere! I knew there'd be something! Come on!"

Jimmy's eyes brightened. They started climbing together. His hands and feet found good holds and to his surprise he kept up with the dog. One large boulder shadowed the slope over him and then he was past it and could see the frayed end of the rope and the base of the tree. The last steps were light and forgotten.

He grasped the rope, his chest heaving, and stared around. To the left, across the top of the slide, footsteps had pushed dirt into a rough path. It lead up through some bushes.

Jimmy stood next to him, looking out over the valley, his muzzle glistening. He tested the rope; the threads were coarse and dry. Then he turned.

His stomach dipped. Forests strained beneath him in the wind, each tree distinct even down to the creek, hundreds of feet below, then blending up into the mountains on the other side. Their summits seemed barely above him; he stood across from where he had first seen the valley, early that morning. Had he done that?

He stared down at the slide. Darkness swept it from a hurling cloud. Who would climb that? Who would come up here?

Mr. Black. Only Mr. Black.

He saw him poised with his hand against a rock, back bent. *Don't be ridiculous.* He was too old –

– The water was cold, colder than the creek. He'd finished it and looked up in surprise. Mr. Black had said something about a camp. *You go to summer camp?*

"Come on, Jimmy!" He almost shouted, waving at the path. "I'm sorry! I'm sorry a thousand times! I should've known where you were going! Come on!"

He nudged the dog's rump. Jimmy looked up as if humoring him and started off. His summer camp – it was a place he built. He went there to get away from the idiots –

He struggled up through the brush, searching ahead, wishing Jimmy would go faster. The ground became hard and rocky again, with many dead trunks angled across the path; the rotten ones were worn down where it crossed.

Above, not far but at the limit of where he could see, there seemed to be a level place.

A strange nervousness touched him. He approached slowly.

The whole valley opened before him. In the far distance it made a big turn and was lost in the mountains. There was a huge ravine that way; he could see the other side, like another mountain, and the ground dropping off. It fell to his left, too, down to some rocks. Beyond them were tops of trees. He couldn't see whether it was a cliff, or another slide. Straight ahead, there were a few piles of angular boulders in the dry grass, and above them a small level area. It was a place where one could sit and think, and lose track of time. If one weren't starved.

Jimmy trotted up to the level place and stopped, waiting, as if he intended to go on –

He searched the ground. It was broken by a number of intersecting paths, most of them leading down to the edge on the left. A small campfire ring looked almost unused. Beyond it, towards the ravine, the trunk of a pine was split by a blackened crevice.

He stood, suspended. It was the sort of place Mr. Black would like. He'd sit on the edge, one knee drawn up with his arms around it, knowing the secret places along the bottom of the valley where he could catch a glimpse of the creek. No one would bother him –

He turned to Jimmy. Of course. He wouldn't build a shack where people could see it. Anything here could be spotted from across the valley. "Go on, boy! Go on!"

Jimmy happily obeyed. Following, David found himself on a well-used trail. It led from the level place into a stick forest of young fir. Their spindly trunks crowded him into a darkness of moss and dead growth and it came so quickly on the great sweep of the valley that his spirit buckled.

But then it was before him: a little cabin. He knew at once that it was Mr. Black's summer camp. The door faced him; it was partly open, the inside dark. He imagined the old man appearing there but didn't believe it enough to call out.

He approached the door slowly, his stomach taut. Alone, closed around by the dark fir, clouds flying overhead, it seemed a thing of the mind; but as he drew near he could see the thin, crude logs it was made of and the cracks smeared with mud. The roof sagged; it was covered with scraps of sheet metal. He saw his own house, its reflection in the swimming pool. Had he reached the far end of the earth?

Before he could stop him, Jimmy trotted up to the door and slipped inside. A lapping noise came; there was water. He peered in but it was too dark.

He pushed the door back. Wooden shapes emerged in the path of the dim light: a bed, a table. He remembered stepping into Mr. Black's house but this wasn't like that; it was small and cluttered, like an old shed.

His eyes were not fully used to the place before he saw them – round and shiny, crowded on some boards against a wall. He rushed at them, almost tripping over Jimmy, and snatched one down. He held the tin can up, away from the door; the pit of his stomach lurched and he salivated. It was beef stew. One board had cups and plates and kitchen stuff on it; he found a can opener and dug it into the lid. The blade was dull and kept coming out and when he'd gotten it three-quarters open he bent the top back, ripped down a plate, and banged the can against it. The gravy flowed fast then the hardened part oozed out with a sucking noise. He shoved his hands in and ate, cramming the chunks of meat and potato against his mouth, chewing just enough to swallow. When there was only gravy left he smeared his fingers across the plate and licked them.

He searched the cans, turning their labels to the light, shoving aside green beans and pear halves until he found a tin of ravioli. The opener kept slipping in his hands but he scooped the can out with a knife and hurried the congealed globs to his mouth. As he fed he became conscious of how savage the ache in his gut had been and how it gave way to a spreading warmth and fullness, sensations of unimagined pleasure.

They were followed by thirst. He started to look around for a sink but realized, in a moment, that there couldn't be one.

Jimmy had stopped drinking. He was sprawled out near the bed, working at a matted clump of fur on his leg. David looked for a bowl on the floor and was startled instead to see a cooking pot, under a big covered object at one end of the room.

He approached it. The cover was a black garbage bag. He lifted it slowly.

Underneath was a big water bottle like in offices. It was held upside down in a wooden frame so that the neck was well below the rim of the pot. The level wouldn't go down unless Jimmy drank. It was less than half full.

He took a cup down from the board and tilted the bottle back, but he couldn't get the cup under it. He tilted it again, further, and pulled the pot out. Water gushed onto the dirt floor; he quickly filled the cup and pushed the pot back with his foot.

He drank it in one swallow and stood staring down at the puddle. He'd wasted a lot but at least he didn't have to drink after a dog.

The food and water changed him; the world felt less hostile. He looked around the room. The table and shelves were on the long wall to the right as you came in, and the bed was opposite them. There were only a couple of steps between it and the table. That much he'd taken in; but there were things he hadn't noticed: a dusty pile of tools stacked behind the door; some old coats and sweaters hanging in the corner by the bed; and a bunch of pictures and a rag on the wall, over the table.

He went up to it and touched it. It was thick like a blanket and hung from two nails. He undid one end; light struck his face. It was a curtain over a window.

The room brightened, just enough to see how old and junky everything was. The glass was dirty but it didn't matter; there was nothing outside but the stick forest.

He stared down at the filthy plate and the mangled cans. He had food, water, shelter – things that had seemed wildly improbable just minutes ago; why then did it hurt again so soon –

The pictures were cut out of old magazines. They were taped on pieces of cardboard that were bigger, to make them look like frames. The one that caught his eye first was a woman kneeling in the surf at the beach. There were palm trees and the ocean foamed around her and the stiff cups of her bathing suit were bursting. She looked old-fashioned, because of her short hair and the way she leaned on one arm and challenged you with her eyes. He thought of what he could do to her with a felt pen.

Last year a kid called Josh had shoved two balloons up his T-shirt. Jeff popped one with his Swiss Army knife. Everyone roared –

He gasped for air. The stuff ran into his mouth.

– The other pictures were different. One was a city in the Middle East. It had those high, thin towers; they shimmered, distorted, in a blood-red sun. There was a castle high up on a rock over a river and, half-protruding from the thick mists of a pine-covered mountain, houses with weird curved roofs like they had in Japan . . .

He felt a sinking. The pictures weren't like Mr. Black. The place could belong to anybody.

And what difference did it make, if Mr. Black was dead?

His eyes wandered around the room, idly hoping that something would give him an answer. Jimmy stood near the water bottle, watching him. At the sight of the bed he suddenly ached to sink down into it and sleep. It was unimaginable – a real bed, with pillow and blankets, in the middle of nowhere. He remembered the filthy carpet, the futile tugging and squirming to try to shut out the cold –

He lay down on it. A surge of exhaustion shuddered against his eyes and they shut. The musty scent of old blankets enveloped him. He sought release –

His mind slipped through layers of wrecks. As if trying to stop him, a kid stood up at the front of the mess hall. He didn't even know him. He wore thick-rimmed glasses and his voice was wheezy. "Hey man – what are you? You bust in here, you pork out, you make a mess, and you crash. Could it be – is it possible – the world's first shit-encrusted Goldilocks?"

He shot up. Alf guffawed. Kids cracked up. Slop struck his face. He glared through the heap of dusty junk behind the door, a cry rigid, motionless in the air –

For an instant there was only a gleam of steel and then he recognized it, the curve of the handle. A terror of possibilities swept him. It was an ax.

He stood; the room veered and he reached for a wall. He held on; there were bursts of darkness. The room slowed. He edged towards the corner.

He worked it out of the pile of tools. It was an ordinary old wooden ax but well sharpened, the head dark except along the blade where it had been ground shiny in a smooth arc. He gripped it with both hands. Images rushed past him, just out of seeing. His voice came, taunting. *What are you going to do? Play a prank? Throw a rock?*

The tips of his fingers rubbed the smooth, worn wood. There could be an end – an end to all they had done. It would just be to scare them. Within an inch of their lives. To see their faces stupid with fear . . .

His hands tested its weight and balance. To hear them plead. To hear stupid words stumble out of their ugly mouths. *Hey man we're sorry we didn't mean to*

And after that to hear the real begging. The final stuff at the bottom. To hear that, as they had heard him . . .

To have the power. The power to undo it, to take it all back. To make it as if it had never been –

He stood, huge gray places opening in the cluttered shadows of the room, convolutions of fear and longing. It'd have to be carefully planned and timed. He'd wait, a day or two at least. He'd move into position just before dark –

He raised the blade, just to the light of the window. The dog made a noise. He wouldn't even touch them. But there would be an end.

His eyes closed. The room and its ugly junk were gone, then the encrusted touch of his clothes. He was standing on the soccer field at school. Some guys from his class were coming up to him. He rolled the ball deftly back and forth on his foot.

They couldn't wait. When they were still the width of the crease away Steve called out, "David! Is it true? Did you really do that?"

He smiled, enigmatically, and flicked the ball up into his hands.

They came up. Brent looked at him in awe. "Those guys must have been scared shitless!"

His eyes opened. He stared around, at the layer of dust on the tin cans and the cardboard that tried to look like picture frames. They blurred –

His wrists locked on the ax. He went out. He didn't know what he was going to do but his steps were deliberate, hurrying him through the stick forest. Its feeble trunks were as hateful as the room but they were not what he sought.

He came out on the level place. The clouds were thicker and darker and the wind had a chill of distant rain. He started down towards the edge. To his right was the pine with the blackened trunk. He cut towards it. In the seconds before he raised the weapon his mind sought an image. There were many that would do but it was Jeff, his voice swollen to madness. *You're condemned to die man –*

He swung. The ax struck the tree hard, at an angle. A piece of bark flew past his head. He worked the blade out and swung again; the yellow-white flesh grew in the cut and he thrilled at the force of it, at the helplessness of the thing. Alf writhed in the dirt. His face was piss-yellow and crazed and he tried to squirm away, his thigh bleeding horribly. The blade cut deeper into the trunk, into the white heart of it. He circled the helpless lump of flesh. His throat was hot and thick and the voice that forced its way past was powerless with rage. *Who's gonna die now, huh? Who's a fuckin piece of shit now? I'm going to trash you, man, I'm going to trash you like no human shit's ever been trashed*

The kid clawed the dirt, straining to pull himself away, his high gasping noises piercing the night. He drove the blade into the tree, white chips flying, slicing deep into its flesh, maddened by the gap between the reality and the image, tightening his eyes shut, straining to slip the last way –

An arc cut the yellow glare of the slope. The impact and sound exploded through him. He brought the ax down again and again.

At last, in some cold cell of time, he realized that the noises and movements had stopped.

He saw. The tree was deeply gashed, hacked by random blows. It would probably die.

He turned away. The mountains, the clouds, the distant veils of rain sweeping down from them seemed unreal. Slowly, he walked towards the place where the land fell. He wouldn't really do it. But he would see the terror of it in them, see them stripped to nothing, hear them beg for their lives. If he could just do that, he could be free . . .

He approached the edge. It was a cliff, maybe fifteen meters high. Angular blocks of stone covered the slope below, far down through the trees. It was like a fortress.

He stared across the valley, towards the camp. The forest was dark in the rushed shadows of the clouds. Here and there the sun came through, casting random pools of light.

They were laughing. In the hang-loose squalor of the bunkhouse at the end of the day they were flaked out on their bunks, everyone begging them to retell it, shouting each other down.

And in the shadows of the corner, maybe even Greg would smile —

He tried to throw it away, to stop the hot mess in his eyes. *Nobody loves me . . .*

That's right. Nobody loves you. But you've got an ax.

He stepped to the very edge. The rocks swayed. The wind fretted the pine. He raised the blade between himself and the camp.

His voice came, out loud. He hadn't planned it. It was strange, solemn and fierce.

"I proclaim this place the fortress of death!"

It swept out across the valley, jolted on the wind.

"I tried to do what you want . . . I tried to be what you want . . . I tried so hard—"

No. Only strength. Only words that can't be taken back, ever. Like the fall of the ax—

"My name was David, David Ashton. You tortured him. He's dead.

"I'm nothing. This is my fortress. And from here I'll rain death on your shitkicking world."

Elaine Ashton hurried towards the big fake Tudor building. A few kids were strolling down to Silver Lake and they stole strange glances at her as she pressed through them. Behind her, she overheard a girl say, "Maybe that's his mom!"

It didn't touch her. They were on the other side of a barrier, a barrier between herself and the whole world, as if the life and meaning had been sucked out of everything and concentrated in her anguish. Cars swept by on the highway; dust billowed up behind her Acura in the valley of Peachland Creek; she almost overshot the camp. It was all happening without her. Nothing broke the grip of hope and fear.

Two police cars, one a station wagon, were parked outside. They were the only sign. It was quiet, so quiet. The wind blew dust up against the building.

She entered the mess hall. Some people were standing around a coffee urn, a table littered with Styrofoam cups. They turned and stared at her. A woman with big earrings put down her coffee and started towards her, her face changing to a gentle smile.

She searched the room. Joseph had said he was in the director's office, in the mess hall. Where?

"Excuse me, are you Mrs. Ashton?" Her voice was kind and it was not until a man behind her hoisted a television camera to his shoulder that she understood.

"– I'm sorry – I've got to find my husband – can you tell me where he is –"

The lake stabbed at her eyes and darkened. There was an alcove in the corner –

"I know it's difficult, Mrs. Ashton, but what have you heard? Do the police have any leads?"

"– I can't talk to you now – I've got to find my husband –"

"Is it true that David didn't want to go to computer camp?"

She turned and hurried towards the corner. Behind her the woman's heels accelerated. Panic swept her – that there was nothing left but cruelty and grief –

"Mrs. Ashton! The public wants to help!"

The bottom tread of a stair came into sight. If she could just make it –

The heels slowed. She gained the stair and glanced back, once, before starting up. The man was still filming her; but the woman had turned back to the others, shaking her head.

At the top there was a hall, an open door at the end. It must be wrong, it was so empty –

He came into view through the doorway, slumped back in a chair, his eyes shut, encased in shadows.

They opened at the sound of her approach. "Elaine?"

She stopped at the edge of the room. "I had to come – I had to, when you told me that they've found where he's been –"

She'd expected him to be mad, but he said nothing. His shirt was limp with sweat, his chin stubbled. A terror seized her.

"Is there any word?"

He stood. "No."

She jabbed her hand at the room. "Where are the police? What's happening? Is there anyone here except those reporters?"

"There are a few people in the next room. The rest are searching."

"You haven't heard anything more? You've sat here, alone, all this time?"

"Mr. Mahon's taking a nap."

She tried to grasp his tone. He came up to her. In the exhausted depths of his eyes she sensed something, waiting; then it was hidden. His voice was soft and terrible. "Elaine, this wind's no good. They've tracked him to an open area and it's making it hard for the dogs to follow the scent. If it rains, it could be gone completely."

Her hands knotted; she placed them against his chest. Her voice strained up. "Why did they wait?"

He didn't answer.

"Tell me what they found – tell me again –"

"The house is over a mile from here. It's boarded up and for sale. Under the porch there was a scrap of an old carpet. The dogs went straight to it. He must've tried to sleep in it."

She wept.

"There wasn't any blood on it. If he has injuries, they think they're minor."

"– But he wouldn't just keep going, he'd come to his senses –"

Joseph hesitated. It wasn't necessary that she know everything, yet. "He may have left the house in the dark. He might be disoriented."

"He'd shout – he'd call for help –"

He said nothing. He was too quiet, like the stillness outside the building. They wouldn't find him. Another night would come, another sleepless waste, her grief dulling in the long hours until, touched by a memory, it would savage her –

She pressed herself to him. "They have to find him before dark."

"It's hours until then." He held her but she knew something clawed him. Was it the wind, or was even that not all? Were they lying when they said he wasn't hurt?

She looked up at him, into the sunken pits of his eyes. "Promise me – promise me he's not hurt –"

"There's no reason to think it –"

"They beat him, didn't they?"

He broke from her; she felt him tighten before they no longer touched. He went over to the window and stood staring out of it, the light painful on his face.

"Tell me, Joseph –"

He spoke firmly, without looking at her. "There's no reason to believe he's injured. He could not have gone that mile in the dark."

"Where are those boys?"

"They've been expelled."

"Is that all?"

His voice cut through her, steel-gray, powerful. "That's all the camp director has the authority to do. But that's not the limit of what is possible."

She retreated. "If they'll just <u>find</u> him – nothing else matters –"

He stood at the window, silent; she knew there was something he wouldn't say. David wasn't a name-caller, a troublemaker. Why –

"They're coming."

His voice carried the knowledge of the first glimpse; yet hope is such that she rushed to the window. A group of searchers was descending the slope towards the mess hall, silent and weary. They were impossible, ants against a storm; yet in the next group, almost hidden by the big man whose hand he held, there would be a boy . . .

A police officer walked down to the station wagon. A few searchers came after him. That was all.

Her hands were against something, keeping her up; the figures dissipated on the dusty lot and above them the forest heaved in the wind. That first day, she'd let him out on the parking lot, the engine of the bus running, he hadn't wanted to go –

Joseph caught her; she stood void in his arms, the eyes, the voice, the touch of her child devastating and sustaining her, obliterating the room, surging over the relentlessness of the seconds. David was alive. He was stricken, terribly, driven by pain she couldn't grasp; but he was alive. The certainty of it struck her like a jolt to the heart on the edge of death.

Joseph drew back from her. He turned to face the door. The voice of the reporter carried up the stairs, then footsteps.

She pressed herself to him. His chest was like a wall.

The officer entered the room, then a tall man with glasses. The officer's face changed at the sight of her and he rephrased what he was going to say. "Uh, Mrs. Ashton, I'm Corporal Reddick. We've gotten into some meadows and open country and the wind's slowing us down quite a bit. The dogs keep losing the scent, picking it up, losing it again. It's possible he double-backed –"

Joseph cut him off. "I'm through with excuses. You wouldn't have this problem if you'd had dogs here before six o'clock this morning, nine hours after my son went missing –"

"They were being used in a criminal –"

"What criminal investigation, sir? What was it?"

The officer hesitated. "A homicide."

"And yet you knew at ten-thirty last night that there was a missing child. Were you searching for the killer or the corpse?"

Elaine shook against him. "Joseph –"

Briehoffer stepped forward. "Wait a minute. The dogs have to be fresh. They were brought in from Vernon as soon as possible."

"Yet do you deny sir that if you had had them here, in the night, they would have led you to the porch of that house as they did this morning?"

Briehoffer gritted his teeth. "Hindsight's never been wrong yet, has it?"

Joseph Ashton separated himself from Elaine and stepped towards him. "You would have found him. Now he could be miles in the bush and you can't track him. If you ran a business the way you've conducted this search, your creditors would be changing the locks! My son was huddled in a rag, only a mile from here, and you did nothing! You've done absolutely nothing to justify any confidence!"

The woman clutched the soaked folds of his shirt. "Please Joseph –"

Briehoffer faced him, controlled, professional. "Look Mr. Ashton, go home and get some rest. We know the general direction – we're going to start a line search. We'll go through the night if we have to –"

"I will not go! I will not entrust my son's life to your incompetence! I demand the commitment of every available resource! I demand results, now!"

The officer started to intervene. "Mr. Ashton, these people are volunteers –"

"Oh well now, that excuses everything!"

The woman rocked against his shoulder, her voice breaking into sobs. "Joseph, stop – please stop –" He barely noticed.

Briehoffer held in. "I just want to say one thing. I've been here before. I know what you're going through –"

Joseph Ashton brought his fist down on Mr. Mahon's desk. "Don't patronize me! Your competence is the issue – and if you don't believe me, sir, continue to perform as you have!"

The tired lines of Briehoffer's face hardened. He turned away.

"I'm not finished!" He steadied himself against the woman's hands. She pulled at him, her fingers dug against his flesh, her choked sobs maddening –

"David . . . please . . . God, my baby . . ."

"You will hear me, sir!"

Briehoffer turned back, just at the door. His voice was quiet, quiet as the emptiness in front of the building between the gusts of wind. "Mr. Ashton, I've heard enough. I know now why your son is out there."

Towards night it rained. Through the long afternoon and evening the wind-driven clouds closed ranks and darkened until, just as night fell, a hard rain swept down across the valley of Trepanier Creek, lashing the long-needled branches of the pine, pelting the scraps of sheet metal on the roof of the shack. The water ran to the earth, filling the dark room with its cold pouring.

David stirred from a restless sleep. The rain intruded on a dream and at first, as he awoke, it was as if the dream continued. He was in a room. It was like the living room at home but the scene outside was different; the lake was close, like Silver Lake. He moved through the room and the things outside didn't move with him; it was as if they were pictures attached to the glass. This seemed perfectly normal; what bothered him was the television. It was squat, black, and ugly.

He moved away, into another room. Kids were sitting around a table, making paper things out of kleenexes. There was a door, a real one. He asked why they were doing it and one boy said, "Oh, just for fun." They began gathering them up. His heart skipped and his voice grew weak and high in his throat. "Don't take them outside—"

In the first light it would be silly—

The rich mustiness of the old blankets suffused the dark. He huddled in them; it was no darkness he knew but a night more intense than even the night under the porch. He clung to the odor of the blankets and the downpour. If he hadn't found shelter—

There were candles and matches, lots of them, in an old cookie tin. He'd left it out on the table.

He didn't move. The night held him. Its totality was almost a physical presence, as if the solidness of the world had been swallowed up and only its sounds and smells lingered. He reached out a hand for the wall. The logs were there, rough and cold . . .

"Jimmy! Where are you, boy? Jimmy!"

There was a stirring near the table. "Jimmy, come here!" He called out with relief; since he'd attacked the tree he'd noticed a change in the dog towards him, a wariness.

He felt in the dark; his hand found the dog's head and stroked it. "Sleep up here with me, boy. It's warmer—" He patted the blanket. "Come on up!"

The dog jumped onto the bed and settled in, curling himself into a warm ball against his leg. He pulled the blankets up to his neck. There was only the drumming of the rain and the soft rhythm of the animal's breathing. He tried to concentrate on them, to ward off a nameless anxiety which seemed to grow from nowhere, out of the dark. He felt the vast isolation of the cabin in the night; the brutality of what they had done; the slash across his mind of another way they could be made to suffer. But none of these were it. It had no source, except maybe the dream.

Paper things out of kleenexes. Don't take them outside. Who'd be afraid of that? No, it was something else. Like why this had happened to him.

There ain't no why. Mr. Black had said that. Then he'd gone into the house. He'd followed him into the dark room —

And now it was boarded up, cold and empty, and it didn't matter to anyone.

Maybe that's how it was. A lot of pain and shit and you get dragged through it and it seems like a big deal at the time, but in the end it's all covered up and forgotten. Maybe every life ever lived —

He felt for the dog. His fur was long-rippled and he shifted contentedly as he was caressed.

"Do you miss him, Jimmy?"

His voice sounded small; it didn't stir the animal's peace. He wondered whether to love or hate it.

"It's all the same to you, boy, isn't it?"

Of course there was no answer, only the rise and fall of the dog's flank. He stroked him a little longer then drew his arm back under the blankets.

The rain had softened. He lay staring into the dark. Tears started in his eyes. No one would miss him either. Except to crap on and make fun of.

His mind drifted towards sleep, wandering in and out of things, somewhere beyond them a huge longing, unaccountable . . .

In the wake of a far gust of rain a sensation touched him, that he had called out someone's name.

He awoke in the night. He shot up on his elbow, intense images streaming into nothing, and hung on the dark; had he heard something, or was it only in his sleep?

The rain had stopped. For a moment it seemed quiet; then he became aware of something like a vibration, a resonance of a sound already gone. When he tried to fix its source or direction he couldn't catch it at all.

It was just from lying on one side. The noise was in a dream.

He was about to slump back down into the bed when he realized that Jimmy was no longer on it. The dog was standing somewhere in the room. He knew this, yet no sound or form disclosed it. He pushed his voice through fear. "Jimmy! Where are you, boy?"

A soft whine came from the dark, tripping his nerves. It wasn't the noise he'd make if he was hurt; it had a wanting —

"Jimmy? What's wrong?"

The whine came again, not quite from the same place. He was pacing, agitated.

"What is it?"

He strained to listen. The ax was at the foot of the bed. Jimmy had stopped, his fur bristling, his whole body tensed –

A static charge gripped the dark; there was a pressure, a pain, like the drawing of a first breath. His mind tore –

"David . . ."

His arm struck wood; he backed up against it. A cry stopped short of sound; no mass or form of thing –

The dog moaned, his love unhuman. He hurled it back beyond the wall, a night thought, debris of sleep –

"David . . . What are you doing to my home . . . the place I love . . ."

He scrambled out of the bed; his stomach hit something; cans or plates clattered to the floor. He twisted away, flailing for the door, almost tripping over the dog. It wasn't him; it was all inside, like a thought, but it wasn't him. He groped for the latch, his breath shallow, his eyes wild.

"I'm sorry, boy – I didn't mean to scare you."

His hands fumbled at the door but it wouldn't open. He remembered the ax; the handles of the tools were jumbled in dust and he shoved among them, frantic for its sleek grip. Jimmy circled behind him, his noises maddening –

"Take it easy. I can't hurt you."

Don't answer. Don't answer or you're insane. He seized it and hoisted it up, turning into the room, crying out on the verge of sound. *It will go away –*

"Where should I go? This is my home."

He held the ax at the ready, even as the realization transfixed him that he hadn't spoken. It was answering his thoughts.

A voice shouted for calm. *What you're experiencing is not possible. No matter how real it seems it is not possible. It will stop.*

"Light a candle, boy, before you or Jimmy gets hurt. They're in the cookie tin."

The lowest common denominator of 35 and 63 is 7. If Jack drives east from Chilliwack at 40 km/hr and Jane drives west from Hope at 30 km/hr and it is 36 km from Chilliwack to Hope. IF R<M THEN GOSUB 1000

"I can't help you with that stuff. I had a hell of a time balancing my chequebook."

He lowered the ax but still clutched the handle, his eyes shut. *Think of something else. Anything. You're not crazy. It will stop.*

He sensed the dog very close to his feet, ears lifted, muscles taut. *You've gotten him excited.* "Settle down, Jimmy – it's nothing –"

"You're right. Go lie down, boy. I had to come on strong for David here."

He felt the dog move away.

Who are you? He caught the cry and tried to stop it.

"Why, it's me, Harold Black. This is tougher on you than I figured –"

The ax fell back into the corner. He waded through the dark, sweeping his hand in front of him until it touched the table, then the cold roundness of the cookie tin. He pried off the lid, found a candle and matches and struck one. It flared up and in the trembling afterglow the half-familiar things took on their shapes, soft against their shadows but unchanged. He lit the candle and held it up to the bed, the shelves, the water bottle. There was no form, no ghostly image of any kind.

So this is what it's like to be insane.

"Insane? Jimmy knows I'm here. Is he crazy? Hell, he wouldn't hang out up here all alone."

His hands clamped the edge of the table. He closed his eyes, concentrating as if to drive each word beyond the light. *Go away. I am not insane. Just go away.*

"No, you're not insane, but you're stubborn as all get out. You could stand someone to talk to."

He forced his mind harder, fighting panic. *I am in control. It's not happening it's not happening*

"That's why you came up here."

His forehead quivered. He stood bent, choked with denial, the words grinding. "Stop – it's got to stop –"

It did. He waited, expecting the voice to return, but seconds stretched towards a minute and nothing broke the tension. He let go of the table and lowered himself in a heap onto the bed. Jimmy stared at him, uncomprehending.

He sat, stunned, in the shabby dimness of the room, his hands twisting the blanket. Where was he? A junk heap somewhere in a forest. It might as well be Mars. Everything, everything was gone, blown away – his home, his mom and dad, his friends. Was it any wonder that he'd lose his mind too?

No. It was just the last step.

He dug his face into the bed, thrashing for a release, an end. Insane. To see things, hear things, to be at the mercy of – To yell at no one and hack at trees. To lose the last defence . . .

Jeff and Alf, Mahon and The Dick rampaged in triumph, their faces glossy and swollen. The ax cleaved deeper into the white heart of the tree. It started to lean with a sickening creak. They hooted and shrieked –

Stop it! You made that up –

Could he have made up the voice, too – even though he felt, intensely, that it was not his, that it was no more his than if Mr. Black had said those things, standing in the room? There were crazies who did that – who invented other personalities, and kept them apart –

But you were still you while it spoke. Nothing took you over.

Whatever it is, it's crazy. You could stand someone to talk to. That's why you came up here. *Only a nut would say that.*

He pulled himself up against the wall. His hands tried to unwad the blanket. *Jimmy's nuts too. He was whining before you grabbed the ax, before you even heard it.*

Who's talking? Who's saying "you"?

The question unnerved him. It was the sort of thing that only crazies asked –

Jimmy's not crazy. And neither are you.

He sat very still. The shadows of the things in the room pulsed gently on the walls. Mars. The last step.

Tears started to well up in his eyes but, unaccountably, they stopped. Jimmy stood, waiting, eyes sharp, teeth just showing. Thank God for him.

He didn't know what he was going to do. His mind passed through a blankness, refreshing, like a sleep. He was aware of it only after.

He glanced around. "Mr. Black?"

"I'm here, boy."

A thrill swept his flesh. His body felt lighter, not slumped against the wall. It wasn't possible –

"Where's 'here'?"

"With you."

"I don't see you."

"I don't have a body. It wore out. I've still got sort of a feel of it."

"–Are you dead?" He stumbled on it.

"Well, more or less – in a manner of speaking – yes. As a doornail." The voice laughed, a laugh of pure mirth.

David tightened. *That's funny?*

"It'd be a knee-slapper if I had one."

He clutched the blanket. He hadn't meant to be heard. He realized that he spoke out loud because it gave him a feeling of separation, of control; but he was actually naked, defenceless –

"I had a tough time getting used to it too. I like privacy, keeping off to myself, you know, just Jimmy and me and the cat."

"I like privacy and now I don't have any."

The voice seemed to hesitate, as if it stopped itself from saying something. "I'll go if you want. But you've gone to a mess of trouble to come here –"

"No! Wait –" The candle threw the shadows of the cans deep into the shelves. "How do I know you're Mr. Black? How do I know I'm not crazy?"

"Do you feel crazy?"

"– I don't know. Yeah, I do, talking like this."

"What's crazy back in Kalamazoo ain't necessarily in Timbuktu."

"What?"

"You've come a long way, David, a long way to meet me. And I don't mean miles or kilometers or whatever they're teaching you now. That day you showed up at my place, that meant something to me. No one ever came just to visit. I didn't forget you."

He leaned forward. "– You didn't? I wasn't there very long – I was only a kid –"

"Time and age have nothing to do with it. We made a connection. You remembered me when you were hurting, when your fear of that camp got too much for you. I started to pay attention –"

"You mean you've been reading my mind?"

"No. It's not like that. You're not all closed up like you think. On the bus, being carted back up there, you sought me strongly. I picked up on the trouble between you and your dad. You felt like you do now – helpless, powerless. It's not so. I know. I felt the same way about all those rowdies that came tearin' around. It's one reason I died."

His fingers worked the blanket. It was real. It was solid. It could be trusted. "You sound like Mr. Black, but the things you're saying are crazy –"

The voice laughed heartily. "Black is cracked? Then spy through the cracks, David! It's an opportunity! Did you ever do that, spy on a strange house through a hole in a fence?"

He dug into the blanket. "I don't understand! I don't understand anything you're saying! Please, just go away!"

There was a long pause. Jimmy turned, ears and nostrils taut to the room. When the voice came again, it startled him a little; it was more like the man he remembered. "I'm sorry, boy. I've never been any good at explainin' stuff. Everything's so different from what I thought – the words are no damn good but you have to use them. Why don't I just tell you what Jimmy and I did after you left."

He hesitated. "OK."

"I wanted to come up here, to my summer camp. I wanted to sit and feel the wind moving through the arms of the big pine, go hikin' with Jimmy down into the stillness of the valley, not even broke by the hammering of a woodpecker. I wanted to lie at night on that bed where you're sittin', pulling memories out of the past like old-fashioned candies that you could suck on for hours. I wanted to say to hell with the soreness and weakness that had gotten so much worse in the spring, and go on living. But I was sure I couldn't make the climb – not with the supplies. The weeks and months slipped away. The leaves turned and the frost came and I ached. One day in October, I couldn't stand it. I drove out here. It was one of those blue fall days when the light is so soft in the distance, but sharp if you turn right into it. I drove along the creek, to the place where I'd start to hike.

"I never got out of the truck, boy. I sat holding the steering wheel, staring up at the mountain, at the ravines and slides and the steepness of it, and my heart folded. It would be worse to try and to not make it, I figured. I drove home."

He listened, picturing it, remembering how he had stared up at the jagged plane of the slide and the big pine at the top, its branches swept back in the wind, and though he was still aware that the voice was inside him, it did not seem so crazy –

"The snow came and I hibernated, my feelings for the place all closed up. I wanted it that way. I was afraid of the spring. When the sun broke through raw old March and bare patches grew in the clearing, it started eatin' at me again. I cooked up a scheme for getting the supplies up, instead of packin' them in once a week like I used to. I'd build a wheelbarrow track and switchback it up the mountain. I actually thought I could do it, as long as it wasn't time yet to try.

"I don't know that that time would ever have come, except for what happened in May. It was the long weekend. Kids started tearin' around in their four-wheel drives, campin' any old place they pleased with their screamin' ghetto bombers. Friday night I woke up with a start, that stuff blasting outside. I went to the window. A big pickup truck's sittin' right outside the gate, headlights and spotlights glaring at me, engine running, the whole house, the whole clearing throbbing with noise. I stiffened up, scared as a rabbit; I couldn't do nothin' but stand there, hopin' they'd go away. One of 'em got out and started fiddlin' with the gate; he wasn't nothin' but a blotch in the headlights but I could see he was too damn drunk to even pull the wire up. He yanked at it, the rest of 'em in the truck hootin' and shoutin' obscene things at him, till finally he was just jerking the gate back and forth in his hands, the tin cans clanking like lunatic cow bells. They shouted louder and he crawled back in the truck. I could hear 'em all yellin' and swearin' like their music.

"They gunned the engine. I prayed they'd leave; when they didn't, a terrible fear grabbed me, that they were gonna ram the gate. But they didn't. They started leanin' on the horn – can you believe that – as if they expected me to come out and open it. I got mad – more mad than scared. The noise by now was enough to wake the dead. (Think about that, David. If we're asleep, doesn't that mean we can dream?)

"I pulled on my pants and shirt and shoes and stepped out the door. Jimmy wanted to come with me but I told him to stay back on the porch. Walkin' into those blindin' headlights, the noise booming out of the ground, my legs almost seized up. But I kept goin', trying not to look scared.

"I was over halfway to the gate before they stopped honking. That's when they must've seen me, 'cause the driver threw his door open and swayed out onto the running board. He had something in his hand; he raised it to his face, waitin' for me to come up.

"I stopped short of the gate. Words were pushin' and shovin' inside me and I don't know which ones would've come out, 'cause the guy shouted down at me, 'You're blocking the road, mister.' Actually, every other word he used was the same obscene one, but there's no sense repeatin' it.

"'What road? This is my driveway. It doesn't go nowhere but here.' My voice was all stiff-edged.

"The guy went on like he hadn't heard me. 'We're going up to Wilson Lake. We're gonna meet some friends. Open the gate.'

"'I told you this isn't a road. It's my driveway and it stops right here at the house.'

"He let loose a blast of filth like I never heard. 'If I have to climb down off this running board you're gonna be a whole lot worse than sorry, old man. You'd best open the gate, now.' He took a gulp from his can.

"I was real scared, but I was also burnin' up that he wouldn't listen. He gunned the engine. My chest tightened up like he'd put clamps on it and I saw myself reachin' for the wire. But the next moment a reckless feeling came over me. I looked straight up at him and the words just came. 'You can swear at me all you want. I'm not opening it, because if I do, you're just gonna tear around my yard till you find there's no way out, and that's not gonna do either of us any good. You've taken a wrong turn, mister. There's a turnoff into the bush about a quarter of a mile up the road, maybe that's it.'

"He came down off the running board, hanging on to the mirror. One of the others hooted at him from inside the truck, 'Hey Grant, what are ya gonna do, beat up an old man?'

"The guy swore at him to shut up. He kept on comin', bulging into the headlights, his face yellow where it was lit from the side. For a second I was wired to get back to the house but I didn't move.

"He threw himself up on the gate, slipped, and stumbled back. The other guy stuck his head out of the truck and yelled, obscene, 'Grant, what if he's right? What if you turned off too soon? They didn't say nothing about a gate.'

"The guy was trying to steady the rail, actually thinking he could climb it. He just stopped, and for once he didn't swear.

"'Stop playing on the monkey bars – we're missing the party!'

"He stood there, hunched over with the beer in his hand, and I knew he was boiling inside. The other guy shouted at him again to get back in the truck. Finally he looked at me, hate and humiliation glistening in the pits of his eyes. 'Yeah, OK . . . Sorry, mister.'

"I was about to nod, full of relief and gratitude, when the can hit me in the face. I stumbled back, beer sloshing down my neck, runnin' into my shirt, the headlights tearing into me and their music shrieking up into the dark. I tried to wipe the stuff out of my eyes, afraid that the guy was comin', but he'd hauled himself back up on the running board.

"What happened next, I don't know how to describe it. I was so mad I couldn't move or talk, boy; I just stood there, trembling, like my blood was about to bust through my skin. And through all that stinging blinding light and noise I could hear 'em laughin' and catcalling stuff more obscene than I'd ever imagined.

"The first instant it let up the guy turned down the music. Then he was leanin' against the cab, a fresh beer in his hand, grinnin' down at me like he was almighty. 'Next time you lip me, old man, they're gonna wheel you into the old folks' home. You'd best keep that in mind, in case I drop by after the party.'

"He slumped down into the truck, gunned the engine a couple of times, screeched the tires around, and left—"

"Mr. Black—" David fought, for only an instant, the sensation of speaking to an empty room. "Could you—could you please stop for a moment—"

"Sure."

He sat, clutched in the lights and noise and sloshing cold violence, not realizing the energy he used to listen. They should die—

"And they will, too. No doubt about it—"

"Please—"

"I'm sorry, boy. I'll shut up."

He pressed himself against the wall, the blanket wadded in his hand. Jeff came out of the cans, holding the bucket out so it wouldn't spill on him. Their mouths were locked open, making inhuman little moans, as they sank into the heaving filth. He looked on, solemn. Death. Vengeance. Plan it.

Suddenly he challenged, "You wanted to kill them too, didn't you—"

"Yeah. For most of the next day."

"Time doesn't have anything to do with it."

"Neither does death, David. But let me tell you what happened after that. No one—no one in the time and place where you're at—knows why I died. I want you to know."

The candle thrust softly up the rag over the window. Behind it was utter darkness.

He felt a surge of fear. It was starting to feel familiar—the insane, the impossible.

"I went back into the house. I didn't sleep that night. I could hear their noise way off, pulsing through the dark. The wound bled and bled.

Somehow I'd make it up here. I'd live here all summer, no one but me and Jimmy and the big pine sweeping down across the valley so you couldn't see a road. The whole screwball human race could scream up and down the highway. I'd had enough. But I had to get enough supplies up. I gnawed on it like a bone, David, all that night, and every time I was ready to quit I'd see that guy grinnin' down at me, see myself standing there, soaked in his horse-piss.

"Morning came like an old dog with a limp. I knew there wasn't any way to do it but straight on, up the mountain, haulin' it in on my back. You can't have it both ways. You can't get off to yourself by sittin' and pushin' a pedal. But I thought of that October day and how I hadn't even got out of the truck, and I reached into myself hard.

"I got my hiking shoes on, and my canteen and backpack, and Jimmy jumped into the truck and we drove to Peachland. At the grocery store I bought too many cans but I never sat down to a meal that wasn't meat and potatoes and gravy. And of course Jimmy had to have his food. By the time I was done the backpack was unnatural, and I knew it was going to take three loads. But I kept telling myself that I had to do it, that I wouldn't have any peace as long as those punks could get at me. I pictured myself sittin' out at the edge here, the cans all in the pantry, my back against that mossy log, and my eyes lost in the valley bottom, in the stillness of midday and the sun drifting on the wings of a hawk. If I could just get here, all the bad stuff would stop.

"Even before I left the pavement my hands held on tighter to the wheel of the truck. I crossed under the power line and saw it stride up over the mountain towards home, and I thought to myself, *They've pushed you out. The goddamn human race has shoved you right out of your home.* And the powerful voice of those preachers came to me out of my brother's pamphlets, how all men would reap what they sowed in another life, and I clutched those words and held them, the trees blurring into the road—"

"Do they? Do they get what they deserve?"

There was a silence. Finally the voice came. "There ain't no other life. There's just one. You're bigger—you're way bigger than you think."

The blanket crumpled in his fists. "If there's no other life then who are you? Who's speaking?"

The voice seemed to catch. "I don't know any way to explain it, except by what I've done. This thing called time, David, is like a scaffolding— something you set up so you can build, so you can create. That's at the heart of everything. I went inside it with a bunch of ideas, emotions, beliefs. I lived them. They brought me to a deserted road, running from my home, with my dog and a backpack full of tin cans. So I guess you could say I deserved it, what came after. But that run at things, that wasn't the limit of what I am. What point would there be to it, if you couldn't take the defeats, the triumphs, the lessons, and work them on?"

The voice paused. "I suppose you can tell, I'm kinda stewin' on how things went. The whole thing could stand to be reworked. That's why I'm hanging around . . ."

He held on to the edge of the bed, but it wasn't enough.

"Did you die – or did you escape from Riverview?"

The voice laughed softly, just as he imagined Mr. Black would have done, sitting on his porch. "I have to admit, there's some resemblance –"

"Please – just tell me what happened –" The room seemed smaller, its four walls lapped by the candle. Hearing the voice wasn't, by far, the last step . . .

"I got to the place where I parked. I got out, struggled into the pack, and entered the forest, with just one look up. The flats were bad enough with all that mess of brush, but when the land started up I felt it. Soon I was stoppin' every few dozen steps, gasping, the straps of the pack cutting into my shoulders. I resented how the sun was so inexhaustible on the bed of the forest. That's what I wasn't ready for – how small and old and alone it made me feel. I kept telling myself it would go away, if I could just make it to the top.

"You know how it gets, how you're finally down to each step. I needed more than a breather. I'd come to the top of a slope that was mainly dry grass with a few big pine. It was dabbed with flowers. I'd twisted out of the pack and slumped down in a patch of shade when a huge pain hit me square in the chest, fierce, like it wanted to ram me into the ground. I fell over, clutching myself, starin' into the yellow blades of grass, moaning. It couldn't have lasted more than five seconds but I thought I was gone. When it stopped, I just lay there. I can't tell you all the stuff that went through me, waiting for it to hit again. How would they find me? Who was gonna feed Jimmy? Had I cleaned the sink?

"There was an orange cat, sprawled out on some bricks, washing his paws and switching his tail in the sun. I went towards him; a big pair of hands grabbed me and held me back. I cried. I was real mad.

"Time broke up. I fell through it. Its passing doesn't take from anything.

"Finally, real slow, I sat up. I only felt tired. If it was a heart attack, wouldn't it have been worse? At first I just wanted to ease back down the mountain; but the longer I sat there, stroking Jimmy, the pain gone, the more it seemed possible to go on.

"I couldn't go back. I had this idea that they were drivin' me out, that there was nothing else left. I tried dragging the pack up the slope, a few feet at a time; after a few tries I took some cans out and stacked them in a pile, and eased the pack up on my shoulders. The pain didn't come. I thought maybe it was just a muscle spasm.

"I crept on, taking three or four steps and stopping, on and on. If I hadn't been so afraid, I would've seen the world in its own time.

"I made it, David. I lowered myself to the ground out by that log, my shirt stuck to my chest and the backs of my legs shaking. I looked out over the long bend of the valley and I thanked God for letting me see it. Now they could shriek and gun their engines till the moon turned red. I was free of them. They had no more power over me.

"Long before dark I was asleep. When I awoke the sun was sharp around the window. Jimmy was curled up on the bed, twitching his ears and dreaming. I got up. I was sore in the legs but there was no pain. I threw open the door and walked down the path, barefoot. The forest was warm with May. I breathed in deep, that blessed concoction of pine and moss and wildflowers, and near burst with joy. That was the happiest day of my life. We were both ravenous, so I made pancakes and fried up some back bacon. Then we got to work. The most important thing up here is water. You gotta haul every drop of it from the bottom of the ravine. There's a spring down in the rocks there. It's small but steady. Don't damn it up, let it keep flowin'. Are you listening – you're gonna need to know this –"

The water gushed onto the dirt floor as he filled his cup. Jimmy stared at him in amazement –

"Hell, you didn't know, livin' in that mansion with six bathrooms –"

"It's only got four!"

"Never mind. The important thing is that you catch it runnin', not stagnant, in those milk jugs under the pantry there, and bring it up here and cover it in the big bottle. Go every other day. Use that stuff that's in there now for washing. Go first thing in the morning, when it's cool. It was a hard haul back up here, with two gallons, but I made it OK. And that pretty well decided me, that that pain had been some sort of fluke."

He stared into the candle. The light lunged at the cupboard. "But it wasn't, was it?"

The voice slowed. "No. It gave me that day. I draw on it now, hiking up out of the shadows of the ravine with the water jugs bouncing against my thighs, the warmth of that May morning soakin' into my forehead. I started carving a bench with the ax. It was gonna have a curved seat and a backrest. The anger and fear that had driven me eased off my heart. I knew that I belonged here – that I had as much right to be here as the tallest trees. I hadn't felt that in a long time – it was like the first day of getting well after you've been sick. But I couldn't stick to it. That very evening, as I sat out by the ledge and thought how I had to go back for the next load, I imagined headlights lurchin' up my driveway. I pictured the inside of the house and a feeling of dread came over me. Maybe they broke in –

"I slept well. In the morning I fixed up the water for Jimmy and told him he could stay if he liked. I was glad when he wanted to come. The sun was just over the mountain when we started. The grass was wet and the slopes were like long dark corridors down through the trees. The backs of my legs got shaky from stoppin' me. I thought about taking every one of those steps back up. By the time I got to the truck, I knew I'd have to spend one night at the house.

"I crept up the driveway and got out to open the gate. From the moment I saw the porch, I felt as if I'd been gone a lot longer than a day. I stood at the door for a moment. Everything looked the same, but old, unused, like nobody lived there.

"I poured myself some juice and slumped down on the sofa. A newspaper was starin' up at me. Oil was gushing from a tanker into the sea. People were dying in droves somewhere in Africa. An economist was predicting a recession. I threw it on the floor. I saw myself – I practically felt myself – get up to start packing the next load. I knew it was crazy – I knew I couldn't do it – but I wanted to so much. I thought about those punks – how they could come boomin' out of the dark, their headlights sweepin' the windows, any second in the night – but I really didn't believe that they'd come – it was like I was lookin' for a reason, for this grief that suddenly filled me. It took in everything – there wasn't nothing outside it, not even my summer camp. It bore down on me, huge, silent –

"I tried to stand. The room slipped out from under me in a rush of shadows. I grabbed at a chair. Pain seized my chest. I held on to the back of the chair. Jimmy got up. The pain eased then drove down my arm. I called for help. I knew what was happening. That was what was so different from before – I had time to know, to think. And I knew no one would hear me.

"I looked at Jimmy. I was about to send him for help when the pain shoved me down. My forehead hit the back of the chair and I clutched at the wood to keep from falling. I felt it slippin' through the cold sweat of my hands. That terrified me – I was terrified of dropping to the floor. It didn't let up now. I clawed at the wood. I felt myself slippin' towards a thing like a funnel and I cried out to God. My knees hit something; I shook against the chair, hanging from it. It skidded across the floor and I dropped.

"The surface was cold. I twisted against it, fighting to breathe under a huge weight. Jimmy's paws were in front of me. Ugly noises came from my throat and I was agonized that I couldn't call out to him. The pain intensified; I struggled like I was pinned under it. A dark curved thing came over me; I'd worked my way under the table. I saw the room through a barrier. Things weren't filmy or blurred but they'd lost their solidness, stripped right off them like plastic wrap. I tore down past them, a little point of something hoping, wanting nothing now but an end.

"It was sometime then, David, that I became aware of the tearing loose. I didn't understand it; I only knew the pain would be pressing me hard, then suddenly go off a ways, then come back. I had the clearest thought that it was letting up, that it might even stop like the first time; then it grabbed my whole neck and chest. My arm hit a leg of the table and I tried to hold it. I didn't know if my fingers were really clutching it. I saw them, for an instant, as if I was standing looking down – frantic gray things, fumbling at the leg of the table. That terrified me. I was thrown back under a wave of pain, and then another. I jolted through them, a helpless lump of a living thing on a butcher block.

"But I wasn't helpless, not even then. That sensation of looking down – I sought it. I sought whatever it was inside me that could do that. I feared it, yet I sought it. I strained to free myself. Why is it, David, that our bodies have to be battered to the ground before we learn that we are not all flesh, that our being can act?

"At first it was useless. The pain wound on through endless corridors. I labored to breathe under it, to get from one second to the next.

"Then, suddenly, I was over near the kitchen. An old man lay on the floor, his body twisted half under the table. The skin of his face and hands was gray and his eyes were clouded. His arms moved slowly, as if he didn't have control of them, reaching for something to hold. A dog stood over him, whining, stricken.

"I'm not telling you this to scare ya. I want you to know, I want you to know more than anything else, that there's nothing to fear."

His hands felt for the bed. His voice trembled into the empty room. "– How can you say that?"

"How can I not?"

There was a long silence. The candle washed gently against the shadows. He strained to imagine –

"Seeing myself down there, what I'd thought was me, the life almost drained from it, I was frantic. Maybe I was seeing my last seconds. Maybe when he stopped moving – I was swept by terror to go back –

"Something held me off. The hands clenched a little, then stopped. I watched in disbelief. What was happening on the floor – that must be death. I'd gone through it. There was something on the other side. I was stunned; a deep ache of joy seized me. I am that joy, David, and so are you. But I didn't know that. I was too confused. I had the sensation, the feel, of a body, but it was on the floor. I didn't know who I was, what I could do. Time seemed to pass, but it was in the room. Everything was changed. The sofa, the chairs, the fireplace – they had a vibrancy. The stones are granite, yet they resonated as if with some kind of energy. It seemed to grow stronger as I thought about them, as if I could feel inside them.

"I clung to the room. I hated the sight of myself on the floor but I was afraid if it stopped I'd be nothing. Jimmy stood with his head lowered to the body. I felt a surge of grief go out of me towards him. That's when it happened –"

The voice stopped. David waited. The silence stretched too long. "Mr. Black?"

"– I'm here, boy – I – I just don't know if I should tell you this. You must be near swamped by what I've said already –"

"Tell me what?"

"– You know how I said – that you don't have two separate lives, a life and then an afterlife – that there's just one?"

"Yeah, but I don't understand."

"I don't know if this will help or make things worse. You have a body and I don't . . . but you're no more tied down to time and space than I am."

His hand fumbled for the blanket, its mustiness rich and dark in the candlelight. "What are you saying—"

The voice halted. "Across the room—as Jimmy stood over me, my face and hands looking more like death, and I cried out to him—across the room, over by the window, there was a pounding or swelling, like something hitting a piece of wood. It seemed a long way off; but suddenly a person came right through it, shedding things like tassels. His body was vibrant like the things in the room, but even more intense, as if his flesh, his form, was being generated by incredible energy. I was stupefied—but suddenly, I felt safe. I—I asked him if he was an angel. He smiled and said, 'Why don't you call your dog?'

"I did. I called him. It was a thought—a thought powerful with love. I saw in the room that Jimmy lifted his head from the corpse, listening. I called him again and he stepped back, his body tensed. I felt his longing. I was wild with joy—"

The voice strained to collect itself. "David, that being was you. You came to me when I was lost, in the most terrible confusion. In the wake of death—"

He stared into the flame, numbed.

"Like I said, you're bigger . . . you're way bigger than you think."

Softly, almost out of hearing, the rain beat against the high windows of the Ashton's living room. Earlier in the night it had lashed the panes, driven on a sudden gust of wind across the lake, but by eleven o'clock it had long since tapered off. The streaks hung on the glass, reflecting the lights of the room.

Elaine sat huddled on the sofa, kleenex wadded in her hand, staring emptily into the dark. Joseph stood, waiting. Somehow, he'd managed to sleep a little in the afternoon. She tried not to resent it.

All evening the phone had rung: business associates of his, friends of hers. After the relentless instant of hope the conversations were brief, awkward, painful; they became a weary ritual. Yet each kept note of who did not phone.

The suddenness of the rain, battering the windows in the dull twilight, had broken her. She'd wept uncontrollably and he'd held her, telling her it was not hopeless: that he'd found shelter the night before and could do so again – that the search would go through the night – that in the direction they believe he'd gone there was a gravel road that led to a number of houses –

She'd twisted in his arms, her eyes fierce. "There was a road right there – right at that house –"

"He's afraid of being found by people from the camp."

The evasion in his eyes had been almost imperceptible. Her hands strained. "I just don't – just don't understand why he would keep running."

She'd already forgotten what he'd said – some meaningless reassurance. David was somewhere out there – cold, alone, starved. And there was little chance now of the dogs finding him. He must be lost, stumbling in panic through an endlessness of forest, night, and rain.

Her fingers dug into the kleenex. What was driving him? Was it some confused notion that he'd be punished – that she and Joseph would not cry out in an agony of joy at the sight of him? How could he doubt that?

Or was there something they weren't telling her?

She'd sensed it in Joseph at the camp, when she'd asked what had been done with those boys: he'd reacted at his tensest – rigid, totally concentrated, the few words he spoke deadly with meaning.

She hadn't wanted to know, then: but now she had to – she had to know anything that would explain why David would choose this, rather than come home –

She rose, shakily; he didn't seem to notice. He stood, half turned from her, staring out into the dark.

"Joseph – promise me – promise me he's not hurt."

He turned, startled, light piercing the crevices of his eyes. He didn't speak at once.

"They found no sign of it –"

"But he could be hurt without bleeding."

He didn't answer. She stepped towards him. "They can't be sure – those boys could be lying –"

He looked at her in a way she couldn't grasp. She clutched the kleenex to her stomach. "Joseph – if there's anything – anything being kept from me –" The words trembled through her dim reflection in the glass.

His eyes ravaged her, weighing something in great pain. When he spoke the words were measured; but they became edged with something she knew and feared. "I didn't want to tell you at the camp, with all those people. I knew I'd have to, but I thought there'd be a better time . . . There was a witness – a boy who didn't go to the movie. He stayed behind, in David's bunkhouse. The police have questioned him very carefully. There's no reason to doubt what he says." He turned away, towards the dark columns of glass; within reach of one, he faced her.

"What they did to him was not primarily a beating."

She stood, suspended in fear. "What do you mean?"

"Jeff – the honor student – knew that a thug might be useful to him. He cultivated an acquaintance with this Alfred Spittal. There's nothing unusual in this, if you know the type as I do. The business schools are plagued with them: flippant young men, oozing daddy's wealth, breezing through their courses on flying carpets. Occasionally one of them gets short-listed and I have the pleasure of watching him unravel. While pretending to be irreverent, iconoclastic, etc., they're actually the worst sort of panderers – 'sucks' I believe they're called. Their deepest fear is that someone will expose their lie. David did that."

"How — how do you know this —"

"Mahon wouldn't say it of course — he's one of Jeff's admirers. But it's not hard to piece together. Jeff surveyed his domain — saw David off to himself, working hard, serious, intent — and knew that he'd found the perfect foil. The easy target. He hazed David in class and in the bunkhouse. But the persecution was too easy — it bored him — so to liven it up he arranged for Spittal to bully him on kitchen duty. They made camp hell for him. It was all in fun until David did the one thing Jeff never imagined he could do — he saw through him. He called him a 'suck.' Suddenly it wasn't a game. David had to pay — he had to pay so terribly that he'd run from the camp, taking the truth with him."

She stood, very still, the creases of her face deep in shadow. "What did they do?"

He wondered how much they would endure.

"They waited until it was dark and everyone was at the movie. They thought David was alone in the bunkhouse, depressed and outcast. Another boy was used to lure him to the washrooms. There's a place there, dimly lit between two buildings — oh yes, it was well planned. The Jeffs of this world make it their business to acquire underlings, connections, debts owing —"

He stopped. In some other world or time the boy stood across from him, the glare of the sun off the lake burnishing the surface of the huge oak desk —

His throat almost closed. "— He tried to defend himself but he was no match for the two of them. Spittal held him pinned while Jeff taunted him and struck him in the face. But a simple beating couldn't satisfy an ego the size of Jeff's. A bucket lay waiting in the washroom — a bucket of human excrement. David didn't beg for mercy until it was placed in front of him —"

Her head fell to the gnarled shadows of her hands. He thought she would cry out and fall against him; but she wandered slowly by, to the darkness of the glass. She clutched a mullion, her face hidden from him, the streaks of rain stopped, motionless on the pane —

"While Spittal held him, Jeff shoved his head into it, again and again. They told him he was condemned to die — they held him in it until his lungs gave out —"

The huddled shape twitched.

"God knows how it would have ended if an instructor hadn't heard them. They ran. David fled into the bush."

He waited; she didn't move.

"Mahon didn't volunteer this. I pried it out of him, and made—"

She cut him off, her voice heaving, her face twisted up at him gouged with wrinkles, her fingers dug against the wood like claws.

"Kill them! Kill them!"

Day came to the valley of Trepanier Creek on a soft memory of the storm. The wind was still but a few clouds lay scattered along the ridges, their undersides inflamed in the dawn. It was long after that the sun broke over the summit of Mt. Clements into the dark, rain-soaked forest on the eastern side. The rag over the window of the shack held the warmth of late morning by the time David stirred.

He awoke slowly from a vast sleep – a sleep powerful with impressions of vanished dreams. He felt regenerated, as he hadn't thought possible; he stretched out in the bed, luxuriating in it. Jimmy waited for him to stop, then settled back in at his feet, unperturbed.

He was hungry and had to pee but he didn't get up. The sensation might end –

The events of the night seemed close, as if their presence filled the room. Shortly after he'd described his death, Mr. Black had said he needed his rest, and that they'd talk again tomorrow. He hadn't objected. Listening exhausted him; but it was also that the voice and what it was saying were at once so familiar and so bizarre that a thousand questions wouldn't be enough.

And it was still possible that he was crazy. He didn't think so, but what lunatic did?

An idea came to him. He could test the voice with questions, things that he, David, couldn't know –

But how would he know the right answers?

They would have to be things he could find out.

The possibility made him nervous. What if the voice flunked? Wasn't he crazy, then?

He pulled himself from the bed and stepped outside. There was a question: where's the outhouse?

He almost smiled. It was a beautiful morning. The air had that freshness that it can only have after a rain, delicious to breathe in. Patches of sun glistened along the path. Jimmy wandered out the door and stretched.

He thought of making his way, barefoot, down to the level place, the valley opening into the distance . . .

They were all in class. Jeff lolled in his seat, a contented grin on his face. Radcliffe called some kid up to the blackboard. The chalk squealed across it –

He stepped aside from the path and peed. Jeff thrashed as it splattered him.

– He turned away. His stomach felt light. He'd tell the voice why he was here. It'd try to talk him out of it but it wouldn't. Maybe it would be like the good angel over your shoulder in a cartoon. A bleating wimp.

He went back inside. There was nothing but cans in the pantry. No granola bars, no Pop Tarts, no cereal – just cans, and two boxes of crackers that had gone stale. He wouldn't last long –

He smeared jam on the crackers and opened a can of pears.

They did this to you

As he ate he remembered that he had to get fresh water. He took the milk jugs out from under the pantry and wiped their dust on his pants. Jimmy made an eager sound and started for the door.

"Hold on, boy! Let me finish and get my shoes on."

– Mr. Black would understand. Those guys who threw beer on him – they killed him. They made him desperate to climb the mountain.

The last pear slice slid into his mouth. He tugged at the caked runners. If the voice was Mr. Black, it would help him. It would tell him where Jeff and Alf were, any hour of the day or night . . .

To know their thoughts, right up to the instant he struck –

He stepped out into the morning. Jimmy trotted around him and took the lead. At the level place he turned towards the big ravine. It got steep fast; a trail descended the slope at an angle. The fir and pine were well spaced and he could see the faint scar of the path here and there among them. It had been well traveled once; he remembered what the voice had said about going every other day. Drops of water hung on the long needles of the pine and a fragrance stirred from the earth.

The milk jugs bounced against his thighs. The path took him towards the head of the ravine; across it was a big rock slide. He thought of how he'd fought straight up, and gotten stuck and scared, and something inside had told him to just climb. Could that have been Mr. Black? Could that have been yesterday?

The trees, the stones, the scent of rain from the earth – they'd all been loosened from themselves.

A thin band of aspen crowded the bottom of the ravine, seeking water. He saw where the trail entered the tangled brush. It was just like at the creek.

A strange thought came to him. All these trees – they knew what was best for themselves. The pine sought the dry, open slopes – the aspen the low, moist places. The fir could live in either. Why couldn't his life be like that? Why couldn't he just know what to do?

He kicked a rock off the path. Some nerd would write a gooey poem about it and the teacher would make it into a poster and out on the playground nothing would change. People weren't trees. They made shit.

Jimmy entered the brush. As he approached he heard the dog's tongue lapping water. He came up to him at a rocky place surrounded by saskatoons and aspen. A narrow sheet of water slipped from one ledge to the next. It was mossy around the edges but clear in the middle. Someone had carved a channel in one of the ledges so that you could fill a container.

He sat down on the rock. He didn't feel like just filling the jugs and going back. It was time to plan it. He couldn't live here very long. But if they confessed, if he came out on top – maybe Dad would listen. Maybe he'd believe him then, when he told him what camp was really like. But he couldn't fail. They would have to be stripped to nothing, their faces white as cat turds, as he stood over them with the ax.

He tapped the plastic jugs against the ledge, alternating them. It swelled to the rhythm of a drum. *They have to bleed. Why don't you admit it? No terror will be good enough. They have to groan in their blood.*

His hands clenched on the handles. They stopped. *Just do it*

Was he waiting for the voice to talk him out of it?

He glanced around. The bare slopes of the ravine rose over the tops of the aspen, glaring in the sun. Maybe just one cut. But where, how – in the middle of the night, in the bunkhouse, with twenty other kids around?

No. He had to have a plan. Jeff would drop to his knees in front of them all and say that he had done it because he was the world's biggest suck. A total faker who'd fooled everyone, used everyone. They would all swear to tell Mahon –

It was that, or hack him to pieces, alone at night in the cans. *You're gonna die man*

His body stiffened against the rock. *They'd find you. They'd hunt you down. With dogs, helicopters –*

He pulled himself out of it. OK, it'd just be to frighten them, make them confess. Then Dad would listen. Then he'd destroy them.

What do Mom and Dad think now? That you ran away just cause you couldn't hack it?

His hands bore down on the rock. No! It would be swift, decisive, terrible – one moment Jeff would be all smug in his bed; the next –

He drew himself up. Finally he knew what to do. The endless mucking with grief, pain, hate – instead there would be one cold, clear purpose. All he had to do was plan it. The voice, the stance, the position of the ax. The shock on their faces as Jeff struggled stupidly out of the sleeping bag. The first gleam of joy in their eyes as Joe Cool started to beg . . .

He glanced around vacantly. Was the voice listening?

No breeze stirred in the bottom of the ravine. The water was silent except for the faintest rush in the air, that might have been imagined. He didn't like waiting, wondering if he was being overheard.

He closed his eyes. "Mr. Black?"

There was nothing. He said it again and there was still nothing and it made him afraid. He thought how strange that was.

Maybe he's doing other stuff.
Maybe he's spying on you.
Maybe you just made it all up.

He'd try again later. What was the hurry? The voice would just say he shouldn't do it.

He stood. Jimmy had gone off; he could hear him somewhere through the brush. He held one of the jugs to the water. It flowed into the plastic and he saw that it would take forever.

He shifted from foot to foot. Minutes passed and it was still mostly empty. But he didn't have any choice.

He sat, stood, leaned, stopped, and started again. If he held the jug almost straight the water made a soft drumming. The sound faded and came back as he moved, like the patterns of sun on the rock.

His mind wandered. Malcolm was rolling on the grass. Radcliffe straightened his tie, smiling, the way he always did just before he reached into his desk for the quiz . . .

Mom sat on the edge of the sofa, her back turned –

The jug felt heavy. Jeff would confess every last thing. How he got the idea on the bus, when he got in trouble with The Dick. How he made friends with Alf and planned it with him. How they even had a name for it, Geek Liberation Day –

He shoved the stupid thing against the rock –

David, the connection between us

The jug dropped and slid down the ledge, gushing; he scrambled after it and caught it. His eyes swept the ravine. "Mr. Black?"

It was very quiet. He felt the growing warmth of the sun on the rock. His voice echoed sharply. "Mr. Black!"

. . . On the edge of silence the water flowed.

He sat down in a heap and covered his face with his hands. To be certified nuts. To be caught between two worlds and not understand either of them. To be pestered by crazy, impossible things when you know . . . that all that matters is to win . . .

The silence pulsed. It faded gradually and there was nothing, nothing except the faint slipping of the water on the rock. His mind drifted against it. It was a restful, idle sound and he let himself be carried along.

Suddenly, the rush of the water was immense. It was as if he'd become a part of it – a vast, aching cold stream emerging from the earth, many layers deep, all moving headlong down a creviced incline of stone. At the end of each ledge they plunged, the layers staying together in midair, a structure of ever-changing parts.

Gradually the water slowed. The layers separated into individual things like blood cells, or blurred points of light on an escalator, moving in creative unison out of the dark. He watched in awe. The rock itself was a matrix of tensioned energy, a pattern of something projected into time. It too consisted of particles like lights, vibrating, the cells of water endlessly jostling against them.

Like the stream emerging from the dark, the voice entered. "David, the connection between us isn't like a phone . . . I reach you through parts of yourself you don't believe exist; you meet me there. You wouldn't do it except for the trouble that's driven you off the beaten path. I wanted you to come down to the spring, like I did with Jimmy. It's a place you can feel how things really are. The water and the rock – do you think they're so very different from each other, and from you?"

He stared deep in the stream of moving lights. He didn't know what to say.

"They're energy, David, they're energy that's thrust itself into this thing called time, in a creative burst. That burst is the thing in time; it goes on and on. Nothing's just created and then done. Nothing could exist where you are if it weren't boisterous with that energy, that thought. When I came down here with Jimmy on the morning of a hot day, I'd sit and listen to the water before heading back, and sometimes I'd get lost in it and get some notion of this. But it wasn't until I saw myself twisted under the kitchen table, turning gray, and could feel the granite stones of the fireplace like they were alive – that I knew life and death weren't what I thought."

The particles fluctuated, the symmetry of their motion hypnotic. "So now you're telling me that rocks are alive."

"They're <u>acts</u>, David, like you. They're energy exploring the possibilities of time. The jagged peaks of the Rockies started out as mud on the bottom of an ocean. It got hardened and pushed and shoved this way and that, hitched up with a bunch of islands from across the Pacific, and finally thrust up ten thousand feet. It's called seduction – a guy I played crib with told me about it. Does that sound dead to you?"

He locked his fist into his other hand. "If I'm an act, I'd sure like to know who's doing me. He screwed up completely."

"How do you know? It's not over."

"I wish it were."

There was a silence. The stream accelerated. The particles started to blur together.

"Do you feel the water, David? I talk about seeing things but I can't see – I can just remember, and feel things from the inside, I guess you'd call it. I was hoping the water would give you some notion of the immense pouring of energy into time. It takes countless forms – rocks, trees, people – but they're all <u>knowing</u>. You were starting to feel this about the trees on your way down here – how each type knows what's best for itself, how to flourish. A pine knows how to be a pine. It trusts itself. It's as conscious as we are, but we don't choose to recognize it."

The points of light stretched, moving ever faster, until he could no longer make them out. For an instant the stream appeared again as moving layers, folded down the rock; then he was seeing it through his eyes. He stared at it, confused; it was a little film of water, insignificant.

His fist tightened in his hand. "What do you want with me? You don't sound like Mr. Black! He came up here to get away from people. He knew they're assholes. He knew the world's sick and rotten. He didn't spout any crazy stuff . . . If he could hear you now, he'd bust his gut laughing–"

He stopped, somewhat afraid; to his surprise the voice didn't seem offended. "I guess you're right. He'd lean against one of the porch posts and laugh till his side ached. And it would do him good."

"Then who are you?"

The voice hesitated. "I asked the same thing about that boy, who told me I could call my dog."

He thrust an arm straight out against the rock. "You made that up!"

"No. I made myself up. And that's no joke. I'm not too happy with some of it. Some of the ideas I was goin' on didn't do me much good."

He pushed himself to his feet. "So now you're trying to make up for it by telling me this weird stuff! I don't want to hear it. – I know what I'm going to do. Nothing you say will stop me."

"What are you going to do?"

"You don't know?"

"I picked up on some of it but it's not too clear. You're going back to your camp with my ax. Are you gonna give those kids who hurt you one chop each in the bunkhouse, or are you going to make soup out of one of them in the john?"

His torso stiffened.

"I'm not poking fun at you, David. I'm not automatically plugged in to everything you're thinkin'. The stronger you feel something, the better I can sense it. And your emotions about those guys are very strong. You want to kill them."

"No! – I – I'm just going to scare them into admitting what they did! Right now Mom and Dad think I took off because I'm a wimpy little loser who couldn't cut it! Jeff and Alf have bragged to the whole bunkhouse – maybe the whole camp – but no one will talk! I've got to get them – I don't care what you say!"

He picked up the jug and saw, angrily, that he didn't have enough water. But to have to stand and listen –

He shoved it under the stream. Adults. We know everything. We know what's good for you. When you get to be our age you'll understand . . . that you were just a stupid kid –

The jug trembled; water ran down its side. He fought to stop it, idiotically, while the great voice on the other side of the desk calmly battered him . . .

No! Not here. Not anymore. No one could tell him what to do. Least of all a dead guy –

But the voice was silent. The drumming of the water deepened. He was glad at first, but as the seconds stretched he was tempted to call out. Jimmy poked his head through the bushes, enthusiastically. His ears were wet.

Finally the voice answered. It startled him; it was unsure, even nervous. "You're right, David. I can't make you do anything . . . It's just that I'm takin' a hard look at what I believed and where it got me, and it's shaken me up–"

"What have you turned into, some sort of shrink?" The mouth of the jug veered back and forth across the stream. "I'll save you the trouble – all my life I've been treated like a little geek. I've never been good enough for anyone. I guess God or someone decides if you're Cool or Not Cool, In or Out. If you're Out you get shitted on." The jug tipped violently and he saw himself slamming it against the rock. He glared through the stillness. "They plotted to make camp hell for me. They beat me up and shoved my head into a bucket of shit. And you're telling me I shouldn't go back up there with an ax?"

He'd started to triumph in it when the voice asked, "Wouldn't it just happen again?"

"What?"

"If you're Not Cool, won't you just get crapped on again?"

"No – they'll be scared. Word will get around –"

"But what if you move away, like to Vancouver?"

He hesitated. "– No . . . If you've got the guts to do something like this, you'll be changed –"

"You're right. And people will know it. They'll feel that you're unafraid and they'll treat you differently."

He stepped back from the water, baffled. "Wait a minute. Are you saying now that I should do it?"

There was a pause. He sensed, again, that the voice was unsure, feeling its way. It disturbed him.

"There are other ways to create that change –"

"No! There's no other way! I've gone through it over and over! It feels like years! – If you're Mr. Black you'll understand. You'll help – you'll tell me where they are and what they're doing."

He felt a jolt.

"– David, I've been trying to explain, I don't know everything –"

"You know where I am. You knew where I was on the bus."

"But you were trying to reach me. I was trying to reach you. It wasn't easy."

He stood, absolutely rigid, clenching the jug, another voice trembling off, its cry sucked into nothing. "Listen to me. I don't know what you are.

I don't know what I am anymore. But I have to do this. Maybe where you are it doesn't matter – maybe it's all some kind of game or joke. But it matters here. I've got to get them. And if you're Mr. Black . . . if you care about me . . . you'll help."

The air seemed hard, sharp as an edge of steel. He stood on his side of it.

Twice he thought the voice was about to come. He grew impatient and picked up the other jug.

It answered abruptly, as he was on the verge of starting back. "There aren't many things worse than staring up at a mountain, then just getting back into your truck . . . I'll do what I can. But I'd like it, if you could give yourself a little time."

"Why? So you can try to talk me out of it?"

"– Because when it's done, you'll go back to the life that you know, and it'll be the end of our talk."

"Oh." The idea stirred his feelings. He was anxious, then relieved – he'd be home again, and sane, the terror of their stinking faces seared into him for life. He had an advantage like no one ever dreamed. The power of it seemed to charge the stillness, more than he could grasp –

"You're overrating me, boy. Your own power brought you here. And nothing else will get you back."

He reacted angrily. "What do you mean? I've never had any power! That's the whole point –"

There was no answer. He waited, testing the silence. It was unfair to get the last word in and then vanish, like a bickering old man –

Come on. He gave in. He agreed to help. Think of it –

He started along the trail, forgetting to call Jimmy. Wasn't anything possible now? He could catch Jeff in the cans. As he dropped to his knees he would suck in the smell of the floor. The urinals – he could be forced to face the urinals – the ax raised to the level of his neck –

The trail started up. The slopes were drying out from the rain and the pines were tall in the sun. The earth was charged. The water rocked back and forth in the jug. As the path steepened he became aware of something in the far distance – a pressure in the air.

Lick it, shithead. Lick it, or –

No – he'd confess – in front of the other kids –

Something shot past him. It was Jimmy. He bounded off the trail ahead and began sniffing around a fallen log. The sun glanced off his coat and for an instant it was like the spring, the infinite points of light flowing over the rock –

Something ached. If there was all this power, and it was so creative, why —

Your own power brought you here.

He shoved it aside. *Dad and Mr. Mahon — they have power. Not a little geek of a kid — unless he grabs it with an ax —*

The thing was almost tangible in his hand when the pressure broke in on him. It came from across the valley, or beyond, a low swelling. Jimmy stood motionless, ears lifted.

He labored up the slope faster. Through the rise of his breathing he thought it might be gone.

He didn't stop until he came out on the level place. He set down the jugs and walked towards the edge. He strained to listen over the pounding of his heart.

The valley opened below. He could see nothing unusual. The sun had lost the translucence of morning and lay heavy on the tops of the trees. But beyond the far ridge he felt a violence in the air.

It burst towards him suddenly, the noise far outweighing the sight: a helicopter, coming directly towards him from the camp. He stood, fixed by the hollow drumming of the blades, contradictory motions shooting through him. The first was to hide; then he saw himself waving with both arms.

It banked and turned in a broad arc.

A fierce pain rose in him. Of course Dad would make them look. He and Mom must be so worried. But no one else cared. They made jokes —

The impact broke towards him again. He stiffened with fear, straining to spot the thing against the opposite ridge. He caught it, swooping high over the trees. They were searching the other side of the valley —

Impulses churned inside him, half-formed images of humiliation —

He turned and ran towards the shack. The firs tossed wildly in an unnatural wind — there were shouts —

He stopped before the door. The scraps of metal on the roof lay hot and bright in the sun.

Quickly, through a furious corridor, he snatched the ax from its place and began chopping branches from the trees.

As he weighed his words, Inspector Burton's hand stroked the ribbed velour fabric of the chair he occupied in the Ashton's living room. He was a big, muscular man with a square face, but there was something in him that gave Elaine hope that he cared. Maybe it was nothing more than his eyes, their soft blue . . .

"He's got to have found shelter. With the overnight temperatures up there, and the rain and wind and the way he was dressed, it's very important. But that wouldn't necessarily be difficult. That house where he was has quite a pile of stuff behind it. He could've found something there – a sheet of plastic – an old coat –"

But if he didn't – She sat clutching her stomach, afraid to say.

Joseph stood facing them. His suit was fresh but his face was locked, gray. She knew he was waiting . . .

"We're expanding the search into the valley of Trepanier Creek. It's heavily forested; the helicopter might spot him but the only way to really cover it is on foot. Normally, it'd be easy to orient yourself there; the valley goes down to the lake, and there's a road at the bottom. But he may not have gotten that far and we're not discounting the possibility that he's doubled back."

Her grip tightened but there was no flesh, only a void of fear. "He may not have gotten that far? What do you mean?"

He stopped his hand. The firmness in his voice terrified her. "Mr. and Mrs. Ashton, I have to consider every possibility . . . One of them is that David has panicked. People alone in the bush can become totally confused and afraid. They've been known to run from the searchers –"

She shuddered at the edge. "You think he's been overcome by exposure, don't you –"

"There's a good chance that's not the case –"

She shot to her feet, savage. "David's alive! I don't care what you think – he's alive! And if you give up Joseph and I will search those mountains step by step!"

He looked up into the dark shadows of her eyes. "We're not giving up, Mrs. Ashton. We have two hundred people searching. We don't know what condition he's in. That's one of the reasons I'm here. Anything that would give us a clue to his mental state might help."

There was a silence. He broke it. "Did David ever threaten to run away from home?"

Her hands clutched at each other, raw. " – No – never. Why do you ask –"

Joseph advanced to her side. "Inspector, you're not going to subject my wife to this. You're not going to put her through more torture to cover your mistakes. David didn't want to go to camp. That's not unusual in a boy of his age. He had some academic problems last year. I discussed them with him and we reached an understanding. If you want clues to his 'mental state' focus on what was done to him by that scum."

The man's jaw hardened; his hand stiffened against the chair. Joseph felt a glint of pleasure that he managed to control it.

"Sometimes I have to ask questions I'd rather not ask. David's attitude to camp and home could be the key to finding him. I've been interviewing some of the students. Their stories agree that he was very unhappy, that in his eyes he'd been forced to go and he could never live up to what was expected of him."

Joseph's lips barely moved. "Children exaggerate."

"Possibly, but there was that incident last year. I know it may not have seemed important at the time, but it is now. Has David every told you where he went that afternoon, what he did?"

Gray, hollowed, the man and woman stared down at him. Finally Joseph demanded, "What are you talking about?"

"– You don't know?"

Elaine's voice rose. "No, nothing – what incident?"

The muscles of the inspector's face drew taut. "I'm surprised you weren't informed. David ditched a canoeing session last year. He left the camp and returned late in the afternoon. He was very tight-lipped about it, even to the other students. He said he'd just wandered around the forest –" He felt Joseph Ashton standing over him, motionless. "I assumed Mr. Mahon –"

Joseph's hands clamped down on his chair. His eyes, up close, were awful. "You mean to tell me that David ran away from camp last year and we weren't even told?"

He tried to hold his ground. "I'll discuss the matter with Mr. Mahon. There may be circumstances –"

Joseph exploded. "Circumstances? What circumstances, sir, could justify not telling a child's parents that he's run off! And what circumstances justify withholding that information now, when the slightest scrap of evidence might save David's life?" He thrust his hands off the chair. With a broken cry Elaine reached towards him – "Inspector, we've been subjected to incompetence, indifference, insult – and we've endured them all in the hope of finding our son! This is the last straw! I'm turning this entire miserable affair over to my attorneys. It's absolutely unbelievable that you'd have to get this from the students –"

Her hands clutched at his suit. "Please Joseph – they've got to keep searching –"

His eyes bore down on the man. "They'll search. They'll search like their lives depended on it."

Inspector Burton pushed himself to his feet. "At least let me talk to Mr. Mahon."

"Fine. Talk to him. Tell him this: that I hold him grossly negligent, unfit to have children entrusted to his care, and directly responsible for what's happened to my son! Now, sir, if you'll excuse me I have a phone call to make."

The cop fought for control. "– Mr. Ashton, my first and only concern is to find David. Your attorneys aren't going to do that. Those two hundred volunteers need your support. One of the reasons I came is . . . Mr. Briehoffer asked me to tell you that he regrets what he said."

"Good day, sir."

Elaine followed him to the door. As he bent to put on his shoes her voice over him was wild, trembling. "Promise me – promise me you'll keep looking."

He stood and faced her, noting the nervousness of her hands and the lost long way into her eyes. "We will, Mrs. Ashton."

"I'll – I'll talk to Joseph. He's very upset about the search."

He hesitated. "People have different ways of handling these things. But some of them only end up hurting more."

She stood, staring up at him as if she hadn't heard. "Promise me."

A huge weight sheared past him. He held to the job. "I promise."

The door barely closed behind him as he walked to his car.

She stopped at the entrance to the living room. Joseph wasn't on the phone; he was leaning against the bookcase at the far end. Noticing her, he moved away from it.

She stepped towards him. "Joseph, they've got to keep looking – these people are our only hope –"

He smiled, terribly. "Don't you see the strategy? They've botched it, but in the end, _we_ will be to blame."

Her voice frayed. "The end? What end? What are you saying?"

"– That even when they've found him, they'll make insinuations to the press, to divert attention from their incompetence. 'Did David ever threaten to run away from home?' Oh, it'll be immaterial that the camp director didn't bother to notify the police for almost two hours – it won't matter in the least that they let a whole night go by, when David was only a short distance away and would've been found by the dogs! And this latest outrage will count for nothing either, because David was driven into the bush by us – his parents – his overbearing father!"

She went closer. Her hands caught at each other. "He was only trying to follow up on what he'd been told –"

"Nonsense!" He glared at her, bloodshot. "It's all damage control!"

She tried to quieten her hands but they wouldn't stop. "Let them blame us, if they'll just find him –"

"No! David's out there because of their negligence and incompetence and they're not going to put it on us! I'm sick to death of it! If you have money you're to blame for everything – unless it was bled from a taxpayer! I should've gotten Cawston on them from the start – if I had believe me, Elaine, it wouldn't have gone like this!"

He started past her for the phone; she caught at his arm. "Why would David have run away last year?"

"– I'm sure it had nothing to do with the director and the students!" He removed her hand; the fingers remained curled, stiff. His voice changed. "Elaine, these people care about nothing but getting out of the mess they've made. If they can bend you double with guilt they'll do it. Please – I've got to handle this."

She wanted to clutch at him or hold him but only stood, trembling. "You mustn't do anything that would make them stop searching."

"They won't stop. They'll search harder."

Her throat stiffened. "– He's right. We made him go."

He fought not to sound exasperated. "As did a hundred other parents with their kids."

She remembered how he'd shoved himself from the back seat of the car, not saying, and the hollowness inside her as she'd driven off. "But maybe this camp was too hard – or he thought it was too hard – and those boys picked up on that and started hurting him –"

"People have to be challenged or they don't excel. If I didn't believe that I'd be down on the shop floor."

He turned away to the phone. A cry tore at her but it had no words. She looked on, pressing her hands to her stomach, as he started to dial.

"No. I won't hold. Tell him it's Joseph Ashton."

– The afternoon sun sifted down through the hanging ferns of her shop. A child bent over a Coromandel inlaid table, drawing a bird. She stole up behind him. It was no copy, no childish cartoon. The creature was tensed on the branch, wings extending, the instant before it took flight . . .

"Tom, it's time you got involved . . . The RCMP were just here. They found out from some students . . . No . . . they assumed we knew . . . they would've helped cover it up . . ."

She turned away, bitterly, trying to shut it out. The lake and mountains bled into each other.

She closed her eyes, straining through eternities of regret and fear. There had to be a way. She called his name, once, then over and over, rhythmically, picturing him that moment in the shop, thrusting her love against impenetrable time and space –

"– I want them to eat, breathe, and sleep knowing they'll be held accountable –"

She stopped, exhausted. There was nothing, nothing but the dread silence, mocking her helplessness.

Long into the afternoon David hung about the level place, watching the opposite ridge, trying to occupy himself. The helicopter swept out of sight and returned over and over, jarring his nerves. He should take the ax that very night, before he could be found –

At last it was gone. He sat with his back against a rock, legs spread, staring down at the drop-off. Why should he wait? It was just so the voice could talk him out of it. When you die you go to a wonderful place where it doesn't matter . . . how much you were shitted on.

– No. The voice didn't say that. It said there wasn't another life. There was just one. How could that be?

He waited, as if the voice would enter and explain it, but it didn't.

Your own power brought you here. He's going to blame you for everything.

The ax drove, a savage blur, into the gut of the tree.

He pushed himself up and stalked into the shack. The table and cupboards and bed loomed like junk but it wasn't dark enough to light a candle. Miserably, he opened a can of stew. For a moment his hand was on the matches. If the fire was small enough, maybe it wouldn't be seen –

He wolfed it down, cold. Jimmy stood looking up at him. He scraped the last of it into his dish.

On the night of the ax, he would have a feast.

After he ate he lay down on the bed. He closed his eyes against the room but he could still feel its weight in the hot stillness. To his surprise no images came of rage and hate – or, they started to form and he slipped past them. He wondered if something was wrong. Then he realized it was because of the plan – the plan and the ax. They were bringing him peace.

A quail cried out somewhere in the valley. He drifted into sleep.

He awoke suddenly, with a feeling of dread. It was much darker. He'd dreamed of his parents – but all he could remember was Mom, sitting hunched over on the sofa, and Dad standing at some distance from her. He couldn't see their faces. It was hard to breathe.

He got up and groped for the door.

He stopped on the other side of it. It wasn't night. The stick forest was dark but over it was a glow, a suffusion of light over the earth. He wandered down the path, seeking it, wanting to get away from the dream.

As he came out on the level place the light expanded to the west. The mountains were dark except for the outline of their spurs and ridges. He made his way towards the edge, staring into the twilight between the trunks of the pine. He felt its huge calm and started to become lost in it –

"When you say you've never had any power, you believe you're only telling it like it is. You feel controlled by the demands of your parents –"

"– Wait a minute –" He leaned against a tree, startled that the voice would simply take up where it left off that morning. It wasn't a good time –

"That's what I want to talk to you about, David – time. It's boxin' you in, like it did me. It's just one way of organizing your thoughts, your possibilities. It's not the only way –"

His shoulders tightened. "I don't understand – please – right now I don't want to think –"

"It's evening, isn't it? Are you sittin' out on the porch, watching the night come up out of the bottom of the valley? I loved that."

It softened him. He sat down with his back against the tree. In the far distance, over the dark headwaters, his eyes seemed drawn towards something beyond comprehension.

"Mr. Black – are you always going to be what you are now – I mean, forever?"

"Forever's a ridiculous word, boy. So's eternity. They both show how tied you are to the idea of time, even when you're trying to get away from it. That's the trouble – you can't open your mouth without implying time and space, and if we want to talk like this, I've got to do the same. But your yesterdays are as immediate to me as what you call now – and so are your tomorrows."

A void formed in his chest. "You know what's going to happen to me?"

There was a pause. "I know that you're a creator – I sense the possibilities you're considering. Remember the fountain? You're energy, thought, thrusting itself into time, deciding what to create. You think you're trapped in it, like a fly in a jar, with little or no say over what happens to you. You feel small and helpless. But how can that be? Thought isn't confined to time or space. Before I died I saw people, events, from fifty years ago, and they were more real than my breakfast. Just now you were thinking of your parents. That thought is known to them, but not necessarily in the same instant. Your energy isn't closed up—"

"Wait—Mom and Dad know what I'm thinking—they know that I'm all right?"

"Yes."

He leaned forward; his voice was shallow in the dusk. "Then why are they so scared?"

"Because of their beliefs about what is real. They try to block out everything that doesn't come to them from their eyes and ears, not knowing how they're sustained by it. But your mother's starting to question. She has a strong drive, like you, to seek out the life of things. You needed that to reach me, and she could use it to reach you."

He saw her bent over the table in her shop. Her hands moved carefully, experimenting with the arrangement of beads in a necklace. "Do you mean we could talk?"

"That'd be hard. We've built some strong walls in ourselves. But you could direct your thoughts to her and she'd become aware of them in some way—a dream, a sudden quirk, a chance remark she might overhear."

He stared into the dark boundary of the glow. "How do I do it?"

"Concentrate. Picture being with her, somewhere you both like. Imagine telling her you're OK. Go ahead, try it."

He closed his eyes. He was standing in the shop, among some tall plants. She was half turned from him at the table. He fought something in his throat; he couldn't say more than her name and it wasn't in the room, it was on the dark mountain. He tried again, saying now that he was sorry, saying over and over that he was no good and he was sorry, but it wasn't real, being in the room, it was all just made up. His hands clenched against themselves as he forced the words into the dark.

He slumped back. It had only been a few seconds.

"Ease up, boy! It's natural—"

"It doesn't feel that way—it feels useless, crazy—"

"You're not used to empowering your thoughts. What do you believe they're good for—keeping track of what's for lunch, what's on TV on Tuesdays? You don't believe they have any power, so you don't try to use them. Yet every night, when you slip free of your hang-ups about time and space, you create worlds with them."

The light withdrew. The line of the dark land softened.

"But dreams are just imaginary."

The voice laughed, softly, as if to itself. David saw Mr. Black sitting back on his porch, shaking his head. It was just like him.

"What's so funny?"

"Nothing – I've got to keep telling myself how hard it is . . . To have a body – to feel all locked up inside it – to be pushed around by heat and cold, aches and pains, sickness – crushable in an instant by any commonplace boulder or tree trunk – to be like that, and to try to grasp that these wandering strands of less than air inside you, are the driving force of everything that is. Maybe it's asking too much – maybe it's impossible, unless people could start livin' like they've been dead –"

It was night, but the line of the earth and sky endured, a pulse across the dark that might have been imagined. His voice sounded small under the hugeness of the pines. "Have I – have I been dead?"

There was a silence. When the voice answered, it was as though it had shaken something off. "Yes – but it's not like that reincarnation business, one life strung out after another. Your energy's too great for that. It wants to create in every direction at once, in and out of time. I'm Harold Black. I worked through that life. But there's no limit to the lives I can imagine. No energy is ever lost, no thought is ever wasted. I'm beginning to understand that it's important to use your power with care, a sort of deliberateness . . . That's why I wanted to talk with you. You need to know what you're up to. You need to know that you're a creator."

He felt his body pressed against the tree and the earth. "You're blaming me, aren't you? You said my own power brought me here. You're saying I'm to blame, not Alf and Jeff."

"I'm saying that your thoughts are the tools you use to build your life. What thoughts did you have about those guys? What did I think of the people who came out my way?"

He hated the feel of dirt in the night under his fingers. "They're buttholes! And that's not just my idea – that's the truth!" The voice hesitated and he jumped on it. "What about all the people in the world who are murdered and tortured every day? Did they think it up? If they'd just thought that the murderers and torturers were nice people, they wouldn't have been hurt?"

The voice was silent and he triumphed in it. When it returned it sounded distant for a moment, like a faint stroke of a mountain on the dark. "Those acts, David, appear very different to me than to you. You decided together – you and your parents, Alf and Jeff, all of you – you decided from all the possible things that could happen, which you'd bring into the physical world –"

His eyelids tightened at the first touch of the fluid, viscous, cold – "You're crazy!"

"I know. It comes with the territory. Give me a moment. This is tough."

It disarmed him. He sat, waiting, little mounds of dirt clawed up under his hands.

Finally the voice came, halting, feeling its way along the words. "Remember how I said . . . that we don't live two separate lives – a life and then an afterlife – that there's just one? The difference between us . . . is that you <u>think</u> of yourself as having a body and being in the physical world – you concentrate your energy in that direction. It's not like you'll die and enter this perfect state, in which you'll suddenly become all-knowing and good . . . I'm no more finished than you are. We're making our way through infinite possibilities. That's what it means to create. If we were perfect, unchanging, we'd have no use for time. But we're not, because the only way to be those things is to not think, not exist. So there's no limit to the thoughts I can have – but I'm also aware of the connection between them and what happens to me in time. I use the physical world to work through my thoughts, to see where they lead. When they cause pain and hate, I know something's wrong . . ." Again the voice seemed to fade to a distance, then return. "Now, there's more to it . . . The more you see physical life as a dead end, the more trapped by it and powerless you feel, the more you're going to either seek power in ways that cause suffering, or be a victim of such people. Cruelty always goes back to threat. They'd be a lot less of it if people could feel their creative power, know that they exist outside of time."

His stomach constricted. "You're still saying that if something bad happens to you, you caused it! I don't believe that – every day you see on TV – drive-by shootings, terrorism, completely innocent people –"

"Yes, it soaks you full of despair, helplessness, and violent saviors, night after night. And then you dream. If you believe that hate is all-powerful, that is the reality you will experience. Yet even then – even at the bottom of the terrors you're speaking of, no life is in vain. The nameless animal in the slaughterhouse cries out to you . . . Out of sight, out of mind, it's nothing. But after countless such cries you will hear and you will change.

The most helpless victim has power, boy – to agonize the consciences of men in the future, and move them to act. That is the meaning you have given time."

He stared into the night. It was warm, the darkness soft. A faint sway of motion passed through him; there must have been a wind high in the tree. The voice soothed him even though what it said wasn't true. Starvation, poverty, all the other crap – no one would choose those things.

His mind drifted out through the night, to where he knew the mountains were.

"Mr. Black?"

"Yes?"

"Tomorrow night I'm going to take the ax, and go to Silver Lake." It shocked him, it sounded so calm; but he'd started. "That's what I've chosen to create. You're going to help."

He felt an intense agitation, a shifting near the edge of his vision. "– Wait a minute. You said you'd give it some time –"

The words shot out of him. "What for? I – I'll never believe this stuff you're telling me –"

"Give it one more day –"

"Every day is torture! You don't know what it's like, sitting up here hour after hour, doing nothing but thinking about it –"

Again he felt it, the energy of the voice changing position, like an electric charge in the dark; it surged at him as if through the dark masses of the trees –

Suddenly it stopped. When the voice came it was where it always was, somewhere in his head. He slumped back against the tree. "I'm sorry, boy – I spilled the lemonade . . . You're right – it must be tough. But you know, what you really need is a rest, a complete break, a vacation –"

He laughed. "A vacation? People don't take vacations from stuff like this!"

"No, but they should. You need a break from me too, all this yappin' . . . Let's see, where could you go . . ."

His arms locked tight against the ground. "You're just trying to put it off!"

". . . I know . . . there's a place on the creek . . . Jimmy and I came across it a couple of years ago. There's this big flat rock, big enough to lie on . . . the water flows around it, the main channel shallow and wide, but the other side through a pool. The sun warms it but the bottom stays cold. Jimmy loved it, he plunged right in. What do you say?"

He wavered. To wash off the grime, the years of stale sweat —
"You won't talk me out of it!"
"I won't talk to you at all, how's that?"
"I'd have to climb all the way back up."
The voice laughed, heartily. "You kids just wanna watch television! Come on, it's summer! I wish I could go — I mean, feel the dust risin' up off the path in the heat, see the sun glaring off the rocks and dry grass, makin' me all hot and tired — and then, when I got down there, to follow Jimmy into the trees and hear the rush of the water —"

He waited for the voice to go on but it didn't. "Why do you want me to wait another day if we're not going to talk?"

"I just think you need a rest. Things might look different after."

His fingers ground the earth. "I won't have any rest. Until I go to the camp."

"You might feel different stretched out there in the sun . . . Your mind gets swept into the water, how it flashes as it swells over the rocks on the bottom . . . There are places where you don't need me."

He gave in. "OK. One more day. But you've got to promise — <u>promise</u> that you'll go with me to Silver Lake the night after."

"I promise. Cross my heart and hope to die."

He didn't laugh. "And don't think that sitting by a stream will make any difference. I've got to grind them to chickenshit. They've got to say lies, stupid lies like they're sorry, like they didn't mean to —"

The voice turned somber. "Jimmy will show you the way." He sensed that he'd wanted to say something else.

He stood. He didn't want to go to the shack so he leaned against the tree, putting it off, the warmth of the night seeming to draw him down through the branches of the pine and out across the valley. It was strange how he could sit and stare at the mountains and listen to the voice, and feel better — but the instant his own voice came again, it vanished.

There was something the voice wasn't telling him. Why? Was it because he didn't want him to know the future?

His stomach hardened. He wouldn't let him go up there, would he, unless it turned out all right? He'd promised to tell him where they were, what they were doing. He'd promised to help —

He stared around. The slopes dissolved into blotches of shadows. The pines twisted spiny arms into the night. How could he stand here so calmly when in reality he was alone, except for a stray dog, on a dark mountain? *You don't really know anything about this voice, who or what it is . . . The only rational explanation is that you are insane—*

He forced it back. What did it matter? There was nothing to do but go on.

Jeff struggled with the zipper of the sleeping bag. He tried to grip the ax's handle tighter but his fingers slid against its film of sweat. They were all staring at him, idiotic, a circle of frozen shock. "Hurry up!"

Jeff yanked at the zipper harder.

"Come on!" Would it never come free or was he faking it, buying time? He jerked the ax, panicking. It was as if they were all locked in that moment, trapped. The words broke out, ugly, bawling down at the kid's head. "Just crawl out of it, fucker! Crawl out of it—"

With the peculiar intensity of a dream, Jeff stopped struggling and looked up at him. He was very scared but his voice held. "No. I won't crawl."

His scream swept into a white flash. There were jagged pieces of walls and bunks and then he was running through the forest, the undergrowth bending and springing back and reality splitting, hurling away at cataclysmic speed—

His hand struck the thing he was leaning against. It wasn't bark—it was chipped, fibrous. His voice flailed over a pounding like far-off thunder in the night. "Mr. Black!"

"I'm still here, David."

It startled him. He clutched at it, a great pain of wanting breaking out of him. "When we go up there—everything will be OK, won't it?"

The voice answered at once. It moved through him like the mountain ridges in the dark. "Yes. Think it, and you will be free."

He pressed his face to the wood. The surface was gouged, bleeding. It was the tree he had attacked.

He held the battered trunk fiercely.

In downtown Kelowna, behind City Hall on Water Street, there is a Japanese garden. It occupies a long narrow space between various public buildings, not fronting on any street, and enclosed by a ten-foot-high stuccoed wall. Many people pass by and don't know it's there; and this is just as well, because it is a place meant for solitude, a place of refuge. Even the entrance is somewhat obscure; the massive wooden gate opens onto a shaded alley. The few people who go there have sought the place out; have known that, passing through the gate, they might escape the disarray of their lives.

It was with desperate hope of this that Elaine Ashton left her husband on the sidewalk in front of the lawyer's office. Joseph was irritated at her refusal to attend; he reiterated that no action would be taken yet. Did she think negligence such as Mahon's should go unpunished?

She had stared into the cauldron of his eyes and known, with a fear approaching terror, that he'd never understand. That it was useless to try to say, that to walk through those oak-paneled doors was an admission that David was gone . . .

She hurried away, her heels striking the pavement, crossing from St. Paul to Ellis to Queensway through a jumble of buildings, all remote and indifferent, like battered props of some forgotten play. And with every step a voice tortured her, a male voice of vast authority and composure, telling her that Joseph was simply facing reality, trying to prepare her for the inevitable . . .

No. He's alive. He's alive! She resisted, fiercely, barely aware of the sidewalk, her hands clutching the twisted straps of her purse. Even the wall of the garden was hidden by pyramid cedars behind the municipal fountain and clock, but she knew that it was there and that on the other side was a bench, the bench where she always sat, in the most private corner of the park. She turned from the street and hurried towards the alley. The house had become fearful, its rooms turned to hollow corridors, yet any object in them, as she drifted past, capable of inflicting sudden agony. She sought the garden for its calm, and in that calm she sought strength, the strength to hold out against time and to believe –

But, passing under the heavy beams and rafters of the main gate, she stopped. The garden was not empty. It was crowded with people, in groups of three or four, sitting on the benches, strolling along the gravel paths, leaning on the arched wooden bridge over the water. She stared around, confused, her hopes turning bitter; then she realized they were city employees, on their afternoon break. They would leave –

A woman with a sharp little face was eyeing her from a bench across the stream. She said something to her companions and they looked, too.

Quickly, she turned and started along the path. Maybe she should go out and wait by the clock until they were gone –

She forced herself on. If only her bench wouldn't be taken.

The path curved gently around a pine and she saw that it was occupied, by a man and woman, talking and laughing together. The strap constricted in her fist. What right did these people have to fill every bench, disrupt the garden with empty chatter? She'd needed so much to come here and now it was a waste, the calm, the order shattered by their millings and bursts of idle noise –

The man and woman were looking at her. She saw or imagined that it was the same look, as if they recognized her in some impersonal way. She hurried past, tears filling her eyes; she almost tripped on the lava stepping stones over the little stream. David was gone and it was nothing to them but idle entertainment. She saw herself standing over the man and woman, screaming down into their stupefied faces, "I hope to God it happens to you! I hope your child is missing or mangled or dead and they squeeze every bleeding drop out of you between two beer commercials –"

To her right was a little service gate opening onto a parking lot. She stumbled towards it and clutched the chain link. Her hands started to shake it like a cage. Damn them – damn all of them –

Resist. It was not a word but a force rising from the very cells of her body. *Resist. Do what you came to do.* She stood for a moment, her fingers crooked over the links in the fence, imagining how they were staring at her back; then she tore herself away. *David. You're all that matters.* The woman with the sharp face didn't bother to avert her eyes as she struggled past. There had to be another corner –

The people on the bridge looked remote, fixed, like in a photograph. Across the water, the square wooden gazebo on the quay was occupied by a young woman, reading. She slowed. Ahead was an empty bench. It was just before the waterfall, a jumble of boulders and trees in a corner of the garden from which fell, in two short plunges, a little stream. She'd never sat there; she'd thought the waterfall overdone, out of proportion, too close to the quay. It was strange, the things that had mattered . . .

She lowered herself onto the bench. Across the path was a low bamboo fence and several trees, a plum or crab tree and two Japanese maples. Past them, at the water's edge, was a gray stone lantern. The afternoon sun angled down its side and over its upturned roof the far end of the bridge was visible through an opening in the trees. She could see the people's heads over the crab tree; they wouldn't notice her. The steady rush of water troubled her until she closed her eyes and her thoughts slipped under it, channeling it between herself and the crowd. She felt the huge depths of the bitterness that had grown inside her—at the merciless reporters, the officials, the friends who avoided her. Joseph—he lay stone-still on the bed at night, as if oblivious to her, her face streaked and her hands clutching his arm, answering her with a word or two if at all. The reassurances had worn out; they were afraid to say them now. Their fear lay slumped on the endless minutes and hours—

No! David—answer me— She hunched forward, barely aware of her hands on the purse. There were stirrings in the dark but nothing came, only the clutter of pain and hope bearing down. She strained under it, seeking something, a barrier to cross—

She could see him. Her shoulders jolted. He was standing with his back to a railing or low wall. She started forward but the image didn't move or change; he stood, remote, untouchable, smiling. She realized that it was a memory—a memory not even of reality but of a photograph. It had been on a trip to Vancouver Island, or Hawaii—

Was that it? Was that all she could reach? Could all the force of love she could hold give her nothing more than a dead picture, a scrap from a photo album?

The male voice entered, serene. *He lives in your memory. You will heal with time.*

No—no— The denial shuddered through her and she wept, wept from the strain of resisting as she gave way. He was dead. The police pretended he wasn't, the searchers pretended he wasn't, Joseph pretended. But they all knew.

It shoved her down. The darkness tightened around her and she broke up and down on it. There were no reassurances, no suppositions, only grief, a pain of separation immense and unanswerable. It tore her through places where no images are, only strands in the dark, vanishing. The convulsions of her throat skewed through them. She hung on them, pierced by them, at the limit of the physical, the one static image appearing suddenly—

Her eyes opened. It had stopped.

Something was different—the light. She wiped her eyes. The sun was softer on the lantern, yet only a few moments could have passed. She looked at the path, the bridge, the quay. The people were gone. There was not another soul.

The leaves of the maples moved, and were still. The trees, the water were intense in every leaf and ripple. The rush of the waterfall seemed to flow through them. It was as if the garden were suffused with an energy, which had been there all the time and she hadn't noticed –

It's because you wept. She tried to feel angry at herself for giving in to despair. *I'm sorry, David –*

The words broke the charged stillness. At once there was another noise – a clatter of dusty creaking from the direction of the gate. She strained to see through the larger maple –

Bicycles appeared, spokes flashing in the sun amid a procession of feet. They were being walked towards the bridge. Bitterness jabbed her. Just when she was alone –

It stopped, suspended. A boy about David's age, or a little younger, dropped his bike by the path, scrambled onto the bridge, and hung his chin over the railing, staring down at the water. Two more joined him. Motionless, heads bent, they seemed fascinated. Maybe they saw a carp.

Her hands didn't know what they were holding. She felt the purse. The leather was wet. That children would come, just when she'd despaired – just when it'd grown so still. It must be a sign – it must mean something –

One of them looked up. He glanced around the garden as if making sure it was deserted. Then he left the bridge. The others watched him. When he came back into view he didn't go onto the bridge but stepped down in front of it. The shore was lined with boulders; there was one lower and flatter than the rest. He stood on it, holding something poised in his hand, intent on the water. One of the other boys began gesturing at him. It struck her, all at once, that he was going to throw a rock at the carp.

She half rose from the bench, emotions pitching against each other. Her instinct was to yell at him but she couldn't. She grabbed hold of the bamboo fence. He had to be stopped.

The other boy was trying to talk him out of it. He swept his hand over the water as if to ask why he'd want to hurt such a place.

At first the one with the rock ridiculed him, waving his arms and pretending to weep in mourning. But the boy didn't give up. He kept talking until the third one stopped glancing at the gate and joined in. The one with the rock turned to them in contempt, but she could see from his body that he was unsure.

She waited, her fingers raw on the rope lashings of the bamboo. It was silly, wasn't it – he'd probably miss anyway. She glanced off, to break her fascination –

Her eyes came back. Her hand leaped off the rail; behind the one with the rock was a fourth boy. He was turned sideways from her, facing the water; but from the instant of his face in profile she knew. It was David.

She shot to her feet; her cry broke over the wall. The three boys gawked across the water at her in shock; she stumbled towards them, dropping her purse, the power of his name wild in the sun. The figure had vanished at once; she seared it into her mind. He'd looked – not sad, but deep in struggle, as if some huge thing disturbed him. The water – there was a connection with the water, he'd stared down into it. And the rock was involved too, the boy wanting to throw it –

One of them started off the bridge; she cried out. *David.* He stopped, probably from the sheer strangeness of it. Her mind flailed; no other word would form, the place, the air where the image had been still taut, the arch of the bridge under enormous tension. She had to cross it to reach them; as she caught at the rail, tears streaming across the curve of the planks, she saw the tenderness of their faces. They waited in fear and amazement of her; she almost laughed. He was alive, whatever else it meant he was alive –

She pulled herself to the center. Up close, they were so young. They would take flight in an instant.

"Please – wait – there's something I –" He'd stared down at the water as if lost in it –

She wrenched her mind back to them. They stood motionless, eyes fixed up at her as if she were some sort of alien.

"Are there – have there been – just three of you – the whole time –"

No one answered. The boy who'd been about to throw the rock started to grin.

"Yes. But none of us is named David." It was the one closest to her. Tears surged through the blurred tangles of her hair and she tried to shove them aside.

"He's here – I saw him –"

The one with the rock made a face to the others.

"– He's alive –" She bent under the release; the next moment it swelled up through everything in sight.

Recognition crossed the boy's face; he almost didn't say it. "Do you mean that kid who's missing?"

"– Yes – I'm his mom –"

They looked uneasy, almost in awe; the one with the rock mumbled, "I hope they find him."

It moved her more than all the adult condolences. Her hand closed on the rail. "He's coming home. There's something he has to do, then he's coming home."

The boy dropped the rock onto the bank. Slowly, they gathered up their bicycles, the stillness of the place closing around them. The wheels revolved, creaking softly, into the shadows of the gate. She watched as, one by one, they passed under it and vanished. Just before he turned into the alley, the last boy glanced back. His face was in shadow, but she heard his thought. *She's not going to tell on us, is she?*

They were gone. Something pulsed against her, like the ebb and flow of the sea. Everything in the garden – every tree, every ripple on the water, every stone on the quay was connected to it. *Tell on you?* She almost laughed. *What we do here, we do to ourselves.*

She clutched the rail, astonished. In the infinite desolation she had never imagined that there could be a purpose; yet in the instant he'd stood there the force of it had stunned her. Nothing had been forced on him. Beaten, agonized, alone, he had chosen to go that way. And he was struggling, head-on, now, with everything inside him that had brought him there –

The current drifted imperceptibly under the bridge. But where he was, it was a torrent –

She staggered under the sensation of leaping.

It was with a strange, out-of-place feeling that David started down, the next morning, into the valley of Trepanier Creek. Jimmy led the way, a faint trail to the north of the rock face; it was so steep that he had to brake sideways, roiling dust up through the dry grass. David's legs soon ached from holding him back; he'd imagined leaving the place for the last time with the ax, and to be doing it for nothing seemed ludicrous. Why couldn't the voice understand that nothing could help – nothing – except to watch them grovel –

Far below, near the bottom, the tops of the pine and fir stood torpid in the sun. It was the sort of air in which a hawk would glide but the valley, from what he could see, was empty. He wondered if they'd given up the search . . .

Mom and Dad know you're OK. His filthy shoe dug for a hold. *What bull. This is just making them endure another day.*

He jolted down the slope, his dust drifting through the lowest branches of the fir, the gray angular boulders and decaying logs and rough red bark of the pines all so still in the sun, as if they lived in a cycle of centuries and he and the dog were too brief to notice. He wondered, oddly, if there was any memory of his passing.

The opposite side of the valley grew closer, its trees sharply ranked. Dirt ground in his shoe. When he stopped, he could glimpse the flat place at the bottom. He looked back up, amazed that he'd climbed it.

He rested there, rather than below; he hated the thick brush. It whipped shadows in his face . . .

He approached it almost hoping he'd have to turn back; but the path continued. The fir on each side had old stubs, where dead branches had been cut. He imagined Mr. Black, working there alone, toiling in the gloom.

Jimmy, as if he sensed his mood, stayed close.

He came out at the edge of the road to a shock of blue sky and flowers. Jimmy broke into a run. The road curved gently downhill to the left and the dog stopped and turned back to him at the bend.

"All right! I'm coming!" He hurried; the road made him nervous. It was not so much the possibility of a truck or helicopter; it was knowing that he could simply keep walking in that direction and be home.

Mr. Black's wrong. You don't have any choice.
What thoughts did you have of those guys?

Jimmy couldn't wait for him to come up. He shot ahead again, ears swept back, as if he were chasing a chipmunk. Once again, he stopped within sight; David struggled after him, his clothes stiff and oily against his body.

On the third lap Jimmy waited, pacing into the brush a bit; if it weren't for David he would've raced on. He caught up and they started into the bush together. Some of it was over his head; his fear and hatred of it grew as he shoved through it. If he just had the ax; he grabbed a piece of the junk and bent it double—

Suddenly he stopped. Why was he so angry? It wasn't the forest.

It's them. *It's got to be—*

He stood, a huge confusion opening in him, a sensation almost of dizziness, like waking up on the edge of a canyon.

Through it came the motion of water.

He held on to the twig. Jimmy looked up at him, eager to go on, his muzzle beaded and glistening. For an instant he wondered if he'd really heard it; but it was close ahead, a swiftness in the air. His anger had shut it out, completely . . .

Could it be that powerful?

He started forward. There was something – something the ax might not help. He remembered asking once, why his life was one long war. That was before – he didn't know when, but it was before –

The sound rushed over him. He came out on the creek. There were two large boulders in it; one of them divided the water into a broad shallow channel and a narrow, deeper one. The other, just downstream, was like a platform, low and flat.

It was the place. Jimmy waded in and drank; then he was swimming for the platform. It was only a few meters; but the current carried him down, paddling, to the end of the boulder. He clambered onto it, his fur dark and dripping except on his neck and head, which were still dusty red in the sun. He didn't shake himself dry; he stood looking across at David, a scrawny mess of pleasure, expecting him to come.

"No, Jimmy – it's too deep –" He found a place to kneel between the rocks. At the edge the stream was a translucent film over pebbles and fallen leaves, but into the channel the lens darkened, and the stones on the bottom were vague and cold. He cupped his hands and scooped water onto his face; at the shock of it his skin came alive with desire and he splashed more on, wiping it over his eyes and forehead and neck, dissolving the encrusted dust and sweat until it ran in streams between his fingers and he swept up more from the endlessness of it, its roar arching over him.

He sat up and pushed the wet hair back from his eyes. Jimmy hadn't moved. He stood on the edge, in a puddle, watching him longingly.

The rock looked warm in the sun. To stretch out on it, soaking wet and refreshed . . .

He pulled off his dust-choked shoes and waded one step into the channel. It was cold but not aching. Little specks like gold shone on the bottom, dimmer until they were lost in the deep part. Maybe it would be up to his waist –

He hesitated, then went forward. The current caught his jeans and he stretched out his arms for balance. A shadow of fear moved through him and swift on it, from somewhere in the light of the dog's eyes, a recklessness –

He plunged ahead; his foot slipped. His arms shot out and his head hit the water. A white surge of cold struck him; he stretched out a hand for the bottom. His eyes didn't close; in the instant before he caught himself he saw the channel, dark near the rocks and algal but over a churning sheet of light agitated by his body. Striking something, he thrust himself up by it through spiraling turbulence –

He stood, tottering in the current, sheets dropping from him, his body astonished. Jimmy was watching, totally enthused.

He wiped the wet hair out of his eyes. "You silly mutt! I didn't do it on purpose!" The sun brushed his soaked skin with a delicious sensation of warmth touching cold. Jimmy kept looking at him as if hoping there would be more.

"All right!" He shoved his hand across the surface and splashed him. He retreated a step and came back to the edge.

David laughed. "Get lost! I'm not getting dunked again for you!"

The dog paced the edge of the rock. He was taking aim again when suddenly Jimmy plunged in downstream. For an instant he was hidden in white; then he was swimming towards him, his head moving in spurts against the current. "What are you doing?"

The dog came up; he could see his forelegs paddling hard under the water. He splashed him, a direct hit.

He didn't know what to expect; but nothing could have prepared him. Jimmy barked – a single loud bark, sharp with joy –

"Jimmy – what the hell –" He stretched out his hands. The dog lunged into them and they fell into the stream, tumbling through frothing undulations of light. He came up amazed, the sun striking down, the rush of water suddenly vast. He held the dog close. "I didn't know you could do it, boy!"

Jimmy panted in his arms as if it were the most natural thing in the world; but it seemed to David that he was pleased with himself.

They climbed together onto the rock. He cast off the heavy jeans and shirt and stretched out in the sun. It flashed down at him through the converging tops of the trees, an humongous generator of dreams, and when in the long channels of creation it had overheated their flesh, they plunged into the stream again, rampaging together.

Far into the afternoon, the sun lost the edge of its warmth. Goose bumps formed on his arms and the chill of the water lingered. He tried to delay it, shifting position on the wet rock, but the light softened in the openings in the trees and shadows deepened on the stream. At last he gathered up the half-dry clothes; he thought of the climb, but without dread or anger. It had all fallen away.

He started to wade to shore through the shallow water downstream; but Jimmy didn't follow. He turned and called him; he stood on the edge of the platform facing the broad channel, his back legs taut, as if he'd heard something.

David walked back to him, slowly, his eyes searching the brush on the other side. There was only the long motion of the water, its sound seeming to originate not in the stream but in the air overhead.

He lingered, wondering what Jimmy had sensed. Suddenly guilt swept him. While he'd wasted another day, Mom and Dad had suffered –

Something caught his eye. It was a banded green stone, just below the surface. It reminded him of the jade in his mother's shop –

He picked it up. His hand closed on it.

I'm coming home. I promise.

He listened, but the roar of water surrounded him.

He stretched out his hand to toss the rock back into the stream.

Detective McNeil, Kelowna RCMP, was about to go home for the night when he noticed that Jack Burton was still in his office. He approached the glass; there were a couple of file folders on his desk and he was reading from one of them. He looked tired.

"Hey Robocop, time to shut down."

Burton barely glanced up. "Hi Doug."

McNeil hesitated in the doorway.

After a moment Burton dropped the folder onto the desk. "Come in. I need a break."

"You need to go home. You're making me look bad."

"You're not on this case."

McNeil slumped into an uncomfortable little chair in front of the desk. "Thank God."

There was a silence while Burton crumpled the corner of the folder.

"So what's keeping you here – anything?"

Burton looked straight into him. "We got a couple of more tips from psychics. One of them is kind of intriguing – it's from a lady in Sonoma, California. She senses that David is in a house – more like a shack – the shack's alone in the forest. He's unharmed. She felt a very strong 'presence' with him."

"What?"

"'A presence.'" He glanced down at the folder, reading. "'An entity outside our physical plane.'"

McNeil laughed, thinly. "You mean a spirit – a ghost? Bloody hell!"

"Yeah, I know. But the idea that David's found shelter in the forest – that interests me. We've searched every house, every barn, every shed that he possibly could've reached – so if she's right, it's a shack we don't know about."

McNeil leaned back in the chair. "I know these people have their use, but if you ask me, they're fruitcakes."

"I didn't ask you. This one's supposed to have a very good batting average. Some of the rest I'm not so sure about. One of them says he's with a dog."

McNeil grinned. "Oh? Is it Lassie or The Littlest Hobo?"

Burton didn't smile. "The trouble is, you get all these bits and pieces, and you have no way of knowing which are legit and which aren't, or how they relate. One guy sensed a very strong connection between David and a metal object. He has intense feelings of rage associated with it. Sounds like a weapon—"

McNeil pulled a loose thread from the cuff of his shirt, thinking. "Wait a minute. That house David was at the first night—it's off by itself, isn't it? And wasn't there a big pile of junk behind it? He could've gotten all kinds of metal objects there. Maybe your lady in Sonoma was just picking up on that place—or maybe she reads *The Vancouver Sun*."

The angle of Burton's jaw twitched. "I know I'm out on a limb. But you tell me what I've got to lose at this point. She had one other thing and I know she didn't get it out of a newspaper. She said the 'presence' is someone David has known." He picked up the folder. "'A being whom he's encountered in this incarnation.' Now the Ashtons don't know anyone in that area—no friends, no relatives, no business associates. God knows they don't go camping. The only way David could know anyone there is through Silver Lake—"

McNeil fidgeted in the chair. "Jack—she's talking about a ghost. You can't be taking that seriously . . ."

Burton seemed taken back. After a moment, he put down the folder and stood. Stepping past the other man, he closed the door to his office. He came back to the desk and stopped with his fists planted against it. The shadows under his eyes looked darker. "All right. Let's forget the psychics. Let's just use reason. David's been missing about seventy-two hours. We've chalked up over five thousand man-hours on the ground and over forty with the helicopters. After tracing him to that house, we've found nothing. So if you ask me—if you ask me what the most likely scenario is at this point—I'd answer that this kid is dead. Dead of exposure, somewhere in the bush."

He paused. McNeil said nothing.

"What are my reasons? One: He was in extreme mental distress to start with. Two: He was lightly dressed, not even a coat. Three: He has no survival skills or training. Four: The camp's at elevation 3,500 feet and the overnight lows have been around eight. Five: It rained. Six: Anyone lost in that area, who still has his wits about him, has an excellent chance of orienting himself and getting out. My guess is that by the time his physical discomfort got the better of his mental anguish, he was exhausted and deep in the bush, and it was too late."

Burton sat. Imperceptibly at first, his voice changed. "Pretty compelling, isn't it? These psychics are the only thing I've got that contradicts it . Every one of them, without exception, says that he's alive. So either their crystal balls have fogged up something awful, or David's beaten the odds. And maybe I'm being a lousy cop, but I want to believe them, and I'll use any scrap I've got, even from fruitcakes, to try to find him."

The other man hesitated, then pushed himself up from the chair, awkwardly. "I just meant the ghost part, that's all –"

Burton smiled, faintly. "It's OK, Doug. We're all on edge . . . I had a rotten sleep last night. It's the idea, that David might know someone – that's what caught my attention –"

McNeil lingered at the door, wanting to break off the conversation and go home; suddenly, a thought popped into his head. "Maybe he did know someone – maybe he knew whoever lived in that house."

Burton looked up at him.

"– I mean, hasn't the assumption always been, that he just stumbled onto that place? Maybe he went there on purpose. Maybe he expected whoever had lived there to help him."

Burton had already pulled another file folder from a drawer of the desk. It was thick with papers and he flipped through them, quickly. "I've got something on the guy but it didn't lead anywhere . . . Where the hell is it . . ." He stopped at a page of handwritten notes. As he read it, it was as if he were trying to pull something out of the words – some shadow of possibility that had eluded him. "The guy's name was Harold Black . . . He was a retired mechanic, aged 78, never married, lived alone. Only known relative is a brother in Calgary. He was found dead in the house on May 19 by a guy who came to read the electric meter. Coroner estimated he'd been dead about twenty-four hours, cause of death, heart attack. He's buried in Peachland Cemetery." He looked up at McNeil. "That's it."

"He had no connection with Silver Lake?"

"I doubt it. Sounds like he was a hard-core loner. But I'll ask."

McNeil turned it in his mind. The possibility trailed off into nothing. "I'm going home. Hang in there . . ."

Burton closed the folder. "Thanks, Doug."

He sat at the desk, alone, for only a moment. The office felt weighted with invisible things . . .

He shoved the folder back into the drawer and stood —

Suddenly he stopped. A loner. Kind of like a kid, who'd ditch a canoeing session, and run off into the forest for an afternoon, and never tell anyone where he'd been . . .

David stood up from the fallen tree. It was far into the afternoon of the next day. And it was time — time to take the ax and start for the camp. All day he'd waited, mostly sitting and staring out across the valley. A couple of times he'd tried to find something to do, but there was nothing of any use. He'd cleaned up the inside of the shack a little, he didn't know why.

He picked his way up through lichen-encrusted gray rocks, towards the level place. The voice hadn't come all morning, and it made him nervous. They hadn't spoken since the day before yesterday.

He knows now that he's not going to talk you out of it. He's given up. The muscles over his eyes tightened. He'd promised to help . . .

The cruelty of it dug into him as he entered the path. But he wouldn't call out. It'd be better, wouldn't it, without any yapping . . .

The shack came into view, dingy in the stick forest. Somehow it was always unexpected, even now.

He stopped at the open door. It'd saved his life. But that wasn't enough . . .

He shoved his way into the room, into the corner where it was. His hands closed on the wood and he lifted it, seeking power, turning the blade until it caught the dull light. He'd grind them to nothing. Their mouths would ripple the puddles in the piss-yellow glare of the cans —

He looked at the things in the room, for the last time. The bed — the table and cupboard — the pictures cut out of old magazines. A hard, determined voice rose in him. *Maybe it's the place you love — but I can't sit here any more.* He went out.

The sky was blue overhead with a few clouds. He lowered the ax to one hand and started down the path. As he entered the closeness of the forest he almost tripped —

"Have you got a coat? It's gonna be cold up there in the night."

He spun around. There was no one. His voice pitched. "– Where have you been?"

"I don't keep very good track of time. But I'm plugged in to where you are now. How was the creek?"

". . . OK."

"It's a nice spot. Too bad Jimmy and I didn't find it sooner. Did you hear the water?"

Of course I heard it. How could I not–

"That water goes all the way around the earth. From Trepanier Creek down to Okanagan Lake, and from there into the Columbia River, and out into the ocean, and up into the clouds."

His fingers pushed against the wood. "I don't care. I'm going to Silver Lake. Will you help me like you promised?"

"Your mom heard it, David."

Tears started in his eyes. He almost dropped the thing, then clenched it tighter. "– Will you help?"

"She's starting to understand why you're here. And so are you."

"I don't believe you! They did it. They're going to pay."

"Yes, they did it. But before every act, in terms of your time, there is thought. You created a thought of love, a desire, at the stream, and it wasn't lost. You can do the same now. That's how I can help–"

The steel swayed at the end of its fulcrum. "You said you'd tell me where they are and what they're doing. Nothing else matters."

He sensed a struggle. It wasn't calm or detached.

When the voice came, it was agitated. "I don't know, boy . . . maybe I've made a mess of this whole thing. I didn't exactly say that, but that's neither here nor there. I'm still strongly connected to where you are . . . so when you sought me, I was filled with worry for you. But I'm also astonished, overjoyed at all that I am, and I wanted you to feel that. David, if you could feel the daring that you are, just once, your world would never be the same."

He clutched the weapon. "Adults treat me like a stupid kid. Kids treat me like shit. That's what I feel – if you're not going to help, leave me alone."

He turned and started down the path. There was only the silence of his feet striking the earth until he came out on the level place and the valley opened below. He slowed, almost dizzy.

The voice broke in. "– All right – I'll tell you where they are. I haven't because it didn't feel right, cutting your feet out from under you – and I was hopin' you'd work through it. But I've meddled in other ways . . . I can't let you go up there like this—"

Everything inside him stopped. He stood, suspended, cradling the ax. "What do you mean . . . where are they?"

There was a silence, then the voice plunged ahead. "David, they were caught . . . they were caught and expelled. I feel it strongly . . . Jeff's havin' a tough time. I guess I should've told you way before now . . ."

It was like a huge, invisible, alien thing, blocking his path. All the planning—all the waiting. A cry of despair and rage coalesced in his being—the ax lightened on the edge of motion—

Then, in an instant, he saw through it. His voice shot out across the valley. "You're lying! You're lying to keep me from going up there!" The certainty of it exploded on the sound. He stepped forward as if advancing on someone. "You couldn't stop me any other way so now you're making up lies! Get lost!"

He veered to the right, to where the path started for the creek, the voice calling his name; he strained to block it out and to his astonishment he could. The words grew indistinct—something about his coat—then they were only a pressure, a disturbance somewhere behind or beyond a black plane. The trees tilted and he started down.

The ground rushed in front of him. Behind his breathing the pressure diminished and he was about to exult in it when an animal raced past him, tearing down the slope. It was Jimmy, bursting with joy as usual at the start of a walk. He almost yelled at him to go home but stopped. He had no home. He would see the end.

Dust churned up from the dog's hind legs. He began fighting the steepness. It was the same path as the day before but the slope ahead looked strange, as if he'd never been there.

Of course it was a lie. How would they be caught? Jeff was too smart for that. He got away with everything. He was making up poems.

Tho' Davey Ashton was sure to fail
He tried to hide in a shithouse pail . . .

He skidded down, braking his feet against tufts of dry grass, the ax hoisted to his chest. The back of the blade smashed open the bunkhouse door. They stared up at him, stupidly, from their sleeping bags. Nothing rhymed.

He stole a glance at the other side of the valley. Blood rushed into the hollows of his arms and legs. He should be in position above the bunkhouse well before dark.

The voice was gone. He tried not to think what that meant but through the jolting weight of the ax the thoughts came anyway. There'd be no more arguing. He'd carry out the plan in silence and in peace. Up to the instant the ax slammed into the door, he would feel nothing but the cold form of his rage.

Your mom heard it. What did that mean?
He was trying to confuse you and make you weak.

The valley narrowed and the other side rose over him, its forest unbroken except for a few rock slides near the bottom. He wouldn't get caught on them – he'd follow the road until he could see to work his way over to the power line. Then it would be a long straight climb to the camp. There'd be no fallen logs and dark brush – only the tension of the wires overhead, serrating the air as he drew closer. The waiting – the waiting at night in the brush above the bunkhouse – that would be the hard part –

Kids were draped over the window sills of the bus. Some made stupid faces but most were nervous. Alf shouted *Snotball* at him. His throat thickened. The Dick was waiting for him in the aisle. He made that remark, *hope you'll stay with us.* He was smiling as he said it, his usual, cheerful smile. He remembered being confused . . .

Maybe he didn't mean it that way. Maybe if you'd just sat down, a lot of things would have been better.

His feet jolted against the path. He slowed, shifting his grip on the ax. He'd expected The Dick to shit on him.

Before every act –

So what. Alf meant it. That's all that matters now. If you think about it you'll be to blame for everything –

He kept going. Pain shot up from his ankles. The valley bottom inched closer. What good was it to shut out the voice if he thought stuff like that. They had to pay. They had to mumble at the floor and be forced to look up at him, at all the other kids. *Louder, shithead –*

Below him was an open place with only a few big pine. He could see Jimmy sniffing around the trunk of one, his fur rich against the pale red bark, but he felt distant. It was as if some connection between them was severed. And only yesterday in the stream . . .

Why don't you call your dog

His hands locked on the ax. When it was done, everything would change. The other kids would crowd around him, eager to hear every detail of how he'd survived, how he'd pursued such an awesome revenge –

No one would speak to Jeff as he shoved his crud into his duffel bag. Two instructors would hurry him down to the parking lot. His honors certificate would be ripped up.

He fought his way down, the back of his legs stiff against the mountain. It would come, if he would just think of nothing else –

The tops of the trees leveled off below. He lowered himself towards them and finally came out on the flats, in the thick of the fir and aspen. No memories bothered him as he wound along the trail – not even when he'd gained the road and passed the place where he'd turned off to the creek. Jimmy knew they weren't going there.

It didn't feel strange to walk along the road with the ax. Once, unaccountably, he remembered the floor of the bus, how the filth stuck to it was magnified by the jolts, how it bulged in the cracks between the metal and the curled-up black vinyl. He'd stared down at it, light and cold –

He walked faster. There was a pressure in the dense growth over the stream. He searched for a glimpse of the power line. Once he was under it he would be OK. He'd think through the words carefully. Everything would be in the right order . . .

Finally he caught sight of the posts, pairs of them scaling the mountain. He hurried forward, anxious for a trail; when there was none he called Jimmy and waded into the brush. He struggled towards the rush of water.

The stream was in shadow. Here and there swellings of silver broke the dark tension of its surface. The dog stood, hind legs tensed, facing the channel. *It wasn't lost.*

He was relieved that there were stones. He crossed quickly.

On the other side the growth was rank. He shoved through with the ax, crawling over and under fallen trunks. The spindly dead growth of the fir he shattered with the blade. Sticks flew into the breathless gloom.

When he broke through to the power line, it was, at first, just as he'd imagined. A long column of posts scaled the mountain head-on, and below them he stepped out into a broad cleared space with a rough road. He'd move quickly now, without having to think about the way. His mind would shape their ordeal.

He thought of resting a little, but the long curve of the wires drew him on and he started. The posts were far apart and their shadows slanted across his path in the late afternoon sun. Now and then Jimmy stopped and looked back for him, his coat fiery red. It was almost as steep as the other side. After three posts he slowed, clenching the ax and breathing hard.

He pictured how it would be. He wouldn't shout; yet his voice would have enormous force. Jeff would struggle out of the sleeping bag and slide to the floor in his pajamas. His eyes would roll and his stupid lies would be silenced. Then it would start. You wouldn't hear anyone breathe. He'd confess why he did it. *You're the biggest suck in this camp and you didn't want anyone to know. Say it. I'm the biggest suck—*

OK, what if I am? What's it to you? I was trying to help you, or have you forgotten?

The mountain jolted to a stop. He'd never have the guts—but it was so real—like he was sitting at the table, the books and papers spread out, the sun going down behind him—

Well?

His fingers rubbed the handle. He'd be way too scared. Besides, it was only because of soccer—that was the only reason he helped—that and to show off—

Jeff looked up at him. He was afraid, but somewhere in his voice there was a calm which he dreaded. *Yeah, I wanted you on the Zorgs. But I also felt sorry for you. After we talked—*

His body bent over the wood. Dry grass huddled in the dust of the road. Shut up. Keep going. Just keep going—

He stumbled forward. Loose rock and weeds were blazoned over him in the sun. Jeff still faced him, kneeling on the floor of the bunkhouse, but the voice that almost crushed him against the mountain was his own self. *Alf threw slop on you. You were furious and you took it out on Jeff because you'd seen them talking. It could have been different*

Shut up! He flung it at the lines of scarred earth. They shifted beneath him and he dug his feet into them to make them stop. The voice—the voice was doing it—but it was all barf and shit. They did it. They had to suffer—

He pulled himself up the plane of broken stone, the ax massive in his hands. Power lines soared over him but he saw only the shadows of the poles. If he could just make it from one to the next—

He closed his eyes. For dozens of steps he kept out everything but the strain of his breathing. When something had to come he clutched what they had done to him. Jeff hurried up the slope from the cans, holding the bucket out from his side. The maddened weight of Alf's body bore down on his neck and when the thing was positioned in front of him he knew that he would beg—

The darkness ripped; a pole appeared. He tried to hold on to it but the distance was wrong and he staggered against it. The impact of the handle shuddered through him. He fought to breathe.

They deserved to die. He'd seen it. Their heads hung between stakes and a thing like a broom was dunked in a bucket of sewage or vomit and lifted, dripping—

Time surged around him. He held on to keep from falling. Something was wrong. Something was terribly out of place. That thing with the broom—he'd imagined it on the bus—the cracks in the floor—

But that was before Jeff had done anything to you. He'd made a smart-ass remark to The Dick.

He stared through the stones of the road. It wasn't a coincidence. He'd imagined it—before there was a reason—

What thoughts did you have

He stood, the ax vague in his hand, every rock and weed above him suffused with slanting light. *I was thinking how I'd flunk, no matter how hard I tried, while guys like Jeff would kiss up and make a joke of everything and pass. I was thinking how The Dick had it in for me. And out of those thoughts—those fears—I imagined it, and it happened—*

A strange lightness spread through him; he saw himself simply let go of the ax and start walking down the mountain. Huge strands of things tore away and dissolved; the whole valley was immersed in the tide below him and his steps were strong—

Just think it and you will be free

Yeah, sure—till the first time someone calls you shithead

The ax pulsed in and out of consciousness. It was true. His whole life he'd been driven by fear. Fear that he wasn't good enough, fear that he'd flunk, fear that he'd be put down, rejected, teased. If those thoughts hadn't controlled him, how different—

He swayed, aching, on the edge of infinite possibility. What if, instead, he'd felt hope—and courage? Would it have happened?

He knew the answer; it had radiated out over the desolate shores of the first ocean. And yet even knowing this, and being swept up in pieces by it, he could not reach the last way into himself, to let go of the ax. They'd prepared the bucket and lured him to the cans. They'd run him down, beaten him, and jerked him bleeding to his knees. They'd rammed him down into it until he lay naked on the floor of a place where there was no courage and no hope. That was real. That couldn't be changed. And they would taste it –

He steadied himself against the pole. It could have been different . . . but wasn't that just proof that he was what they said . . . a mental misfit, a snot-eating spazz –

The ax twisted. Jeff's face shot up in terror. He thrust himself from the pole and started climbing. It was too late. Even if it was all his fault – that didn't take away one instant of it, one second of the helplessness and the fury and the thick cold rivulets streaming down. Blame didn't matter. Thought didn't matter. Only rage –

The filthy stubs of his shoes jabbed at the road. Above him the poles towered against the mountain, their shadows sharp and unyielding across the bare earth. The ax was a dead weight and shifting it from hand to hand didn't help. High up Jimmy bounded through some fire-red weeds at the edge of the cut. *Poor slob. He thinks we're going home.*

There were six poles before the ridge. If it could just be that instant – if he could be standing before the bunkhouse door, under its porch in the dark, knowing they were sleeping on the other side, every particle of his being charged to strike. But it was never that way. You had to drag yourself from one second to the next, through hours, days, until the only second that mattered came and you were wasted.

He ground his teeth. No. He had to do it. His life depended on it – on seeing them huddled below him, their mouths fallen open – on knowing that he merely had to flick back the blade and they would beg, their speech stupid and slurred –

He fixed his eyes on the closest pole and tore into his arms and legs to take something for the next step.

In the calm of the evening, inexhaustible currents arched over the mountain.

Inspector Burton rubbed his thumb across the phone; it was slick and oily. The Calgary detachment had him on hold. Earlier, he'd asked them to have a talk with Harold Black's brother. He wondered if they'd gotten anything.

His thoughts turned back to the rumor, which he'd heard that morning, that Joseph Ashton was preparing to sue everyone connected with the case. He was probably waiting for the search to be called off.

His fingers slid against the plastic. The guy was a monster. He drove his kid to screw up at camp and now he was blaming everyone but himself. He deserved —

What?

But after working on a case like this, to sit in court and be rat-tailed by his lawyers —

He slammed the phone down on the desk. As if in pain, it peeped up at him. "Inspector . . . Are you there?"

Mechanically he picked it up and put it to his ear. The voice on the other end was brief.

"Well, does this neighbor have any idea where?"

His other thumb worked the dogeared corner of the file folder.

"I need you to find him . . . Yeah, I know, but this is important . . . I have a feeling this could be important . . . Maybe he has some friend who knows where he goes . . ."

He barely listened to the objections. When the corner was wrinkled enough he'd start to tear it, a little at first, and then a little more —

"Well don't forget all the legwork we do for you guys. How come you keep sending us all these teenyboppers? What do you think this is, California?"

Somehow he was irritated when the voice laughed. "OK . . . do what you can . . . thanks . . ."

He lowered the phone. Harold Black's brother had gone fishing. He could be anywhere in the Rockies.

He stared down into the blank expanse of the folder. They were being nice. It couldn't even be called a lead . . .

Shit. How long can this thing go nowhere?

He glanced at his watch. On the way home he'd pick up a case of beer and some old movies.

And for one night he'd forget about David Ashton.

David breathed in deeply. Night had finally come, merging bush to bush up the slope from the bunkhouses. The sky still glowed overhead. Everything was as he expected: the lightless bulk of Nos. 5, 6, and 7 broken up by the trees, and below them, a dim backwash of light from the cans. He hadn't come this close until the dusk was well advanced, maybe half an hour ago; in that time he'd heard no one. It must be close to lights out. They were settling down in their bunks.

The ax lay across his lap. He huddled closer against the growing chill, his gut tight to the handle. Jimmy lay at his side, his head down on his paws. He wasn't asleep.

Seeing it again was awful. To stare down at the faint light and know that that was where it was done – it sent a jolt through his blood, obliterating everything that had happened, everything except the plan and the ax. Pieces of the thing came at him, lucid, violent, precise in every detail; he fought to control them. They bled off in shudders of pain. *You won't be able to stop. At the sight of them you'll go mad—*

No. He had to be in command – every word, every action. If he hesitated for an instant he'd end up a fool – a murderer. He had to overwhelm them. The door breaking open, just as they drifted off into sleep – the shock of him standing there like a ghost in the whirling glow of the wood stove – everything was with him if he could just pull it off –

If they give you any shit they're dead. They've got to know that – they've got to taste in their fucking mouths that the only way to get out alive is through total humiliation—

He bent his head. The ax was hard and cold in his stomach. He'd imagined it maybe hundreds of times, yet he hadn't realized that he'd have to go right to the edge –

Kill them. That's what you really want.

— No — shut up —

Jeff will say something and you won't know what to answer and you'll lose it anyway

— No — please — He rocked back and forth, his body doubled over the ax. *You'll blow it. You'll blow it like you've blown everything. Why, for example, do you keep saying "them," when you know that Alf's in another bunkhouse?*

A void formed in his throat, rigid, choking. His arms trembled. He had to hang in. He had to do it. It would be like acting out all the rage — letting it burst into the world, overturning everything before it, but only up to a limit. *Do you have the strength not to cross it*

I don't know

He stood. His body felt weak in the night air. After all the planning and waiting, he wasn't ready. Maybe there was no way he could be ready, for the one chance to take back his whole life —

He bent his head. *God don't let me lose it. I've got to do this. Please.*

He noticed Jimmy, a dark shape at his feet. He dropped to one knee and held him. He'd been there the whole way, from the gray dawn under the porch. He pressed himself to the warm contentment of the animal's flank and he wondered again what knowing was in it.

He took the ax in both hands and started down the slope. It was the way he'd stumbled, the night pitching, shattering. If he could make them feel that — not just the act itself, but the passing of the seconds after . . .

A solid mass appeared off to his right. It was No. 5. His body scraped leaves and branches and he slowed to make it quieter. As the black roof of No. 7 took shape below him a thickness pushed at his chest. There were no sparks from the chimney. If the fire had burned low he'd have to shout, crazily, that he was David Ashton and he had an ax. Someone — Greg — would throw open the door of the stove. Then, trussed in sacks, he'd see their little white faces. *I've come back from the dead — you're gonna eat it —*

The dark void of the porch grew from under the roof and he felt himself drawn down into the pressure. He tried to fix on the words; his hands shifted on the ax, testing their grip. Off to the right was the fire barrel.

He took the last few steps. His hand felt for the low wall; the logs crisscrossed at the corner and he worked his way around them. Then he was under the porch. He moved forward; he couldn't see the door but the pressure swelled towards it. He reached with his hand to find the distance.

Worlds moved past him. He lifted the thing. In a few minutes he would be free —

The ax slammed into the door. It shot into nothing and he followed. No fire swirled away; his voice struck and came back at him.

"I'm David Ashton —"

No one answered. No mattress creaked.

"I've got an ax—"

The sound broke on the walls. He strained through the dark for a human presence, terrors hurling through the silence. "Answer me!"

There was nothing but the cold brief echo of the room.

He swung to one side, holding the ax out in front of him until it hit a bunk. He swept his hand over it. There was no body, no sleeping bag, just bare mattress.

The handle started to slip. He turned back to the void. In some world where he could reach madness the ax bludgeoned the bunk until it splintered in the dark. But the emptiness was too vast; he simply stood, the ax loose in his hand, unable to comprehend that they were gone, that there was nothing. On the outside it was all so unimportant, so ordinary, a bunch of beat-up old bunk beds in a vacant room . . .

Like a wind high in the pines, the voice entered. "I was afraid for you to come up here, boy . . . I was wrong."

Violent surges shook him. The ax fell and he pressed his hands to his face. The words sheared as he forced them into the dark. "Where—where are they—"

"They were expelled. As for the rest, today was the last day of camp. The buses pulled out in the afternoon."

He fought to breathe under the weight of nothing. "You promised to help me but you lied . . . you could've told me before it was too late . . . you could've saved me everything—all this hell—and Mom and Dad too—"

"Yes, I could've told you. And you would have gone home with nothing changed, convinced that you're utterly worthless, utterly powerless. The idea of coming here was the only thing that gave you hope, the belief that you could do something. It's not mine to take that away . . . because it wasn't a lie, boy—and it isn't now."

A bitter laugh racked him. "Oh? Tell me what I'm supposed to do in an empty room."

"Ask yourself why you've created this."

"You're insane—"

"On the way up here you realized that this big scene you had planned wouldn't work. Just now you were afraid that Jeff would get you tongue-tied and you'd let loose with the ax. You didn't come here for that. You're here to take on that guy you came face to face with down at the power line. The one who kept telling you you were sure to flunk, that the smart kids and the instructors had it in for you, that you were the camp joke. The one who taught you to slant and shade everything people said and did, so that the world would always confirm those ideas. The one who's telling you you've blown everything. You haven't blown it. The guy you're after – the one who did this to you – is right here."

His shoulders heaved. "They held me down – in a bucket of shit . . . Can't you understand?"

The voice rose through him, charged. "You're not powerless and you never have been. The power of creation moves through you more intimately than your blood. It's what you are. How could Jeff or Alf take that from you – it's the birthright of all things. And you alone, of all creatures, have used it to degrade and diminish yourselves."

He huddled against it. "You're blaming me for what they did! I shouldn't have jumped on Jeff – I shouldn't have called him suck – but I didn't deserve –" The words reeled off through the dark.

"It was the only kind of end your beliefs would allow. Under the power line you saw how you started working towards it on the bus, and you imagined to yourself, what if those beliefs had been different. That was the turning point, boy – a point most people never reach in their lives at all – the moment you realize you're a creator, and take responsibility for it."

The night washed against him. He remembered that second's sensation of letting go of the ax and starting down the mountain, huge convulsions breaking away, emotions from which he thought he could never be freed, not even by the ax. But what then – what would it be like, climbing the driveway to the house – or to be caught and taken there in the back of a cop car –

He saw himself standing before the door, filthied, waiting for his parents to open it. His chest locked. "You're saying that I can magically make everything better – just by changing my thoughts – But I've still got to face my dad and everyone at school. I've still blown camp completely and been ground to shit. How the hell do my thoughts change that –"

The voice slowed. "Your beliefs got you into this. To your way of thinking, it is neither more nor less magical for them to get you out. You exist in time; you have to work with what you've created there. It is not instantaneous. The beginning will be difficult."

The darkness hovered, protean, waiting. Outside a jolting window the sun slanted down through rising dust. Maybe it could be true – but it was too much to fight. No one cared about his thoughts. He had to take something back with his hands –

The chance was gone. It had never really been . . .

He turned. They would have stumbled on the words. Their faces would have been disgusting. Everyone would've seen it. But now – to stand up to them all with his mind alone – the hopelessness of it gripped him. He backed away into nothing –

"– On the first day there'll probably be fifty kids waiting for me on the playground! This was my only hope – and it wasn't even real –"

It surged over him, thick, cold. He swerved into a bunk; his fingers scraped fabric and he saw the piss stains on the blue and white stripes. He shoved himself away; there was no door, no way to ever leave the room, he'd had one chance and it was a lie. The totality of it burst through the walls of his flesh – what if death was a lie and there was no escape even then –

Words, images, broke under it in the dark. As if from a growing distance the voice called his name. He turned again in the room; the pressure accelerated, driving out from his gut, pieces of Jeff and Alf and his dad submerging into his blood until there was only madness to get out. He rammed into a bunk; his hands closed on the rail, shaking it, the legs skidding across concrete, fragments crying out for an end. Finally he leaned against the frame.

At the far edge there was a shape. He pushed off from the rail and stumbled across the dark; he realized it was the dim outline of the door. He broke through it; a rush of night air struck his face and then he was running uphill into brush.

At once, the sensation exploded through him that it was happening again – that nothing from the time he'd lifted his head from the fire barrel had any meaning, that he'd crawled up mountains and experienced miracles for nothing. His body drove through the thicket. This time there'd be no dog, no rock slide, no glimpse of a shack. This time there would be an end. His lungs fought the slope and cold. He could go back down the power line to the road, and reach the highway, and hitch a ride at dawn and go on and on. It was a lie and he clutched it, to make it easier –

Unseen branches whipped back from his arms. His breathing coarsened and he strained not to slow. The image of the room, of driving the ax at the door and bursting in and shouting at no one, slashed him and he flung himself at the night, bending and twisting living trash while kids shrieked with laughter. He imagined things with the ax, human animals writhing in the dirt, their mouths gaping, but they were a lie too, nothing was left but the forest and the night and the need to stop the pain.

His gut struck something. He caught at it in shock. It was the rail fence at the top of the camp. He pulled himself over it and stumbled onto the road.

He stood for a moment, his chest rising and falling. There was a vibration. He moved towards it and it rose over him, huge, but he couldn't see lines or towers.

Currents shot through the dark. His shoes struck the ground askew and he tried to control them. He was at the power line. It would take him back down into the valley and, in the cold glow before dawn, he would stand numbed by the side of a highway—

His life rose in his throat. He'd tried to find a way. It had turned days and nights into centuries and he'd endured them . . .

—For nothing. For an empty room.

Walls shuddered. The night throbbed, massive.

Endless trees along a deserted road . . .

He plunged across the bare earth into forest, shoving past trunks and branches in total dark, not knowing how he'd made the decision, a voice screaming stop but not enough, the thing gaining power and reality because he'd started. He trampled and thrashed his way forward, straining not to slow and not to think because he knew it was endless and directionless and there would be a point where his thoughts wouldn't matter. His breathing quickened. They saw you got delirious, that you staggered, drunk. After that there was only sleep—

Leaves struck his face and he tore at them, missing, his body dragging against the thicker branches until they whipped free and he stumbled into more, their touch cold and unbreaking. He fought to go faster but the stuff blocked him, dead masses of it shaking, his hands attacking it in clumps, the outrage of his life straining through them, kids waiting for him on the playground, cold noodles and sauce oozing from stacked-up plates, the oak-grained labyrinth of his father's desk—

Wood struck his chest. Blows hammered a sheet of plywood. The night collapsed inwards, frothing—

He stumbled under a fallen trunk. The side of his face struck hard and he squirmed, stunned, on the cold ground. A red blotch of pain pulsated against him but it wasn't enough, he knew even as it bent him that the way was long and only a fool would think it would be so quick—

He raised himself, his hands crushing dead leaves and filth, his face streaming in final hopeless rage. *Drop dead*

He'd pushed himself to his feet to go on when something startled him. It was like a wave out of the dark – an abrupt sensation of change. He searched the faint shapes ahead. Jimmy – where was Jimmy. The path – there was a path – and off in the forest to the left –

It gripped him. Its physical form was nothing – a place in the dark, to the left of his line of vision and a little down. That was wrong – he was going uphill. He stared into it – it was like the night was concentrated there. He'd been that way –

Reality flexed. He was stopped on a path in the forest, in the early morning. He'd lost sight of Jimmy. They'd just met – it was after that first night under the porch. He'd had the feeling that Jimmy had wandered off the path – that there was something in the undergrowth to his left. Suddenly, he'd gotten very afraid, and anxious to catch up; when he'd moved it could have been either way –

He stared into the place. Something welled up out of its stillness – fear, energy, a kind of lifting. It couldn't be the same spot as that morning – why did he suddenly remember it, when he'd completely forgotten –

He approached again. His confusion thrust at the limits of memory. He called out. There was no answer. He had to decide –

In the colliding backwash of time, it came – a rush of images. He left the path and tore downhill through the brush, branches coming faster than he could avoid, the dog's name jolting apart in his throat, the shifting masses of the forest darkening towards him, his panic growing for a glimpse or sound. It wasn't a memory or a dream –

He felt himself drawn down by his gut towards the place in the night, as if a world were concentrated there. He closed his eyes, allured and afraid –

Leaves, branches shot in and out of sight, endless, directionless. He heard his breathing, thin, strained with terror. There was no sun, no sky, no glimpse of anything human. The trees rose and fell and he lost all sense of which way he had come. Finally the undergrowth closed on him, ramming his face and arms; he clawed at it, shreds of his mind crying out to his mom and dad and to God –

In a little clearing, near a fallen log, it stopped. A little ways ahead, huddled in some low bushes, was a shape.

His body stiffened with fear. The object that he'd sensed off in the forest – it wasn't Jimmy. It was this.

He went closer. He reached for something to hold but there was nothing.

He saw, fragments through the bush. It wasn't like he'd thought. He hadn't stared up at the clouds. The flesh was bruised and cut – the hands had clutched at the ground –

He was dead. It was real. He didn't know how but it was real.

His body emptied from under him. His knees struck cold. His eyes searched the walls of the night and the pulsations started in the empty cavity. He wasn't sure which way he'd come. It wasn't a memory. It was going to happen, now.

He huddled against the ground. The place that he called himself slid and tumbled uncontrollably and he saw the edge, a black drop –

He screamed. It choked on the cold odor of the earth. "Mr. Black –"

For a second there was nothing; then he jerked in shock. The voice came from the point in the night; it started there and rose into him, as if it were never really outside him, as if what he was reached into that place. "I hear you, David."

His back shivered. "What's happening –"

"You lost sight of Jimmy on the path. In a split-second decision, you pursued him into the bush. When there was no sign of him you panicked and began running to catch up. Fear pulled you down in there and you never came out . . . Your remains will be found by some hunters in the fall. On a beautiful crisp October day they'll be laid to rest, as you call it, in the city cemetery of Kelowna. Hundreds of people will attend the service. You will have the revenge you wanted. Jeff, forced to sit at the back, will break as the coffin is carried past him out of the church."

His mind trembled in his hands. "– What are you saying –"

"What I've said from the beginning: that you're way bigger than you think. But your creative power reaches further than I've had the courage to tell you. You've been torn all along between different solutions. The choices you envisioned couldn't be pursued in one existence. At that instant on the trail, reality split. You created two different lives." The voice paused. Huge swells moved through him. "There's not much point in dying now, David. You've been that way. You choose death, in that reality, because you can't overcome your belief that you are powerless and worthless. You're where you are because you believe that you can finally cast off those ideas. If that's not true, keep going into the bush. Don't be afraid, you've gone through death a thousand times. It's life that haunts us."

There was a silence. A confusion like he'd experienced on the path rose in shaken leaps through the dark. It was madness; and yet, he knew in himself that what maddened him was to break through the hate and the anger. The words drove, trembling, to the edge of being. "– Who are you –"

The voice hesitated, reluctant. "You knew me as Harold Black. His experiences are close to me and I've spoken to you through them, but they are not the limit of what I am, any more than David Ashton is the limit of what you are. It was not just to put you at ease that I chose this personality; through him we're deeply connected. On the other hand, he couldn't encompass the things I've been telling you; so I've moved in and out of his character.

"The creative energy that we are is inexhaustible. We are driven to create as many and as varied experiences as physical and other realities can accommodate. The joys and terrors we encounter are not haphazard; they well up from our being and in them we confront, and perhaps transform, ourselves.

"As Harold Black I died hauling tin cans up a mountain, trying to get away from people. That was one incident in a long struggle. Almost seven hundred years ago, in terms of your time, I lived in a little village in a narrow mountain pass, somewhere in Asia. It was a paradise of fragrant gardens and fruit trees, nestled in the barren and sun-scorched rock. Like my father and his father for generations, I was purveyor to the caravans that came through there, laden with silk or cotton, spices and almonds. They treated us as ignorant people and I came to resent them, foreign dogs who could afford to pay far more for our provisions. My father said there was nothing to be done about it and when I demanded why, he hesitated, then said they could take other routes. I didn't want to understand. I grew sullen and the valley, with its little cluster of mud houses at the bottom, became hateful to me. In the evening I would climb the rugged sides of the pass and stare, alone, into the far distance, to where the mountains descended into the haze of the desert, like into a sea; but it brought me no peace, because I realized that I envied these foreigners, who traveled so far beyond the limits of my world. At last my father grew old and spent his days in the square with the other old men, smoking his pipe and playing dominoes; I began charging the traders more. They grumbled and accepted it and I grew bolder and more surly. Finally, one of them had had enough; he lashed me across the face with his whip. Stunned, bleeding, I watched as they took what they wanted; when it was done the trader laughed, and tossed a few coins at my feet. Saliva foamed at my lips; but that wasn't the end of my humiliation. The elders, my father among them, called me before them and declared that I must go back to the old ways at once, before I brought ruin upon the village. That cut deeper than the whip; I detested them as cowards, but it was unthinkable to defy them. So I obeyed; but, whenever I could, I climbed above the village and plotted, my mind tormented as the heat of the rock. I resolved quickly to steal from the caravans, until I had enough to leave the village; I planned and prepared a place to hide the booty . . .

"On my very first attempt, I was caught. It was nothing, a barking dog (so you see why I'm so fond of Jimmy). They beat me savagely and bound me and told me that at daylight I would be beheaded. The entire village assembled, hushed, to await the moment the sun rose over the pass; but when I was brought out, it was only to be hoisted onto a camel. Without a word, the caravan left. I'll never forget the depths of my father's eyes as I was led past him; he believed I would be sold into slavery.

"As the caravan wound down from the mountains onto the great floor of the desert, I wept at the fulfillment of my longing. The next day they gave me a drink of water and pushed me off."

The voice caught on a shred of silence; yet the words rose and fell on a great calm. "I concluded from that experience that the answer was to put up and shut up, to endure. But peace can be aggressive, and strength and weakness are not what they seem. I was a baroness once, a young woman of exquisite beauty and refinement. My father, a military man, considered me his prize and treated every young man who courted me with contempt. At first I resisted, tearfully; but slowly, as if in revenge, I grew perverse. I toyed with my suitors, and the more attracted I was to one, the more I led him to imagine, in vain, that he had a chance of success. I kept their desperate letters in a steel box.

"On our estate there lived a family of hired hands. They had a daughter; she was pretty, in a coarse sort of way, and stubborn. I took a dislike to her and began sniping at her in the kitchen; I loved seeing her bite her lips, how her chin wrinkled. The common youths of the district pursued her madly; on more than one summer evening I stood listening behind the curtains of my sitting room, as her laughter drifted up from the twilight of the courtyard intertwined with some young man's. Breathlessly, I waited for their voices to stop. My cheeks flushed. With utmost discretion, I began spreading rumors.

"These divertissements were interrupted by a war. My father joined his regiment, the young men were conscripted, and life grew dull. I read and played piano for hours; but gradually, hardship set in and I had to work. I was weak and clumsy at it and the hired girl watched me with delight. I prayed for victory.

"Winter came and things got worse. My father's letters were guarded, but they led us to believe that in the spring there would be great advances.

"One sunny windy day in April I was toiling in the kitchen when I heard shouts. I hurried outside; one of the young men was back. We began to half-walk, half-run towards him, a lone figure at the far end of the alley. I remember cherry blossoms whirling across the road in the sun and our excitement that we would get some news. But when we were still at a distance, our steps slowed; something was wrong. I stood flustered, uncomprehending; he hobbled towards us on makeshift crutches. His left leg was gone. As he came up, he addressed me respectfully and tried to bow. I fainted.

"He told us that the army had suffered two defeats. A few nights later, we thought we heard cannon in the far distance. Rumors flew; and yet, we were unprepared for the terror, for its swiftness. More wounded soldiers appeared on the roads, huddled shapes with sudden unimaginable eyes; we gave up questioning them. Then, one midmorning, columns of dust rose in the east. We delayed, disastrously, supposing it was our army in retreat; I ordered some food and belongings to be loaded onto a wagon. We were rushing to do this when a low rumble of hooves came from the road. The men had gone into the house to bring out my trunk; the hired girl and I stood alone in the yard as enemy cavalry turned into our alley.

"She wrenched me by the shoulder and we ran into the barn. She hurried me into an obscure stall and we crouched together there, panting, not knowing if we'd been seen. Animals bleated and bellowed. Shouts came from the yard but then there was nothing. I fidgeted with my necklace as it rose and fell, fighting not to weep.

"Then someone entered the barn. His steps were slow and they echoed dully in the gloom of the place. He went up and down the aisles, stopping several times. As he approached our stall my breath locked in my throat.

"He continued past. When he was many stalls away I breathed out, almost silent. The hired girl touched my shoulder; I thought she meant to get up. I started to rise and she pushed me down, madly. I was furious –

"Then he was standing there, towering over us in the half-light of the aisle: a huge man with fierce eyes and jet-black hair. He shouted something in his language. When we didn't move he drew his saber.

"I swayed to my feet. As we came into view his teeth flashed in a grin and the only question in his eyes was which of us to rape. He examined us like cattle; then he motioned me towards the straw.

"I collapsed in terror, imploring him in the name of all the saints to spare me, the words shrieking into nothing because I saw that he neither knew nor cared what they meant, they only inflamed his hate. He came towards me; I couldn't scream —

"Suddenly the hired girl was at my side, scooping up dung and filth from the floor of the stall and smearing it on her face. Quickly I did the same, flinging the cold running muck of the stable at my closed eyes and wiping it down my neck and arms and dress. We befouled ourselves until we were blotched and reeking and then, together, we faced him. As I looked up at him, my terror changed to a strange and boundless courage.

"He glared down at us in astonishment; then he started to raise the saber. I didn't move.

"He swore savagely, spat on me, and walked out.

"We ran out the back and through the birches along the stream until we were well away from the house. Then we washed and embraced each other, weeping. We hid by day and fled at night through the fields, the fires of burning estates ringing the horizon. On the third morning we met a man hauling milk. We burst with joy when he didn't understand us; we had crossed the border and were safe."

David pressed his arms to his chest, fighting the cold. How — how could she have looked up at him like that?

"In that moment, boy, without knowing it, I touched what I am. But there are lives in which I have breathed it. Most are in your future; but one of my favorites occurred very long ago, in terms of your time. A mountainous island rose from a glass-swelled sea. The peaks were naked to the sun but the valleys were crowded with olive groves and vineyards. White-walled cities lined the coast, their harbors gaudy with sails, for these people were expert mariners. In one of these cities I worked a small olive press, and while my oil was clear and light, I'd neither ply the jobbers with wine nor sell too cheap, and so I never really prospered. I was getting on at this, turning white-haired and, according to my family, somewhat cantankerous, when a change came over me. I'd always had a speculative side, but suddenly I felt an intense curiosity about certain phenomena.

"It started one evening as I was walking on the beach. There was a ship far out at sea, coming into port. I noticed that the sails appeared first, followed much later by the hull. An explanation occurred to me, that the surface of the sea was curved. I rushed home and told my wife, adding that it might be possible to calculate the degree of curvature; but she only smiled and said, 'You saw the sail first because it's big and bright.'

"I sulked a bit, but soon began to wonder about other things: why the sun was lower in the sky in the winter than in the summer; why it cast straight shadows down a wall, but a rainbow was curved; why the stars were fixed in relation to each other, but rotated through the seasons, as if they were painted on the inside of a huge black bowl that turned. I devised an instrument to measure the angle between an object in the sky and the horizon, and began to take readings with it; my family grew concerned. My wife demanded why I was doing it, saying the neighbors all knew I was standing on the roof every night and I was becoming quite an object of gossip. I had no answer except that I was curious; but soon after, I hit on a use for the thing so stupendous that it tingled my spine: to calculate the distance to the stars. My plan was this: to measure the altitude of a given star and then, exactly a year later, measure it again, but from another location. The difference would produce an angle and, the distance between the two places being known, someone learned in numbers could determine the distance to the star. I took a series of readings and, a year later, concocted a business trip to a distant island, where I'd heard there were skilled mathematicians.

"The plan failed. The differences were so tiny that my instrument couldn't measure them. I threw the thing away, maddened that I could have been such a fool; and I was about to board ship for home when a stranger came up to me on the dock. He was a foreigner with a long beard. He said he had seen me pointing something at the sky at night; his Greek was awful. I was suspicious, but he wouldn't quit, so finally I told him what I'd been up to. I expected him to laugh; instead he asked me a few questions about my instrument and then, mostly with sign language, suggested some improvements that were nothing less than brilliant.

"Together we built a new instrument. He was Persian; he called himself a trader but I think he was more a smuggler. He said that if I would send him the figures, he would do the calculations; only, he advised me to stick to the sun. I agreed and we parted. I took the first readings and sailed home full of hope.

"A year later I took the second measurements and sent them off. Even with the sun, the angle was minute. Months passed and I heard nothing;

I'd started to despair when the letter came. I sealed myself in my room; the parchment wouldn't be still. At least he'd hired a good scribe. I remember how he began:

> Honored friend, forgive the long delay. I've been in Babylon. The figures you have sent indicate an average distance to the sun of 1,996,000 stadia. However, as the error must be considered in favor of an even smaller angle, the true distance could be many times that . . .

"I reached for a wall, boy. It was inconceivable. He was saying that the sun was at least 229,000 miles from the earth, and probably much further. I went out and wandered the streets that night, and the next day I began talking about it in the marketplace. There were scoffers and jokers, which I was used to by now; but I was met by something I didn't expect. A man yelled up at me, 'Why would the gods put the sun so ridiculously far away?' I tried to explain our methods and calculations but he kept shouting, his face turning red; others joined in. I spoke in a neighboring town and it was the same. They were scared.

"I was puzzling about this when soldiers, members of the palace guard, appeared at the olive press. I was summoned before the ruler of that city. My wife, poor thing, grew frantic; at last I agreed, more or less, to drop the whole matter.

"It was a hot, breathless night when I appeared before him. His throne faced the open courtyard of the palace. Arrayed on each side of him, their faces chiseled in the glare of the oil lamps, were the high priests of all the temples. My heart lurched.

"He welcomed me as the head of an old and honored family; then he began to speak of the rising tide of idle speculation on the mainland, how it was turning men from fixed, Immutable Truth. The universe was a series of perfect concentric spheres, of crystalline composition; the motions of these spheres could explain all apparent anomalies. I need not concern myself with instruments and calculations . . .

"I'd started to answer, humbly, that my work was only concerned with estimating distances, when one of the priests cut me off. 'We know your purpose. Just now, alerted by one of our scribes, we caught a foreigner, a cursed Persian, practicing their black arts and astrology. Before he died he confessed to making an instrument such as yours.'

"I went numb. The ruler was speaking again but the words were swept into the light of my friend's eyes as he fitted the copper scale to the quadrant. The lamps quivered. It had something to do with exile.

"The ruler stopped. He expected some reply.

"I was about to cry out in rage when something came over me. It was like – like that old guy standing in the glare of the headlights. Or those women in the barn.

"I stepped towards the man, then stopped and looked up at the stars. I felt his eyes follow.

"I spoke quietly. 'It's like a river. We're children, forever trying to dam it. It will always overflow us. That's its power and its joy.'

"He banished me from his realm forever.

"The next day my wife, my children and grandchildren fell before him and pleaded. He was merciful; I had only to proclaim, everywhere I had spoken, that all my work was in error. I almost went mad that day and night, but I couldn't – I couldn't do that to my friend.

"The sea the next morning was a hard, cobalt blue; it heaved under a brisk south wind. I stood rigid at the stern of the ship, my wife overcome with grief in my arms, staring out over the piercing white wake until the land vanished into the horizon.

"I smiled, once. The last I saw of my home was the highest peak, radiant in the sun."

The voice broke from the point in the dark. "Your journeys, David, are no less than these. You've suffered injustices and you've imagined them. You've wept in stinking prison cells and in empty palaces. You've begged on street corners, plotted rebellions, stared at death through barbed wire. Through the explosive fission of your thoughts you've joined in creating worlds, worlds so enchanting in their detail and so alluring and fearful in their possibility that wandering them, you've forgotten from where you come. You feel despised and powerless, but even in the depths of that creation, when everything seems to confirm it, you are sustained by what you are." The voice halted. "Do you think you're helpless, a 'stupid kid'? Nothing you create is lost, nothing is wasted. You've molded and discarded countless forms of power. Your mind has thrust through the ages at the limits of thought. You have wrought all grief and all joy. Your children have laughed and your lovers have died in your arms. They enlarged you, and you them."

There was a short burst of silence. "So, if you'll excuse me for asking, why are you going to pieces over one lousy bucket of shit?"

His mouth dropped. He couldn't speak. He stared into the place in the night as if he would be swept into it, as if a thin film separated him from all the lives he'd almost lived—

The voice sensed his confusion. "May I suggest something?"

It startled him. "—What?"

"Rise. It is not I, David, but your own inviolate self, that calls to you to live unafraid. And it's not any power of mine, but the power of your own thoughts, that will decide whether you die in this place, or further the love that brought you here. Love—what I mean is that insatiable thirst for experience, that undying urge to change, to discover, to create, that drives all things. Even Alf and Jeff . . . You went to camp convinced of your helplessness and inferiority. You lived those fears. Your experiences flowed from them so perfectly that you never thought to question their validity. Until they brought you to this . . .

"You are a creator. If this cold, forgotten place is what you've crafted out of fear, imagine what you could do with your desires."

The words stopped. The night moved around him. His breath was stiff, his body empty against the ground; but something—something was stretched, connected in unimaginable ways with the dark, in every direction. He was dead in the forest; but that was just one strand—

He picked himself up. The backs of his legs trembled. He didn't know what moved him. He'd have to face his dad, the kids on the playground—

But what if, in all the world, there was nothing to fear?

It powered through him. The dog plunged into the stream and they rioted in its swiftness, translucent, shouting—

He tried to steady himself. The darkness was intense, the trees obscure. Most people would be afraid . . .

Was it the darkness of creation, awaiting his touch? How long had it been since he had dared to want? When had he last imagined some joy, and thought to himself, I want that to be?

—He didn't believe it. Yet he'd had no trouble believing in the power of malice and cruelty—

Maybe he'd needed them to be huge. So he could stay helpless and small.

The night lapped against him. He didn't know which way he'd come. His body was a thin shell.

He forced the words into the dark. "What do I do?"

The voice laughed, softly. "Why don't you call your dog?"

It took him by surprise. "– Did I say that?"

"We battle in ourselves, David, but not alone. We claw and thrash our way through time in search of who we are. In countless ways these struggles are connected. Our thoughts are all shared. You are sustained by friends some of whom, in time, you've never met. And what you will do helped empower me."

He almost asked what he meant; but he stopped.

He would go back – but never – never the way he came. He'd still be Uncool. He'd still be no good at computers. But those things would not have the power to make him worthless or helpless.

They never did.

He shouted, his voice hoarse in the night. "Jimmy!"

He turned; his hand touched something rough. He remembered the fallen log. He crouched under it and waded into the brush. "I'm over here, boy!" A voice started to say it was silly, he'd left him at the bunkhouses. "Jimmy!" The branches were close. He worked his way through them. He was not afraid that it wouldn't be the way –

Suddenly, to his shock, the trees stopped. He was standing at the edge of the power line, long before he'd expected. Transmissions pierced the silence over him. The place where he'd despaired had been a few steps into the bush.

A few remote stars glistened over the towers. It was like standing before that ruler in his courtyard – going home. He wouldn't hide. His voice would struggle with incredible things. He wondered if his dad's eyes would even follow . . .

He can't make you small unless you let him.

He scanned the rough edges of the night. Somewhere across the clearing was the road. "Jimmy!"

There was a stirring behind him. The darkness snapped; he turned –

Nonchalant, the familiar stroke of the dog's panting came towards him – but from the side of the power line where he'd been. He knelt and called out; suddenly the rich pulse of the animal's fur filled his arms.

"He gets around. Kind of like me. He was near you the whole time."

David thought. "Would he have saved me?"

"You did that on your own."

He held the dog, afraid to say.

The voice changed. "You're right, David. There are no fixed states – whether of salvation or wisdom or peace. You are always becoming. And so is your father. At first you'll feel driven back into the grooves you two have worn. I'd like to offer you some advice for dealing with this – because the situation isn't what it seems. But now you need rest. Why don't you spend the night at my place?"

He hesitated; then his exhaustion and cold sank into him. "OK . . . Is there anything to eat?"

"Well, they cleaned out the kitchen. They found the gumdrops in the night table. But I planted a few things in the garden – maybe there's been enough rain."

"Good . . . I'm sick of cans." The shifts in the voice no longer startled him.

"Jimmy will show you the way. There's a key under the porch, the first post to the right of the steps. You'll be real comfortable –"

The voice stopped. He waited; its presence was weak. It was like he'd dashed off, to get ready for company.

He let go of Jimmy. To his surprise, he didn't move. Finally he said, "Didn't you hear, boy? Take me home –"

For an instant he thought he sensed, in the darkness of the animal's form, a reluctance; then the dog started up the power line. He went slowly, stopping to sniff obscure things. "Please go faster, Jimmy, I'm dead tired."

The dog obeyed. He followed him up the rough track from one tower to the next for what seemed a long time, his mind bent to the trail; then the images started. They surprised him and he wondered that they did.

The house had appeared slowly, an angular concentration of night. He'd known at once but standing in the chilled crust of hate he didn't believe it. Mr. Black would turn on a light. He'd fling open the screen door. *My goodness boy what's happened to you* – This – this was some old barn or shed –

In quick succession he saw the rest: how he'd approached the impenetrable darkness under the porch, telling himself the house was different; how his hand, outstretched into nothing, had finally brushed the mesh of the screen door; the little indifferent click of the lock and the empty table and, at the very end, the plywood sheets on the windows. He'd huddled against them, the cruelty incomprehensible –

He stopped. He'd followed Jimmy into the bush. The trees opened ahead. He'd come this way, the night air scraping his filthied body, madness inside him, just held back by the softness of the old man's voice.

He went forward. Somehow, after all that had happened, it would be changed.

The house came into view, featureless, desolate in its clearing. It seemed a little smaller. He stared at it almost in anger.

He crossed the dry grass towards the porch. *He died. His stuff was hauled away, the door was locked, the windows were boarded up. A "For Sale" sign was slapped on one of them but no one ever came. And that was that.*

The posts just separated from the night. The first one to the right of the steps. He'd shivered there in a rag in that blackness, the finality of it immense, crushing.

He approached it. Huge questions weighted his blood. If there was no key – if it really was all just inside him – was he insane? Or wouldn't he have to be bigger – way bigger than he'd ever imagined – just to have created it?

He reached around to the back of the post. Slowly his hand searched the rough surfaces of wood.

It brushed a string. And then he was holding it – a key.

There was a rush outwards. He caught himself.

A voice laughed. *Lots of people would hide a key there. It's the obvious place.*

He didn't believe it. He felt his way up the steps and to the screen door. It squealed back. The door knob was cold.

The key ached in the lock. The voice had a reason for bringing him here – he could feel it – as if the words were already formed –

The door opened. The darkness on the other side was intense. He stood, wanting but afraid to enter.

The voice surprised him. It was soft, as if the old man's eyes had sparkled. "The light switch is in the obvious place too – right next to you."

He flicked it. The room leaped at him and he shielded his eyes. Images shot back into objects – the wood stove, the table and chairs, the huge granite fireplace. Jimmy was moving about, sniffing.

Nothing had changed. A weariness cut into him. He wondered what he'd expected.

He shut the door. From the inside the plywood on the windows was ominous and he tried not to look at it.

The kitchen was utterly bare. The cupboards and counter were clean and empty and worn. They took the canister with the skunk.

He approached the table. He knew what rose in his throat. Jimmy was standing near one of the legs, staring down at the floor.

That's where he died. He clutched at one of these chairs, feeling it slip through his hands. Then he dropped.

The shadow under the table was solid, sharp. The struggle and terror were there, concentrated inside it – the old man twisted under it, his hands reaching where there was nothing to hold –

He glanced away. The plywood was crooked. It was all lifeless, empty, closed. They'd sealed death into the room –

He'd turned to the door when the voice surged through him, not loud but stronger than he'd ever known. "This was the end, David, for both of us. Persecuted, powerless, alone, we ran until we dropped. My brother's pamphlets warned me to expect nothing but the worst from people; your father's lectures did the same for you. But we took those beliefs and made them our own, in our everyday acts, and they brought us here. You huddled against that board drowned in hate. I tossed the newspaper on the floor and died. We wanted out."

"I – I don't want to sleep here –"

"That's not death you feel, it's stagnation. Death is vital. All life, all consciousness, creatively limits itself in order to enter space and time. Once it has made its choices, developed its potential within those limits, it will not stagnate. Relentlessly it seeks new avenues, new dimensions. Harold Black experienced the wonders of solitude; yet he couldn't free them from his bitterness. I intend to pursue this. Death is the forge of my creating."

The voice stopped for an instant. "He died, alone and angry and afraid, in this room. I am not limited by him. I don't have to deny the beauties and strengths of his experience, or dwell on his failures. That form of pain you sense on the floor is real, and valid. But in the onrush of my becoming I have swept past it."

He reached for the back of the sofa, shaken by what the voice was about to say. "That boy out there on the porch, David, soaked in shit, is real. You don't have to spend the rest of your life hating him, pitying him, denying him, because he is not you. You are the relentless power of creation, poised in one instant of one pulse of space and time. There is not a moment in which you are not sustained by the full dimensions of your being. The very cells of your body are determined to thrive. Do you think that you alone, of all living things, are not designed to flourish?"

There was a break. Then it was as if the force of a life burst through him. "Turn that power around, boy! Instead of struggling to haul tin cans up that mountain – I – I should've made a new sign, bigger and more beautiful than the old one, and set it up out by the road, saying, 'Welcome – Harold Black–'"

The voice fell silent. Without knowing why, David let go of the sofa and went over to the fireplace. He reached out a hand and touched one of the stones. The light and dark minerals of the granite flashed along the edge of his touch.

He turned back to the room. "– I'm afraid to go back, to Mom and Dad. I won't know what to say, to do –"

The voice came softly, from enormous depths. "Sleep, David. Sleep. Trust your being. It's more true than you know, that what you most desire in time and space, you call a dream . . ."

Constanza placed the last dish on the rosewood table and closed the door to the kitchen behind her. Joseph Ashton, seated at the head of the table opposite the big picture window onto the lake, studied Elaine a moment before offering to serve her. "This looks good."

She stiffened against the chair. To say anything about the food – she barely noticed what it was –

She waited, fearful.

He took a few bites and stopped. His hand reached for his water glass but he didn't drink.

Opposite her, David's plate and glass and silver sparkled. She'd told Constanza to set his place, the night before. Seeing it, Joseph had stopped and almost turned away. But neither spoke of it.

His hand worked the stem of the crystal. "Tom's recommended that we retain L. Waterford Jones."

He waited. She gave him nothing.

"I'm sure you've heard the name. He made headlines last year, in *Culos versus Ontario Regional Transit Authority*. The bloated mandarins who own this country have nothing to fear from voters – but they fear him."

The tines of her fork quivered through the little bit of food on her plate.

"He's already examined the case and agreed to take it, on a contingency basis. He turns down over three-fourths of the cases referred to him."

The fork skidded off the edge. Her head dropped in a blur of pain.

" – He's flying into Kelowna tomorrow afternoon. He wants to meet us both. I thought it would be more comfortable for you, if it was here at the house."

The words wouldn't come. They tore at her throat. "You said – you would wait – "

"I'm sorry, Elaine. L. Waterford Jones is on an impossible schedule. He had to get a recess in a three-million-dollar suit, in order to come." He hesitated. "Tom thinks they're playing a game with us now – "

The fork slammed into the table. She rose, her chair screeching back. "For the love of God – they're trying to find our son –"

"I know how difficult –"

"Don't give me that! I'm sick of you patronizing me!" She stood back from the table, shocked. "David's been missing four days and all you care about is your goddamn lawsuits! Suppose you maul every one of them – suppose your big-shot lawyer ruins their careers, strips them to their underwear – you tell me how the hell that's going to help –"

Her hand trembled for the chair. Tears struck the bones of her face, savage.

Joseph drew himself up. "I love David. I'm shocked that you could question that."

"Then give the people who are trying to find him some of that love, that hope! Hate and anger will never bring him home. I know that –"

He looked at her in guarded pity. There was a deep silence. She felt light against the chair but she would not sit.

The edges of his face eased. His voice was measured, calm. "Let me explain why I'm doing this. . . . When we sent David to Silver Lake, we put the director and staff of that camp in the highest position of trust – higher than if they safeguarded our very lives. We expected David to learn, to be treated with respect, to be safe from harm. They betrayed that trust, grossly and repeatedly. They concealed a serious incident from us. They failed to take decisive action even when it was clear that David was being mistreated. Finally and unbelievably, they didn't notify the police that he was missing for almost two hours – precious hours in which, with a proper response, he would have been found. . . . Elaine, every parent of every child in that camp shared that trust. It didn't have to have been David. I am doing this not out of hate but so that some other parents, somewhere, just might be spared what you and I have suffered. What I have watched you endure makes me laugh at hell."

She cried out inside, *No! It had to have been David, no one else –*

The voice heaved. "But the one thing I will not endure – is for those who did this to then say to us, it is our fault. As I anticipated, that will be their main defence. And they will choke on it –"

He stood from the table. His eyes glared through her from their sunken pits. Her body tensed with fear; she struggled against it, the massive creaking of a blood-stained wheel –

Suddenly, she heard herself tear free. "Then you should sue me too."

"What?"

Her hand couldn't hold or let go of the chair. "– I've had hours – years – since this thing started, to think about us and David – to try to understand why it happened. I've felt the things you're feeling – bitterness, rage at the mistakes that were made. But when I've searched for the heart of how this could have been – I've come to us, Joseph. We made him go – but that's not the main thing. Our responsibility goes beyond that."

He stared at her in shock. "– Then you would betray me?"

She struggled, as in the shadow of a huge wall. His voice lunged at her, steel-gray, sharp. "You would give our enemies the final pleasure of watching us writhe in guilt – after they have taken our only son?"

Her hand groped for the chair. "– Our enemies?"

He came towards her. "Yes, our enemies! The obscene establishment that's bleeding this county to death, with its relentless war on anyone with drive and ambition! We have money, don't we? Then of course it's our fault David's missing! We warped him psychologically! Just ask any beaded junior psych professor!"

She fought not to panic. "You think someone takes pleasure in this? Who?"

"Oh, no one much. Just the media and their vast audience! There's no spectacle the masses relish more, than the fall of the rich –"

– She stumbled along the path. Ahead, the sharp-faced woman didn't bother to avert her eyes –

A choking hate bore down on her. She forced herself not to back away. "Have you forgotten the hundreds of volunteers –"

"It's all window dressing, putting in time! Tom's convinced they would've called off the search by now except they know what's coming and they're padding the hours for the judge –"

She looked at him, stunned; then she turned as if to go to the window, but her body simply collapsed to the table, her hands pressed to her face, her back trembling up and down –

He stared down at her, empty, then relieved that he'd said it. She had to face the truth.

Time bled. He saw through a crack in the doorway that Constanza was listening. How much would she be paid –

He waited, rigid in grief. She needed time to deny. When she was through it far enough to accept, he would comfort her – and she would burn with the justice of what he was doing.

But in the long aching he grew uneasy. She was too still. He wanted to touch her shoulder, but was unsure . . .

Suddenly, she stood and faced him. Her flesh glistened with tears but they had stopped. Her eyes were dark, her voice low. It startled him. "David's alive. I don't care what your lawyer says. He's alive and he's coming home. But not to this."

His voice stiffened. "What do you mean?"

"You really have no idea?" She came towards him. He tried to guess to what madness she'd succumbed. "The people who ran the camp are indifferent to kids. They allowed David to be hazed. The police don't care either – except for their PR. The searchers are just going through the motions. The media's drooling to blast us onto the air screaming and crying. Everyone thinks we got what we deserve."

She stopped. He waited, unmoved.

"It's all just an ugly war to you, isn't it?"

His lips narrowed in a tense smile. "I face reality. I deal with life as it is."

She reached across the table, snatched up David's water glass, and thrust it at him. It flashed in the light of the chandelier. "You don't face reality – you make it! That's why you're vice president of the company. And that's why this glass is empty! Look at yourself in it – how distorted it is! You've fought people for so long that you can't see anything but incompetence, indifference, and cruelty!"

"Oh, I see. I made it all up. Their not telling us that David ran away last year – the two hours before Mahon called the police – the nine hours before they brought the dogs. My what a cynic I am to be upset with such trifles."

She lowered the glass to the dark wood, clutching it fiercely. "What did you say to him last year when you told him he was going to the camp?"

It caught him off guard. He tried to remember. "– What any parent would tell his child – to work hard and do his best."

The crystal twisted in her hand. "You were disappointed in his report card. You said we had to get him on track before it was too late. You called him up to your study. After some time I heard his voice, raised. It was so young, so afraid . . . I heard him say, 'Why do you even want me around –'"

His hand closed hard on the back of her chair. "Now really, Elaine, that is enough! To hold me to blame for what a child says in anger –"

"Maybe we should've listened to that child, just once! Before he ran out of the house he stopped and looked at me – I took it then as you do, a child's exaggerated reaction – but that look haunts me now. What did you say to him!"

His eyes didn't move from hers. "The mere truth. That in the future there will be fewer management positions. That he had to excel for the sake of his success and happiness. I don't sugarcoat the world and you needn't try to make me feel guilty for it."

The crystal shuddered; her voice flew on its light. "I don't want you to feel guilt – I want you to feel uncontrolling love! Through all this I've come to know, that that's the only real kind –"

There was a glint of a question behind his retort. "Uncontrolling love? Oh, you mean, go on and get mediocre grades, David, if that's what you want . . . School shouldn't cut into your fun, so do as you like, play Nintendo, flake out in front of the TV, and don't give a thought to your future."

Her eyes fell to the intricate depths of the glass. "Did you have so little faith in him?"

There was a silence. "– Of course not –"

"Then when did you ever ask him what _he_ wanted?" She pierced him. "Don't tell me he didn't think about his future! He's talked with me about it – but not in the last year." She forced herself on. "Maybe – maybe this was the only way he could see, to take his future back into his own hands. It's not that we made him go – we sent him up there deadlocked in fear and despair. I could feel it right up to when I let him out of the car – I knew something was wrong but I didn't listen –"

He cut her off, perplexed. "Despair? How? We offered him every advantage – a private tutor – his own computer –"

"Yes, we gave him everything – but we took something away. Freedom – and with it respect. The freedom to find his own way, no matter how hard. He had to be a manager –"

"I never said that!"

"You didn't have to say it. He got the message. If he didn't aim for the board room he was second-rate, or a fool!" Her voice pitched. "That created quite a problem for him, because he knew that he was not a manager, that if he went that way he'd never measure up. So no matter what he did, he'd never be good enough."

The lines of his face slipped. "I didn't say one word to him – not one word – disparaging that report card! I've always praised his successes. You've encouraged him constantly –"

Her hand searched the facets of the glass. "I've thought about that. He seemed to want praise, but when he got it, he drew back, as if he didn't trust it. Maybe we weren't quite genuine – or maybe it was because the power to praise is also the power to condemn. I think that's what he really wanted, but felt he had no hope of ever experiencing . . . power."

He looked at her as if she were mad. "Power? He's twelve years old!"

She turned and walked to the window. The evening sun played across the lake into the shadows of the mountains. He waited for her to explain but she only stood, her head bent, holding David's glass in both hands, as if it might catch something, a glint of knowing.

Finally he couldn't hold back. The words stumbled, cut. "What kind of power? To decide for himself, at the age of twelve, that computer technology doesn't matter, that he'll do just fine without it, pumping gas?"

She didn't answer. He felt a rush of triumph.

She stared into the glass. The lake, the mountains, the room were concentrated within it, transformed by the refraction of light. Rays converged. He was alive. He was alive only because through every second of her agony, he struggled to be healed –

She turned towards him. The edges of her dress dissolved into the sun on the water. "I guess what I mean is simply . . . the power to grow up. To start making his own vision of himself, even if that meant making mistakes – what we call mistakes. We thought that all we had to do was program him with the necessary skills, the right components – and, like an automated toy, he'd start marching towards success. I think he saw through it. I think through a terrible process he came to the same question I have. We wanted him to be a leader, an achiever. How were we preparing him to do that – if what we really taught him – was that his thoughts, his feelings, didn't count?" A fierce light surged past the pain in her eyes. "He made them count! Don't you see – there is a process here –"

He looked away from her, stunned. Her voice swayed over a silent rift where the shadows touched the lake. "You say you were preparing him for life. But was it enough to warn him about the difficulties he'll face? When did we ever help him reach into himself to search for what he loved? When did we ever try to help him feel the vastness of his potential? When did we ever warn him, that there are dreams that won't let go?" Her voice dropped. "That to act on those dreams there is a power to move mountains?"

He stood for a moment, staring down at the dishes on the table; then he turned and went back to his place. He seemed to glance at his plate. When he spoke, his defiance shuddered against something. "I'm a pragmatic businessman . . . I'm sure there are things I don't understand. But I want you to know that everything, absolutely everything I've done – I believed to be vital to David's future."

She caught something, buried deep in his eyes. *You do understand. All too well.*

It startled her. She approached him, wondering. "<u>He</u> has to make that future, Joseph, we can't do it for him . . . We thought we were preparing him for life. Maybe what we were really trying to do, is protect him from it – from the pain and uncertainty of growing up. We laid out a course for him – a sure route to success. We didn't want any doubts, confusion, mistakes. It would've been fine for some people – but not David." The words staggered out of silence. "He's very talented – that's not the word for it. Whatever he draws, it leaps off the paper, as if its very life surged through his pencil. I have many of his things . . . he was afraid to show them to you. If you'd look at them you'd see a power that can't be held back –"

There was a motion to the silence, a minute fluctuation of the fading light.

Slowly, as if lost in himself, Joseph Ashton sat down. His hands hung from the armrests of his chair except, once, in determination or pain, they started to clench. She couldn't see his face but she sensed, in the sculpted gray lines of his forehead, that he battled a ghost.

At last, as if staring down onto some dark broken plane, he spoke the most terrible words she'd ever heard. "What does it matter now?"

She lowered David's glass to the table and, taking his hands in hers, lifted them and placed them against it. She bent at the lifelessness of his touch.

Layers tore and dissolved. Structures shattered. She held him through it.

Suddenly, she felt his hands press the glass. Light shot off the rim, streaming through the broken bed of their flesh.

When David awoke, it seemed as if a strong current of sleep had washed him up on a far shore. There was a stark, thin line around the boarded-up window; it felt late. He turned on his side; Jimmy shifted and settled. He could tell Mr. Black had let him sleep on the bed. But Mom wouldn't permit it.

On his third try he forced himself up and wandered into the living room. The wooden floor rubbed his bare feet. Slivers of sun crossed it.

He opened the door and screen and stepped out onto the porch. It was broad day. The sun had lost the sharpness of morning and lay warm and solid on the dry grass. Insects flitted through the clearing. It looked unfamiliar, as if he had traveled a great distance. In a few seconds the feeling vanished.

There was a place at the edge of the trees. It was where he'd stood when he'd first seen Mr. Black, sitting hunched over on the porch, mending a shirt. If he had known, then, a fraction of what would come of it, it would have been too much. *That water goes all the way around the earth*

His eyes fell to the railing. Today he'd go home. The paint was worn off at each post. Some of the weeds were higher than the floor. He'd climb the driveway. If the Mercedes was not in the garage it would be angled in front of the gray brick columns. Ordered shafts of light would descend from the skylights over the entry. A great distance . . .

He was about to go back inside when the voice entered. "Good morning."

It felt as if they'd just been talking. "Hi."

"Did you have a good sleep?"

"Yeah."

"Is it a nice day?"

"It's clear . . . hot." He almost asked about the night but didn't. "I want to get dressed. I'm starved."

"I'm sorry, boy. There should be toast and cereal and orange juice. Or pancakes, drenched in syrup."

He almost laughed. "Stop it! You're making it worse."

"They'll feed you when you get home. Till you're fit to bust."

He didn't answer. He went back inside and began pulling on his pants and shirt. They were oily between his fingers and stiff. Mom would have a fit –

He stopped himself. He knew it wouldn't matter. Why was he so afraid?

He expected the voice to say something, but it didn't. He scoured the dark floor for his shoes. He took them out to the porch and sat down on the steps to put them on.

It would be all emotional at first but, after that, they would blame him. For not coming home when he knew the way. For putting them through it.

His fingers stopped on the laces. Grief or anger knotted him; then through it he heard himself, immense, calm. *You had to do it. To come home at all.*

But how would they ever understand that?

He waded into the tall grass, around to the back of the house. Beyond the pile of junk the tangled dry leaves of a few plants struggled free of the weeds. Approaching, he saw that there were green tomatoes and lettuce, but it was yellow and dead. Up close, he found lots of sugar peas; he'd never seen them growing. He knelt and twisted one from its stem. Tentatively, he bit into it; it was crunchy and sweet. He began picking and eating more, suddenly craving their rawness, their pungent juice like nothing ever tasted out of a can. When he was satiated with them he sat back on his knees. The earth underneath was dark. It was the moisture of the rain that had fallen the night the voice had come.

He looked up, over the tops of the vines to the edge of the trees. "Mr. Black?"

"Yes?"

"Last night you said you were going to give me some advice about my dad."

"Yes . . . Are you in the garden? Are those my sugar peas?"

"Yeah. They're good."

"I envy you, boy . . . I'm glad something got eaten."

"Mr. Black?" He hesitated, his fingers making a groove in the earth. "I'm afraid to go home. They won't understand. Ever—"

The voice seemed to gather things in the silence, working them into a form that he could touch. When it came it was soft, intense. "Your parents had rigid ideas about what you should do and be. Don't do the same to them."

"What?"

"This long rough way that you chose—it's been their journey too."

He pulled at the dry stem of a tomato. "They'll blame me for not coming home. I've put them through hell."

The words moved through the warmth of the sun on the plants. "They've suffered terrible pain. Yet long before they drove you to the bus, your mom and dad knew, instinctively, just as you did, that your family couldn't continue the way it was going. Fear – yours and theirs – was tearing you apart. There are other ways those fears could've been dealt with; but the three of you rode them to a crisis."

He laughed. "My dad's not afraid of anything – except that I'll turn out a loser."

"And why does he have that fear?"

He carved a line through the dirt. The dark ground welled up. "Because I like to draw."

"There are many avenues for that talent. That's not the reason."

His hand gouged the earth. "Then why? Why does he want to make me be something I don't want to be?"

"Because there is someone he fears. Himself."

His breath stopped. It was too mad to answer –

The voice eased. "I sense things, obviously, by nonphysical means. You do the same, but you're trained to think that all information must come through the physical senses. I don't know what your mom and dad had for dinner last night – but to some extent I can tune into their thoughts, their emotions – your mom's much more readily than your dad's. I've been able to piece together some things which should be of help to you."

Something moved near the edge of the clearing. He could just make out the golden red curve of Jimmy's head through the weeds. He moved back and forth, following some scent.

"Your father, David, was once deeply artistic, like you. I don't know what form it took; but in his youth he struggled to develop that part of himself. His efforts met with bitter failure; instead of persisting he turned on himself. Over a period of time he literally recreated his personality into the man that you know. But he wasn't content just to change; he reacted to the pain of failure by denying his creative self. He strove to become the opposite of what he'd been. The young man was vulnerable, full of self-doubt; he would be aggressive and overbearing. The youth devoted himself to emotional and imaginative experience; he would be totally concerned with business and money. The youth was powerless and alone; he would be at the top of a large company. The transformation of course was exaggerated; and this was a measure of how deeply he feared the vulnerability which he associated with his artistic abilities."

He listened, astonished; the sun glanced off the dog's fur in the far reaches of the clearing.

"Your mother had an important role in this. Her highly intuitive and creative nature served him as a sort of bridge to his former self. Through her, he could continue to value and enjoy – safely – these qualities which he had rejected in himself. In her jewelry shop the conflict between artistic expression and financial success was resolved, on a miniature scale.

"His fears were not really overcome, however. As your artistic powers emerged, they surfaced fiercely. He was determined to protect you from the bitterness, pain, and defeat which he had suffered; he would rescue you at all costs by guiding you in the direction which he had taken. This is why he's been so adamant, David, so uncompromising –"

The boy's hand trembled in the darkness of the earth. "Do you mean that through this whole thing – Dad was afraid too –"

"Even more than you. That's why I said the situation's not what it seems – that all-powerful figure was driven by fear, running from shadows."

The voice paused. Jimmy wavered in the distance. "He's coming at last to face what's driven him. You've shown him, in no uncertain terms, that he can't control your spirit. And your mother – who was always the mediator between you – has come forward, boy. She'll no longer run a doll's house. In a way, she knew the crisis was coming and she reserved her energies for it. She's shaken the beliefs that controlled him. He's coming to understand, David, that he can't deny you the powers and abilities that are yours. And maybe he'll realize that this defeat which so hurt him had no power, except what he gave it.

"You can help. You can let him know that you are not afraid of the future and that there's no need for him to protect you so closely. Reassure him that you have many choices yet to make and that you won't cast off things that you'll need. Let him feel, for the first time, the strength of your being."

He stared into the shadows of the vines. Could Dad change – was it possible –

"As his fear subsides, so will his need to dominate you. You'll need patience; he's staked his identity on being overaggressive. But if he knows in the depths of your eyes and the calm of your voice that you don't need to be protected from the world by this fixed posture, he will ask himself at last why he does.

"Your mother has started these thoughts in motion. Her intuitive freedom has aided her powerfully; she not only knows that you're coming home, she understands that you could not do so until you and your father had broken the hold of fear and anger on your lives. Through the dead pain of the minutes and hours she has sensed that time is a struggle of thought. They won't blame you, boy; they've grasped too much of themselves."

The soil broke between his fingers. Tears struck it. "She knows I'm coming home –"

"Yes. Ever since you told her, on that rock in the creek."

"But she must think by now it's hopeless, crazy –"

The voice stopped, as if unsure what to say. His eyes swept the edge of the clearing. He caught a streak of red at the far end. "Jimmy! Come here, boy!"

The voice changed. It was more like Mr. Black. "My sense of time's getting rusty. Maybe I've tried to forget, how sharp it cuts . . . I'll go with you as far as the valley."

His hand froze against the ridges of dirt. "What?"

"I guess you've forgotten, with all that's gone on . . . our conversations have to end when you go home. It's just as well, boy. It's time I shut up."

Jimmy's head bobbed up and down towards him through the tall grass.

"– Why? What do you mean?" Cords hurled into the dark. "How will I know what to do –"

"If I don't tell you?"

"– But I won't ask you all the time – just if I really get into a fix! Like what you were just saying about Dad – I'd never know that without you –"

Jimmy came up, his tongue draped between his teeth. He put his arms around him and drew him closer. "I can't face them alone –"

For a long moment, the voice seemed suspended in the stillness of the clearing. When it came, it stumbled. "You're right – that was a fine speech I just made – but it's – I don't know how to put this . . . Our talking like this, David – I've come to see that it was – not a mistake – but risky – full of risks I didn't anticipate. I plunged in without thinking it through. It was only natural – I was still wrapped up in that life, and deeply moved by how you'd helped me. On top of that I was shocked by how much of myself I'd closed off, by how small I'd made myself – and then to find you in that desperate mess, believing absolutely that you were trash tossed on a curb – I remembered how my heart had ached staggering up that mountain, and I wanted to save you from the mistakes I'd made – just like your dad."

The words touched silence. "If I stayed here at your shoulder I'd also take your freedom and power away, but far worse than he did. I came to open you up to the great expanses of yourself you've forgotten and denied. But if you just listen to me, you won't learn to seek those knowing places in yourself, that have been there all along. There are no walls stronger than those made of thought. You'd cut yourself off so deeply from the resources of your being that you needed a breakthrough. But now that I've shaken you up, you'll find your own strength, and listen to voices you didn't know you had. For us to talk at all, you draw deeper on yourself than you ever thought possible. There at the creek, you reached your mom with a motion of your hand."

He clung to the warm movements of the animal's flank. "But what harm would it do, if I could just talk with you now and then, when I'm sad?"

"Jimmy's starved too. Take good care of him."

The sun bore down on the clearing. He waited; at last, his hand still on the dog, he stood. It would be a long way. "Come on, boy." Slowly, he walked around to the front of the house. As the weathered posts came into view, stark against the shadow of the porch, his gut tightened. He'd never see it again. Someone would buy the land and tear it down and throw up a huge stucco box bristling with motion detectors.

He stopped at the foot of the steps. The voice had no answer. He was being abandoned.

He went up to the porch, pulled back the screen door, and stood on the threshold of the dark room. It was a place meant for silences, even when he'd lived there. Maybe they needed that. Maybe they couldn't talk in the middle of TV and traffic and school and—

He knew better. With vacant motions he closed the door and locked it and hung the key back under the porch.

He turned away from the house. Jimmy was watching him, teeth grinning.

"Doesn't anything make you sad, boy?"

The dog looked up at him, quizzical; he almost laughed. "I guess not. But you were sad when Mr. Black died . . . He's leaving me now."

Jimmy seemed to contemplate it. He patted him on the back and was about to set out across the clearing, when he stopped. "I guess you don't have any choice but to come with me . . . I mean, I already have a dog . . . you'll have to be fenced up . . . and Mom won't let you sleep on the bed."

His eyes shone, eager.

It swept him with a cold shock. He started moving through the grass. The dog bounded ahead. Silver-dark water rushed past. He'd stood at the edge, shivering . . .

It wasn't fair. To come and shatter him and drive him almost to madness and turn him inside out, and then decide that maybe it wasn't such a good idea and stop. The voice was outside of time. What difference did it make then if it spoke to him now, or twenty years from now?

Shadows closed around him. He wasn't asking for much – just, when things got tough, that the voice would come and remind him of what it had said. Because it would be hard to think those things when all the world was telling you you were small, that you didn't count . . .

The forest was warm, heavy. He worked his way through it. Jimmy had gone on. The path vanished at every turn –

He stopped, shaken. The air was cold. It roared. He'd tossed a stone back into the stream . . . it reminded him of the jade in his mom's shop . . . Was that what the voice meant? How could that have reached her?

– He'd pressed it in his hand, and promised that he was coming home. But he'd thought that countless times. What was different, there at the stream?

He wandered forward. He could see, a ways ahead, sun striking down through the branches. He'd come out on the power line.

You threw it all off. That's what was different. For a few brief hours you threw off the hate, the fear, and the worry, and it changed everything. This bigger self the voice keeps talking about – maybe it's not some secret part of you, maybe it's what you are, all the time, but the fear of what could happen to you, of what other people could do to you, keeps getting in its way. When you got so caught up in the stream that you forgot to be angry and afraid, you became that bigger self. Places opened inside you, without end or limit. You reached your mom.

A cold surge broke through his flesh. He forgot the path. The darkness of the trees swayed with the light up ahead.

– The voice wasn't there. You – you had the power to free yourself. Because you knew, all along, that the rage to hurt and humiliate and get back at everyone was nothing but your own weakness. That they had no power to harm you and never did. That's what you saw at the spring that first morning, when the trickle of water became huge – That's what you saw when you slipped in the stream and went under and the light was churning over you. You are the stream. You have no beginning and no end.

The trunks of the fir rose over him in their time. Insects buzzed in the brush. To revel in the daring of creation – to make beginnings and endings, orders and meanings, and to outgrow them all without end –

Light sheared off the edge of the forest. He passed through it. The sky opened above him. People talked about miracles and magic—as if they were exceptions to the reality, to suffering, crap, and pain. But what if the power they half-glimpsed was not a world apart? Suppose it suffused him and the voice and Jimmy and the stones of the fireplace, an infinite restlessness of thought, empowering all things?

Then what you love, create. That is the spilling over of the fountain, the outpouring that can't be measured, the release.

The power line descended through a corridor of trees. Jimmy stayed close. He knew there was about to be a change.

As they approached the road above the camp he saw himself stumbling the other way, struggling to hold up the ax. Far off in the depths of the valley, there was a rushing . . .

He couldn't see the place where the valley opened up. His feet plodded down the dusty track under the transmission lines but there were whole passings from one tower to the next that he didn't know.

He would draw. Not timidly as he had drawn, afraid that his dad would see, but openly, freely. Because it could not be done timidly. In the closeness of its thrusts and shadows—there was its strength. Seeing that he really meant it, Dad would respect him.

And maybe even envy him.

Who are you living for, man? Yourself or your dad?

He smiled. Voices.

The land fell off more sharply. Soon he'd be normal again—almost. It would be strange—to feel the creative surge of his thoughts and test their reach, where he had sulked, frightened and hopeless—

He slowed. The far side of the valley came into view, deepening towards him. A little to the north was the big ravine and the rock slide. But the level place was hidden.

As he stared over at the mountain the voice entered, like an echo of his thoughts. "We've come full circle, David, you and I. On the way down here, beaten and hopeless, you sought death. I thirsted after physical life, mulling and stewing over the one I'd just lived. But it's all one journey. That journey takes us through time and space, life and death. We are change, we grow and diminish, on and on, in and out of time, drawing from infinite possibilities. So in that one journey there are many."

He almost asked, *why must you leave me*, but stopped. There was something wrong with the words—

"You are starting to use the creative power that has always been yours, to turn your experience around. You will get discouraged, you will feel surrounded by the great walls we have built in ourselves. They are highly functional, creative limits, but we have come to the point where their massive rigidity is hurting us.

"When that happens, David, know that in a far deeper sense, these walls do not exist. Our communication began as you sat in despair on that bus, grinding up through the dust. Recall the feeling you had when you woke up this morning. No consciousness is isolated, closed. Together we are struggling towards a reality in which we dare to rejoin the sources of our being. What you and I have done is part of that struggle.

"We have all consciousness to help us. Jimmy knows, far more immediately than we, the interaction of his being with all others across life and death. So does the cat. And the mouse in her claws. Cherish them."

The words stopped. Jimmy stood motionless. He thought for a moment that the voice was gone but it came again, almost to his surprise, hesitantly. ". . . A personal struggle, of course, was involved too. The act of creation you knew as Harold Black has fulfilled itself. But that fulfillment did not come before death – it came here, with you. At the end of an increasingly bitter and lonely life, when it seemed there was nothing left but to be done with it, he had what is called a chance encounter. In those brief moments huge connections formed.

"The emotions, the issues facing him, spanned death. It seems to you that his voice came from a dimension of greater knowing, to rescue you – but David, how you lifted him. Through all your suspicions, your arguments and set-tos – he felt an outpouring of honor and concern for your being. He died, bitter, alone, and forgotten. But his triumph was to come. It was to know and love you."

His eyes fell, to the tops of the tall trees far below over the creek.

"And if you face the challenges you've created with a fraction of the courage you showed him –

"Enough. Go and live it."

Seconds passed. The silence of the valley deepened around him.

There was a flash of sunlight below. He searched for the wings of the hawk but couldn't see them. It must have just been a sparrow.

Briehoffer's pencil drifted across the scarred topographical map fixed to the wall of Inspector Burton's office. His voice had the weariness, the somber persistence that had come to grip the search. "Basically, we've covered a six-by-eight-kilometer quadrangle, bounded by Peachland Creek, Trepanier Creek, Lookout Mountain, and the mine. We've used a ten-meter line over most of it. The mine road and the power line cross it and there's a road on the east side of Trepanier Creek. There's lots of chances to orient yourself."

The pencil hovered, then skidded off. "I think he moved out of the ground search area. He kept going, maybe right across one of those roads, because he didn't want to be found."

Inspector Burton strained to keep focused on the map. The contour lines floated off the paper, huge currents and shoals, meandering off into nowhere . . .

"OK. That was the case when he left the house. But how long could you keep going, just into the bush, with no objective?"

The steel rims of Briehoffer's glasses twitched. "If you were worse off than we thought — suicidal? Long enough to get exhausted and panic-stricken, a couple of miles or more from your last known location, on a completely unpredictable course. Maybe he came to the edge of the valley and didn't want to go down. Or maybe he did go down, and used the road along Trepanier Creek to move out of the search area." He stared at the map. His voice was almost matter-of-fact. "If I'd had five hundred people, I might've covered every possibility in time."

Inspector Burton turned away from the wall. As he'd bent by the door fumbling to tie his shoe the woman's voice had flailed over him, trembling off into nothing like the lines of the map. *Promise me — promise me —*

He drove his knuckles against the edge of the desk. The man and woman stood opposite him in the darkened room, waiting, their faces skeletal. *Mr. and Mrs. Ashton, I'm sorry to inform you that the search —*

He looked at Briehoffer almost angrily, knowing the answer yet determined to pierce the steel-rimmed calm of his eyes. "So you don't think there's any point –"

The phone rang. It rang again before he picked it up.

"Burton here . . . Yeah . . . Yeah . . . Hold it – I've got the search coordinator here – let me put you on speaker –" He jabbed a button on the phone and stepped towards the map. "OK – what did he say – don't leave anything out."

A muffled voice filled the office. "Ronald Black's never been there. His brother talked about it once or twice. It's high on the side of a mountain . . . He had to climb quite a ways on foot. The place looks down on a valley with a creek in it . . . That's all his brother really said, how he sat up there and stared down into a valley, with his dog . . ."

The contours rose in ordered ranks from the thin blue line of Trepanier Creek. It was the only valley big enough, close enough –

"Hello?"

"Yeah . . . Hold on . . ." Inspector Burton took Briehoffer's pencil and held it poised over the terrain. "The east side of Trepanier Creek. It's got to be – if he had to climb the valley to get to it – If we project David's last known direction –"

Briehoffer fidgeted. "What's this about?"

The cop's voice drove at the map as if oblivious to him. "That's why he was moving so fast . . . But how the hell – did the old guy give him directions –"

He broke off. "If it has this great view it must be near an open place, like the top of a rock slide . . . Was there anything else – anything at all –"

"No. That's it."

"OK. I'm going to put you on hold."

He jabbed another button on the phone. "This is Burton . . . Bring the chopper in to get me, now."

Eight kilometers after it crosses the power line, the road along Trepanier Creek switchbacks down to Highway 97, just north of Peachland. As David came down, the backs of his legs aching, he studied the orchards and houses and the great glittering bend of Okanagan Lake with a feeling of strangeness, of separation. With effort, he managed to reconstruct that it was the seventh day, probably to the hour, since the bus had swept him past the intersection below. He struggled with it. It might have been seconds or centuries.

A few cars had gone by. The driver of one, a woman, had stared at him; as he'd turned away he'd sensed her thoughts. *It's because you're so dirty.* He'd walked faster, the pavement burning against the worn soles of his shoes.

Just above the highway, he stopped. The cars hurled by, self-contained frenzies of noise and violence, mad to be somewhere else. He stood watching, lost. Far out over the level place, the branches of the big pine swayed in the wind . . .

Finally he took off his belt and slipped it through Jimmy's collar for a leash. Jimmy looked up at him in amazement. "I'm sorry, boy."

They crossed the highway. Nervously, he stood by the shoulder and stuck out his thumb. The cars screamed past. Trucks whipped him in bursts of wind. A few people looked at him but most stared straight ahead.

He started to count them. Ten, twenty, thirty –

But what if one did stop?

"– Come on, Jimmy. There must be some way to get home."

He had a little money; he didn't know if there was a bus. They started wandering along the highway into Peachland. Maybe he could find some pop cans –

They crossed a concrete bridge. A sign said "Trepanier Creek." He stopped and stared down. The water raced, careless of beginnings and endings, the last few hundred meters to Okanagan Lake. He felt a huge and inexplicable gratitude . . .

Jimmy led him down to the bank to drink. It was shallow and the stones ached.

They left the highway and entered the quiet streets of the town. They met no one until they came out on a street on the shore of the lake. People were at the beach, suntanning, tossing Frisbees, playing in the water. Jimmy looked on, his forehead shiny with sweat.

"No boy."

Ahead, some kids were on a dock. Their wet bodies twisted as they struggled to shove each other into the water.

"Buttmunch!"

"Super ginch man!"

"Let go of me you slimy skater!"

"Take the plunge!"

There was a burst of white off the end of the dock, and shrieks of laughter. He tightened inside; then he felt his body pushing and straining on the wet planks, the sun bearing down on his flesh, and he laughed into the other kid's eyes . . .

He stood lost in them, little figures against the vast plane of the lake and the blue depths of the mountains, and he knew that what drove them was ever-changing and indestructible.

"Hey son!"

He turned, startled. An old man stood in front of him. He wore a white shirt and suspenders and an old-fashioned hat. "You sure are dirty."

His eyes fell to the sidewalk, his heart racing –

"That's a pretty dog. What's his name?"

He forced himself to look up. "Jimmy."

"Don't you have a leash for him?"

His hand tightened on the belt. He strained to think what to say –

The old man's voice changed. "Do you need any help, son? Are you in trouble?"

"– No – I've got to get going –" He started walking away, too quickly, feeling the man's stare at his back. When he'd gone several houses he glanced around. The guy hadn't moved.

Ahead there were stores. He hurried towards them, his legs stiffening. The old guy would call the cops. He tried to think what to do. Maybe he should go back to the highway –

Then he saw it, ahead, on the window of a restaurant: a white poster. He came towards it, a hardness forming in his stomach, as if he'd never imagined it yet knew at once what it was. As he drew closer, the picture and the words took shape and he had to force himself through the pounding.

The ink was black, the lettering thick, heavy. It slammed into him, impersonal, hopeless.

MISSING
DAVID ASHTON
TWELVE YEARS OLD
From Silver Lake Forestry Centre
Near Peachland, B.C.
PHONE 911 OR KELOWNA RCMP
865-1267

In the picture he was bright, clean, smiling. It was a school photo. Mom had made him change his shirt—

The words bled. He tore himself away, his throat hollow, the sidewalk and the buildings tilting off into the blue of the lake. He stumbled forward. The next building had a poster, and the next. They awaited him, fixed against dark glass like doors into nothing, and he suddenly knew that the smiling kid was not him but the David the voice had told him about, the one who had died.

It came, choking, shattering the gray plane of the sidewalk. *What have I done. What have I done.*

Shapes moved past him, streaks of color. Two girls eating ice cream cones. He started to cry out to them but stopped. Ahead a woman was unlocking her car. He forced himself towards her. His voice shook wildly.

"Can I—can I please have a ride to Kelowna—"

The woman turned, startled. Her eyes narrowed as she stared down at him.

"I'm not going to Kelowna."

She turned back to her car.

He moved away. More people went by. The posters glared at him from the dark storefronts and he felt invisible, as if the people approaching on the sidewalk could go right through him and not notice a thing—

They must think by now it's hopeless, crazy

He saw his mom. She lay broken in the dark. A stranger stood over her—

There was a sharp jerk at his wrist; he almost tripped. The stores had stopped. Jimmy was pulling him across a side street, towards a gas station.

"Slow down, boy!"

He didn't obey. He tugged towards the gas pumps. An old blue pickup truck was parked at them. A man was getting into it. He noticed them. He was tall and balding and had a sparkle in his eyes.

He thrust past his fear that the man would say no. "Mister—are you going to Kelowna—could you give my dog and me a ride—"

He looked them over. "Aren't you a little young to be a professional mud wrestler?"

"Please—"

"Hey, no worries. Put your pooch in the back." He stepped to the back of the truck and lowered the tailgate. David took off the belt and Jimmy sprang up.

The man grinned at him. "Nice dog, even if he is a little spicy on the olfactory glands. – I'm Gerhard Blonk. I'm from down in Oliver."

The boy mumbled a name. There were centuries in his eyes. The man saw it.

The truck turned a corner and lumbered onto the highway. The man didn't pry. He talked about UFO's and tropical birds and how to thin peaches. As they crossed the bridge and entered the city, five police cars shot by the other way. The man offered to take him home.

He couldn't ring the doorbell. There was a hidden key to the side door to the kitchen. That much he saw. But he barely tried to imagine how he would look at them, what he would say, through the rush of its approach.

"Go over it again – those rock slides just south of the ravine –"

The helicopter banked right. Inspector Burton peered down through the spires of the trees. If it was easy to spot the air search would've picked it up –

The pilot flew in low over the scarred slopes. The granite rubble glared in the sun and Burton thought, *Jeez, you'd have to be motivated –*

"There – just above that rock slide – I want to see that again –"

The helicopter turned. As it came back to the spot, slowing, he studied a level area below the thrashing tops of the trees. "Looks like someone's been down there – see those paths?"

Mere strands of bare earth, they wound between weathered boulders and sun-bleached logs. Most led towards a drop-off. *You'd have a view of the whole valley –*

"I'm going to look around down there."

The helicopter descended into the clearing. The terrain was too rough to land so Inspector Burton had to lower himself from the skid gear.

He motioned up at the pilot. "Give me five minutes –"

The helicopter rose and moved off. He stood, the convulsions of the trees subsiding, swirls of dust drifting across the clearing. The pressure of the blades diminished.

Towards the edge a pine was split by a blackened crevice. A dead tree rose above the drop, its branches contorted against the depths of the valley. A feeling came over him; he pushed it back.

He walked along beside one of the paths. There were broken prints of a running shoe.

Suddenly he knelt. There was a complete print. The shoe was the right size. But it was not that that swept through him in shock. Beside it was a footprint of a dog.

McNeil grinned. *Is it Lassie or The Littlest Hobo?*

There were more prints. He moved on, down to the edge. They stopped at a fallen log. The land fell away, a fifty-foot drop.

He saw the boy sitting there with the dog – Harold Black's dog, who somehow had found him and guided him here from the house, beyond the far side of the valley, across miles of rough terrain. He told himself there was no evidence for it. But he knew.

Slowly, he walked along the edge of the clearing. There was a small campfire ring. He was making his way towards it when something caught his eye. The pine that had been split by fire – it had a deep gash on one side, about four feet up. He went towards it. Something formed in his gut.

It had been done with an ax. Details shot at him, scraps of logic – the height of the cut, the fresh chips on the ground, the wild, glancing blows to the sides – but it was as if they came out of a knowing that was already there. *A connection between David and a metal object . . . intense feelings of rage –*

He fought it. *What's next – the bloody ghost? Flaked out in the shack, waiting for you?*

The drone of the helicopter bore down on him, throbbing. *You're not here to investigate – Maybe he took off when he heard the chopper –*

He didn't call out. David was gone. He realized that he'd sensed it even from the air. A bizarre sensation came over him, of having been connected all along . . .

The paths converged at a dense forest of young fir. The shack would be hidden there.

As he entered the stick forest, feelings came, pulses in his blood. Torturous hate, exhaustion, fear – there had been all that – but something else too, something the boy probably didn't recognize – a foreboding –

No – it's you – that ghost stuff's –

Suddenly it was before him. It was darker and more run-down than he'd imagined. The trees crowded around it and branches had been cut to hide the roof. He tensed. *Somebody ought to give this kid a good licking –*

They already did.

The door was closed. There was a break in the throbbing before he opened it.

A dim light fell into the shack. He stepped inside. Objects took shape, formed of shadows: a bed, a table, shelves with tin cans, a black thing on the floor against the far wall. He went up to it and lifted the garbage bag: water, rigged so that the dog could drink, without anyone to help –

The bed was made. The table, the shelves, the floor were clean. Not like a kid, a crazed kid with an ax –

The cop in him told him to get back to the chopper, to bring detectives, searchers, dogs . . .

He sat down on the bed, his big hands folded in the half-light of the door. Something was wrong.

There were pictures on the wall, cut out of old magazines: exotic places, a 1950's bathing beauty. Forlorn dreams of an old man.

The ghost was gone. What had the lady in Sonoma called it – an "entity" – yeah, "an entity outside our physical plane." Fruitcakes.

And yet, something had happened here. The boy's murderous hate and agony had met something – something powerful enough to at least temper them –

And that alone probably saved his life.

His hands rubbed against each other. Almost seven thousand man-hours searching on the ground – over sixty hours in the air – the relentless pursuit of every possibility that reason and logic could suggest – all had failed. Yet somehow, a woman a thousand miles away, who'd never heard of Kelowna, saw David on this remote mountainside, in this shack.

How could she do that? Was it luck? Did she have powers normal people didn't have?

A being whom he's encountered in this incarnation. A scrap of New Age babble. There was nothing else, nothing, behind the series of wild guesses that had led him here.

His hands clenched. *Up to the minute you saw those footprints there was not a shred of real evidence that David Ashton had ever met Harold Black. Not one.*

Hey, get off it. You have a folder full of tips from psychics that didn't check out. Time's wasting –

He started to rise. The bed creaked. Time. Molecules, chemicals and stuff, doing their thing, one second after another, on and on, for billions of years –

Come on. The chopper's waiting –

We leaped it. A bunch of nerves, tissues . . .

He stared around at the objects in the room, still, silent, utterly physical. Something was wrong.

A black Jaguar stood before the house on Clifton Road. The face to the street was guarded, withdrawn: the Ashton's cars were locked in the garage, the vertical blinds at the entrance were closed; this had become usual. But on the west side, facing the lake, the curtains of the picture windows were also drawn.

Constanza had been given the rest of the day off. The house was empty except for four persons gathered under the great windows. Elaine Ashton sat upright in a chair by the entrance to the dining room. It was the chair in which she'd been reading a magazine, when the phone call came that David was missing. She thought of that, her eyes lowered from the others: why, when she had been broken to pieces in an instant, did it take so very long, the bleeding to death . . .

Joseph sat at the end of the sofa nearest her. Minutes before the lawyers had arrived, he'd gotten up and closed the curtains. She hadn't asked why. They couldn't look there anymore. But a strong light came in around the edges.

At the other end of the sofa was Tom Cawston, the Ashton's attorney. Normally gruff, he sat intent and subdued, yet trying, perhaps, not to appear overawed in the presence of his famous colleague.

L. Waterford Jones stood before the bookcase at the end of the room. He was tall, with narrow features and white hair parted not quite in the middle. His three-piece suit, tailored by a little shop on the Via Monte Napoleone in Milan, appeared impervious to the long flight. His eyes were steel blue.

The introductions were over. L. Waterford Jones spoke with a natural elegance and Elaine's hands involuntarily started to ease on the kleenex wadded in her lap. She caught it, shuddering, resisting. "Mr. and Mrs. Ashton, I wish to emphasize that I would rather not have come here, at this point in time. The trial in which I'm engaged presented no alternative. It is my fervent hope that David will be found alive; and yet, with the search now into its fifth day, we must face the possibility that this may not happen.

"Mrs. Ashton, I understand that you especially are present, as it were, under duress. While there is a chance that David might be found, the matters we're about to discuss are necessarily painful and offensive. I am fully aware that spiritually, there is no possible compensation for the loss you face. I am also aware, more keenly than you, that those guilty of negligence use that spiritual truth to their material advantage."

She sat stiff in the chair, her eyes driven through the dark patterns in the carpet. *He's alive. You saw him.* She groped at the image in the garden, struggling to reenter the white flash point of that instant, to sustain its reality against the endless attrition of the minutes and hours –

"Judicial tradition and practice in this country, in regards to the wrongful death of a child, are appalling. If you, Mr. Ashton, were to be maimed for life in a car accident, the largest of the courts would be considerable, in light of your income. But a child's future earnings are problematic; no one has suffered a loss of support; and too often the courts have wielded such a callous yardstick that, even when pecuniary losses have been determined, they have deducted what the parents will save, by no longer having to raise their daughter or son."

Her head bent. The words struck like an echo off a cliff. It was the voice, the male voice of vast authority and composure, assuring her that she was merely running from the truth . . .

"The courts have focused so narrowly on gross monetary issues that in our fight to make the negligent truly accountable, we've been reduced to arguing, for instance, that the value of a child must at least equal the amount the parents have spent on it. How desperately all of this misses the mark. Grief – accountability for the infliction of anguish – these are the real issues. Many a counsel for the defence has chided me over lunch that I'm out for blood. This is my reply: as a direct result of the historic judgment in *Culos versus Ontario Regional Transit Authority*, twenty-two million dollars in state-of-the-art safety equipment will be installed in Ottawa subways."

Lucid, grand, the voice encircled the battered shell of her being. She huddled against it; and yet it began to work its magic.

Give up. Why do you torture yourself. This man is offering you a cause –

L. Waterford Jones stepped away from the bookcase. "I believe that we have the potential here for a similar precedent-setting action. A judgment that at last will establish the principle, that the greatest loss a human being is capable of suffering may not be inflicted with virtual impunity. A judgment, moreover, that will send a message to the institutions to whom we entrust our children, that nothing less than the highest standards of professionalism will do. That is what interests me in this case. David is not a victim of a split second of carelessness, by an ordinary citizen in his car. He is a victim of the arrogance of institutions – an institution charged with nurturing his young life's potential, which instead, through repeated failures of responsibility, may have destroyed it. In a tragedy like this few consolations have any meaning. I believe this is one: that as a result of your loss, such pain may be prevented from happening again."

Thoughts tore like flesh. She struggled. *They'll drag you down into a hell of accusations and denials.* Yet might it be a way of letting go – making the pain crass and public? Would it not all become more distant, dignified, manageable? She saw herself in the courtroom, somber, devout –

No – to sit posed, day after day, immaculately wronged, while lawyers grubbed for money –

But they are *guilty. They deserve* –

David. The force of it had blown her hand off the rail, exploded through the objects in the garden as if the very stones of the quay were tensioned energy. He'd stared down into the water, lost in struggle. Had he wanted to toss the rock? Was it anger?

Or had she in love and desperation mistaken –

The vaulted ceiling closed over her. The lawyer's voice sounded in a room where all echoes died.

Maybe he was struggling . . . to say goodby.

It swept her into places where there was no will to cry out.

" . . Take time and consider carefully . . . the risks are high . . ."

Who could've missed it . . . his tossing a stone back into the water . . . to sink into the dark . . .

". . . More than stamina will be required . . ."

That alone had kept her from being pulled under – a single instant, like a fragment of something much greater, shot through time and space. And instead of pursuing it she had enshrined it.

The lawyer's voice drove, distant, passionate, a pressure of dead air –

There was nothing left – nothing but imaginings and regrets. How lucky Joseph was, to smother them in rage – and believe in it –

She glanced up, just enough for the sofa to come into the edge of sight.

He shocked her. The nerves in her hands reacted –

He'd been withdrawn, as usual, since the night before. The scene at dinner – the sense she'd had, as he'd collapsed into his chair, that in his long battle with David he had fought some remnant of himself – she had prepared herself that it would make no difference. Whatever had stirred in him, he would silence – because there had to be someone to blame, to take action against. That had always been his way –

And she had thought, almost with guilt, *if that is the only way he can get through this, would you take it from him?*

– She had forced herself into the room, expecting the lawyer's eloquence to lift him back up, to recharge him with wrath and purpose. It was with shock then that she saw him slumped against the sofa, the hard lines of his face gray and unresponsive.

A cry racked her. *Forget what I said, Joseph – so that one of us has something –*

". . . There is a reason I am laying such emphasis on this. The courtroom is a cruel arena. As Mr. Cawston has anticipated, the defence will be based on an argument of contributory negligence. They will say that you forced David to go even though he was so embittered towards you and the camp that he was at risk of running away. That you were so mad for him to achieve success in your eyes that you sacrificed not just his feelings, but his very safety."

The voice dropped. "Mr. and Mrs. Ashton, this argument – so facile, so irresistible – will prove their undoing."

Her body tightened, a shrunken scaffold of pain. Joseph rose from the dining table, his eyes bloody pits. It was the thing he'd said they would choke on –

But he showed no reaction. He sat, almost as if he hadn't heard . . .

L. Waterford Jones approached them. "I know the devastating impact this must have. I mention it because I want you to understand, from the very start, what to expect . . . I assure you it will not succeed."

A silence hung on the light around the curtains.

"You are concerned, involved parents. This would be true of anyone who sent his child to a prestigious summer computer camp – in most cases, I suspect, against considerable opposition. You were not trying to dictate David's future – you were providing him with the technological skills you knew he would need in our dramatically changing society. That his academic strengths lay elsewhere is not unusual; in fact, such students are encouraged in the camp's promotional literature. He'd already attended last year. You had no reason to believe that there was anything more to his opposition, than a twelve-year-old's reluctance to give up a week of summer, mixed with some normal academic jitters."

He stopped on the stairs. The crystal ached in the joints of her hands. *What did you say to him*

Joseph stared into the dark folds of the curtains, the edge of his jaw tensed —

The lawyer's voice crescendoed over them. "You had no reason to believe that, because Futuristix Inc. did not inform you of critical events which would have alerted you to the seriousness of David's mental condition. His running away last year is the most notorious but not the only example. Mr. Cawston has learned that David was no sooner on the bus than he refused to take his seat, and demanded to be let off. An instructor had to order the driver to pull off the road; yet apparently he didn't even report this incident to the camp director —" Joseph's hand clutched the crease of his suit. L. Waterford Jones hesitated, then drove on, overpowering. "You were not advised of any of the incidents leading to the attack. The more defence counsel argues that you should not have sent David to the camp, the more glaring will become their client's failure to safeguard him. For it goes without saying — if you had known of even one of these things — you would've gone and talked with David, possibly pulled him out."

She slumped against the gray hollows of Joseph's face. She would have thought there was nothing left to fear —

"They never gave you the chance to help him — to respond to the numerous warning signals that were there. For Futuristix Inc. it was business as usual, right up to the moment David stumbled into the night."

The lawyer stopped. Joseph's eyes had fallen to the sofa. His hands lay bent, still. His final words slid past her, a mad cry of hope. *What does it matter now*

Somewhere, the stillness brushed a door.

— He'd stared down into the water. Faint ripples obscured its surface. But where he was —

L. Waterford Jones waited. She felt his energy — concentrated, focused, unsure.

Tom Cawston leaned forward. "There's lots here to think about. You may want to take some time —"

"Mr. Ashton." The voice was sudden, decisive. "If you had known that David ran off last year — if you'd been informed of his demanding to get off the bus and the incidents that followed, as it was the camp's responsibility to do — would you not have brought David home, or at least sought counseling for him?"

He didn't move. Cawston started to say something but stopped.

"If there's a weakness here, admit it, and we'll deal with it."

Joseph didn't look up. The lines of his face stood tensed as if under the weight of ruins. At last he spoke. "Weakness?"

"Yes."

". . . I wouldn't call it that. I had the power and I used it."

Words bent through her. *What kind of power to decide for himself*

He pressed a hand to his brow, then forced it away. "To answer your question . . . I believed David's attendance at the camp was absolutely vital. His feelings were not at issue. Had I known of these incidents, I would've spoken to him, but the outcome would not have changed. In your profession, sir . . . is it not true that in the end, the only thing that matters is to win the case? Then you will understand how things were between me and David."

Silence weighted the room. A madness struggled through her, unspeakable—

"I knew what was necessary for him to be happy, to be successful . . . to not live at the mercy of . . . our changing society. His resistance was a child's stubbornness, it meant nothing. I was right, in regards to the facts." The words shuddered and dropped. "I thought that was all that mattered."

L. Waterford Jones moved off towards the bookcase. He turned and stood, one hand in a pocket, deliberating—

She stumbled up the arch of the bridge, tears slicing the rail and the astonished faces of the children and the place where he'd stood. He battled, now, with everything inside him.

Joseph there is a process—even now—

In the darkness of the house she caught a stirring, so hushed it couldn't be . . .

Gray, fissured, he entered places where he would be lost. A cry broke the tensed angle of her hand.

"David was a victim of my arrogance. I wanted the best for him. I never—I could not—question what that was. I've always despised people who make excuses. I accept responsibility . . . for his death."

The lawyer fumbled to object. Madness overwhelmed her. Her hands tore from the chair. *Joseph he chose to go that way—I don't understand—I just know there's something in him we couldn't hurt—and he sought it—and death isn't the end of that search—*

He turned to her as if she had spoken. The cry shattered, impossible. She watched him collapse, the light of his eyes swept away. "I am a toy... of anger, hate, and guilt. I could endure them... if I could feel for an instant... that I ever knew my son."

A silence fell, that no word could ever lift.

Behind her, in the dining room, there was a change in the light. She started to turn—

David took his arm from Jimmy's neck. His reflection played across the posters and a thought shot through him, that he would enter the room and no one would see or hear.

There ain't no other life. There's just one. What we do here, we do to ourselves

He pushed forward. A cry stopped in his mother's throat. He approached the huddled shell of his father's being. His voice trembled, not with fear but with the power of the release.

"I am not a victim. Everything that's happened to me—everything—I DID."

The famous lawyer's face turned ashen.

Joseph looked up. He caught the swiftness, not of time, ever running before—

The man and woman leaped into the arms of their son.

Kelowna, British Columbia
January 8, 1990 – April 23, 1996